THE WAY WE USED TO WALK

THE WAY WE USED TO WALK

MEGAN ENGELHARDT

MARK BEALL

For our own found family, the Retrograde Orbit Society. We love you nerds.

Published in the United States by Creative James Media.

www.creativejamesmedia.com

978-1-956183-06-1 (trade paperback)

First U.S. Edition 2025

PROLOGUE

Smitha locked her office door and turned away for the last time that semester. She wasn't done with work, goodness no—the briefcase full of papers and USB full of research proved that—but it was nice to think that she'd have some time away from students, away from scheduled classes and meetings and office hours. After three years of teaching, she'd gotten a handle on things, mostly, but a break was always welcome.

In the next few weeks, she would have plenty of time for researching. Plenty of time for making merry. And plenty of time with Thomas.

She narrowly dodged a snowball fight that a few students had started outside the red brick building. Spirits were high all around at the end of the semester. Happy voices followed her down the sidewalk.

Smitha turned left out of the wide driveway that led into campus and began walking down the mostly broken sidewalk that led into town. It wasn't a long walk from campus to their house, even in the snow and cold. Always an attentive husband, Thomas urged her to just take the car, but Smitha liked walking.

Smitha followed the road around a small bend and turned into a residential street, brick-paved and lined with tidy homes shining white lights from windows and orange lights from streetlamps on the humps of snow-covered bushes. Smitha picked up her pace as the large house, too large for her and Thomas alone but just right for the family they wanted someday, came into view.

The curtains were drawn. Thomas's shadow passed by the lighted window once, twice. He would be getting dinner ready, something warm and filling. The piquant smell of it floated out to greet her as she drew closer.

Another shadow appeared through the curtain. It was tall and thin, with sharp angles and pointed edges. It flickered, sometimes obstructing the light, sometimes allowing it to shine through. It was not a person, could not be a human.

Smitha didn't know what it was, the thing in the window, but just the form of it caused her blood to chill and her stomach to bottom out. She began to run but slipped on the snowy sidewalk. She fell to her knees, dropped her briefcase, cried out.

Behind the curtain, the strange shape grabbed Thomas. The shadows clashed, swayed, began melting together. The attacking shadow grew darker—Thomas's shadow disappeared. There was only one shadow now, solid and sharp. Smitha realized there had only been one shadow from the beginning; a trick of the evening light fooling her into thinking there were two. Then even that was gone, as the streetlight outside the window flashed to life and washed it away.

Smitha shuddered as a wave of cold washed over her, so intense that for a moment she could think of nothing else. It left her feeling disoriented, sitting on the ice for a long moment trying to remember how'd she gotten there and what had seemed so important that she hadn't stood back up. It was something about a shadow, she thought. She blinked several times in rapid succession, squishing her eyes closed and giving her head a hard shake each time she opened them; a trick she often employed to kick start her memory when she lost focus. Nothing. The itch at the back of her brain persisted for a few seconds and then faded away. If she'd forgotten something important enough, she reasoned, she'd remember it later. Probably when she was trying to sleep.

She struggled to her feet, complaining under her breath about the city council and their failed promises.

"Salt for the sidewalks, my foot," she said.

A window was open near the back of the house. Smitha didn't remember leaving it open, but she must have. Sometimes the old house's heating went into overdrive, and she had to crack a window to get the temperature normalized. She wasn't worried about a break-in, not in this sleepy little town. Anyway, it was clear no one had been in the house but her: nothing was disturbed, nothing was missing.

She checked the stew that had been cooking in the crockpot all day. It smelled delicious, warm, and filling. She would eat some later, alone as usual at her table with a book and maybe some soft music in the background. A simple, quiet evening.

Smitha had been single her whole life, and she was used to it. Sometimes she wondered what it would be like to have someone waiting for her when she got home. But really, she didn't mind being alone. Plenty of time to get some work done, to read and research and grade. She'd call Charlie on Christmas Day, chat with her best friend for a few hours, and that would be enough.

Outside the snow began to fall again, large white flakes filling the dark night sky, settling on bushes, trees, unsalted sidewalks, and the spiky, pointed outline of a monster that made its way stealthily back to campus, to slink unseen into the abandoned building that housed the rest of its kin.

PART ONE
PRESENT DAY

CHAPTER

ONE

Charlie used to believe in magic.

Not the unexplainable, mystical kind—no, he knew that existed, and he hated it. The mundane kind of magic. The beauty of sunsets. The ability of music to encapsulate one moment in time. The crash of the ocean at night. True love.

But the soft colors of a beautiful sunset were a result of pollution and music these days was garbage. The ocean was full of plastic, and true love, like all good things, did not last.

"Maybe it's because I'm older now," Charlie said. "I mean, not like you guys old. Not that there's anything wrong with that. Grey hair is a crown of splendor and all that."

His audience said nothing.

"But you know, I'm thirty ... five? Six? How old am I? Whatever, it doesn't matter. I'm not a child anymore, and I've put childish things behind me." He wagged a finger at one of the old men who slumped in a wheelchair. "Don't look at me like that, Leonard. I know what you're thinking. 'But Charlie, you seem so cheerful and full of life!' That, Leonard, is because I'm a good actor."

Sandra bustled up, arms full of noisemakers.

"Thanks for filling in, Charlie," she said. "I can't believe traffic was so bad!"

"Not a problem. We've just been chatting."

"You're the best. Want to stay and have some fun?"

And he did want to, so he did, helping the residents shake their noisemakers to the patriotic music Sandra played. He even started up a parade around the Hickory Glen Assisted Living and Memory Care Facility community room, drafting other residents and workers to push a few wheelchairs until he and Leonard were at the head of a long chain. By the time music therapy was over, he had made three nurses and two residents giggle and even Leonard had cracked a smile.

Charlie spent his lunch break sprawled across the back seat of his car, eyes closed, letting the early autumn sun shine on his face. Then he went back inside, ignoring the rubbery-faced, open-ribbed monster stalking the parking lot. A few more resident visits and some paperwork later and he was done for the day.

The monster in the parking lot was still there. Charlie still ignored it, as best he could. It wasn't easy. The hatchet sharp face leering out of the not-quite-there body chilled his bones with fear if it got too close. He wasn't sure which was worse— the hungry, spectral bodies of the unreal beings or the monstrous, solid forms they took after consuming someone and stealing their place in reality. He hadn't seen a Real Boy in years, but they still haunted his nightmares.

He didn't want to go home yet so he drove to a nearby park. The sun was out and even though there was some bite to the air the park was full.

Charlie walked the paths, not really paying attention to where he was going. No monsters at the park, thank goodness, but there were lots of young couples, which was almost as bad.

Well, not really. But it still wasn't easy to watch.

"Grim today, Charlie old boy," he said to himself. Unfortunately, himself was not being a good conversationalist.

Alone with his thoughts. This walk had been a bad idea. Today wasn't a good alone day. He needed noise and lights and distraction. Maybe he'd change and hit the clubs. Did he even have to change? He glanced down at his work outfit—close-fitting black jeans, sleeveless gray cardigan, lighter gray dress shirt with the sleeves rolled up.

"Hey," he said, turning suddenly and surprising a rollerblader who looked to be a few years younger than he. "Is this a good club outfit? Maybe if I take off the cardigan?"

To his surprise she sneered.

"Aren't you a little old to be hitting the clubs?" she asked, and zoomed past, leaving only her mean laugh behind.

"What the hell?" Charlie asked, genuinely shocked.

His phone rang. He checked the number—the Professor —and answered the call.

"Smitha," he said, "someone just called me old!"

"We are old, Charlie."

The Professor's voice was calm and familiar, a cool hand on his fevered soul. He always answered when the Professor called. She was the only thing about the past that made him feel good.

"True," he conceded, "but it was rude of her to point it out. So, what's up? Hey, wasn't your date with Beau today?"

"It wasn't a date!" Smitha protested. "We just got lunch together, that's all."

"Uh huh. Just throw him over your desk and kiss him, Smitha."

"Charlie! I could never do that. And it wasn't a date, really."

Charlie mouthed *it was a date* as he walked past a little girl jumping rope. "So how did your not-date go, then?"

Smitha told him all about her not-date-but-totally-a-date

and Charlie listened and walked, walked and talked, until the sun was nearly down.

"I should let you go," Smitha said eventually. "You probably have plans?"

She was digging, her voice indicating that she hoped he did have something lined up with someone.

"Tons," Charlie said, which was a lie.

Smitha started to say something but stopped herself.

"Well, have fun," she said finally. "Be safe. Be good."

"Always, Prof. Always. Love you."

"Love you too, Charlie."

A monster was waiting outside his apartment building, so he kept driving and ended up at his favorite club. He took off the cardigan and went inside. According to a very friendly young man named Frank, his outfit was just right.

SMITHA ENDED CLASS TEN MINUTES EARLY.

She wasn't in the habit—the students had paid for this class, and she was going to give them every minute of value—but there was no point in continuing. Money, Credit, and Banking was right after lunch and it was a struggle to keep the kids awake on a good day. A beautiful day like today? Impossible. A full third of the students had skipped class to spend time in the unexpected warm weather. The other two-thirds had at least shown up, but they kept casting longing glances out the large classroom windows. When her projector remote malfunctioned Smitha gave up. She tossed it down on the podium and said "That's it for today. We'll finish up next week."

There were no objections.

The classroom was in the Fine Arts Building and her office was across the lawn in Bohm-Bawerk Business Center, so she enjoyed a leisurely stroll in the sun. Students sprawled on beach towels or just sat in the grass, chatting and laughing. Smitha smiled, full of nostalgia for her own college days. She remembered many days of sitting on that same lawn with her friends.

Back in her office Smitha put down her briefcase and pulled up the day's schedule on her computer. She had a section of International Economics at 3 p.m. and there was a guest speaker in the evening that she and Beau were meeting up to see.

On a whim she clicked on the 9 p.m. box and added "Coffee with Beau". Its casual inclusion made her smile. How nice it would be to make it a recurring event, coffee with Beau every day. A little time set aside for talking and laughing together, a little oasis in the day.

She deleted the event.

"Dr. Pillai?"

A student from her Money, Credit, and Banking class stood in the doorway, looking sheepish.

"I know it's not your office hours, but I have a question about today's lecture ...?"

"Come on in," Smitha said. "I have a few minutes."

The rest of the day passed as it usually did, grading and talking with students and giving her lecture, snacking out of her top drawer until she had a chance to run to the student union to pick up something to eat. She was finishing up a chicken tender wrap when Beau knocked on the door.

"You ready?"

Smitha looked up and met his broad smile. Beau had a great smile, huge and bright and focused right on her. She quickly stood and walked around her desk to greet him.

"Yep, ready! Let me just grab my bag and we can head over."

Beau wandered around her office while she closed her computer and gathered her things.

"I love your shelves," he said. "They're filled with whimsy and surprise."

"And economics textbooks," Smitha pointed out.

"Yes. But look at this!" Beau lifted a small figure off a shelf. It was a ceramic tiger, sloppily painted in orange and black.

"My nephew made that. He's six."

"It's great. I love it." Beau replaced the tiger and moved along the shelf. "Is that a God's eye? And what kind of fossil is that?"

"It's a footprint from an *Alwalkeria*. It was a small theropod ... it lived in India. Late Triassic. I'm ready. We'd better get going."

Beau turned from the shelves.

"Okay, let's—hey. You've got a little—" He motioned to Smitha's cheek. "Here, let me."

Beau grabbed a napkin off her desk and reached out, gently wiping away a smudge of ranch dressing. His hand lingered near her face just a little longer than it needed to.

"How embarrassing," Smitha muttered, looking away. She was trying very hard not to remember what Charlie had said about Beau the last time they talked.

Beau cleared his throat and stepped back a pace. He threw the napkin in the trash.

"Well," he said, "let's go." He offered his arm with a smile which teetered between friendly and flirty, and Smitha took it. They walked together to the lecture hall and sat side by side, legs touching at the knee, elbows brushing.

CHAPTER

TWO

L ater that evening Smitha and Beau strolled down the sidewalk, talking animatedly. The campus streetlights painted everything with flicking orange and pale yellow. It was growing colder, a crisp fall evening. A few students were still out, bundled up and walking quickly or standing in pairs or small groups talking.

Smitha and Beau reached Smitha's car in the parking lot but continued to talk for several minutes until the conversation reached a natural pause. Suddenly, in the quiet, they each realized they were standing too close. Smitha broke the silence.

"Well ... thanks for going with me. To the speaker. It was good."

"She was a good speaker," Beau said. "Thanks for inviting me."

For the hundredth time Smitha wondered if she should ask him out for a cup of coffee, continue the night in the small all-hours cafe down on Main Street. For the hundredth time, something stopped her. It wasn't that she didn't want to, it was just— she couldn't.

"Well," she said again. "Class in the morning. I should get going."

"Yeah," Beau agreed. "Same here. So ... goodnight."

He started to lean down, definitely giving out kissing vibes. Smitha really wanted to kiss him, but again—she couldn't. So, she squeezed his hand and gave him an apologetic smile.

"Goodnight, Beau," she said. "I'll see you tomorrow."

She got in the car and started it, because she knew Beau wouldn't leave until he was sure she could get home. Then, after his taillights had disappeared around the entrance bend, she turned off the car and got out. She needed to take a walk.

Ravencrest College was divided into two parts, colloquially known as Upper and Lower Campus. Upper Campus was where the academic buildings clustered, fine arts, science, and engineering all staring each other down in a rough boxy standoff. Lower Campus housed the various dormitories, the chapel, and the main administration building.

When she was in college and needed to think, Smitha would circuit around Lower Campus, from her dorm past the chapel, past the creepy bronze statue of the founder, around by the flagpole, up past the admin building and back again. They all took walks, the whole gang, at any time of the day but most often, it seemed, at night. Any heartbreak, or failed test, or bout of loneliness, any bad thing at all would see two or three of them perambulating in the dark, allowing the easy movement and cover of night to free up whatever words needed said.

She walked by herself now. Most of the time she didn't mind the solitude, but occasionally, like now, she wished Charlie or Alice or Mona were there to give her some advice. Mona would have been good—she was always straight to the point, able to get to the heart of the trouble with incisive quips that somehow managed to seem compassionate and truthful.

"What's on your mind, Professor?" Mona would have asked with no preamble. "Got a problem with Nerd Charming back there?"

"No problem," Smitha muttered. "He's a good guy. Good company."

"So snatch him up," Mona would have said. Smitha could imagine the sideways look her friend would have given her, eyes narrowing through purple-hued fringe. "What's stopping you?"

"I don't know," Smitha said, talking as much to the phantom of her dead friend as to herself. "He wants to—*I* want to. It just doesn't feel right."

"Why?" Mona would have asked. Smitha repeated it. "Why?"

Her feet thumped the pavement. From the parking lot, up past the administration building, across to the chapel, and again, asking herself and the shadow of Mona "why?" Past the flagpole and ask "why?" Skirt the parking lot, not ready to go home yet, and head to the chapel again, asking "why?" Pass the bronze statue and—

Smitha stopped at the bench where the creepy statue sat like some old-timey Ronald McDonald. A memory slid into place the way memories sometimes do, and Smitha frowned.

"There wasn't a gate here before, was there?" she asked.

The ghost of Mona stayed silent.

Whether there used to be or not, there was a gate now, rickety iron hid between two overgrown bushes. When Smitha approached and peered through it she could see, like Alice at the keyhole, a garden on the other side. While Alice's garden looked delightfully inviting, however, Smitha's looked— rather boring, actually. Very normal, with bushes cut in very ordinary shapes and low beds overgrown by the most mundane plants. Smitha found herself so uninterested in the garden beyond the gate that she would have walked away and never thought of it again—if not for the persistent worry that the garden had not always been there. It looked as if it had been abandoned for decades, but Smitha couldn't shake the idea that only a handful of years earlier something else had stood on the other side of the hedges.

She tried the gate. It clacked, sticking, but when she pulled slightly it swung open. She stepped through. The gate swung closed behind her.

The garden was enclosed by huge trees that arced overhead, a skeletal ceiling of branches. A few lamp posts burned orange, providing just enough dim light to make you see things that weren't actually there. A large shape resolved itself as Smitha walked closer, into a greenhouse covered with old vines and new fallen leaves.

Smitha shivered in a sudden cold gust and rubbed her arms, peering closer at the greenhouse. She frowned at it and blinked, for a moment seeing another building overlaying the greenhouse. A building that looked just as old and abandoned, one that was long and low-

"The pool house?"

She blinked again and the overlay was gone, but the feeling, that of a building out of place, remained.

And when the creature appeared around the corner of the greenhouse, it felt like Smitha herself was thrown out of place and time.

It had an angular face, coming to a sharp point at its nose with one large, watery eye on each side and a row of terrifying teeth through which a tangled mass of tongues lolled. Beneath its face, the faint outline of a robe fluttered open around a set of barbed and barbarous ribs. It turned its head to one side and looked right at Smitha.

And suddenly she remembered everything, and she turned and ran, stumbling over the detritus on the garden path, fumbling with the gate. It would not open—*it would not open*

—-and she knew that the monster was right behind her, and then the gate swung open and she bolted through. She ran, past the bronze statue, past the flagpole, to the parking lot and her car, where she dug for her keys, looking and looking behind her but seeing nothing. The car unlocked. She jumped in and turned on the ignition, locked the door behind her, flipped on her headlights, and sat for a moment, catching her breath. The thing, the monster, was gone.

She remembered. She remembered *everything*. The monsters and the pool house and Mona—poor Mona. Fifteen years later and she finally remembered, and with the memories came the realization that they weren't done. Her family still had work to do.

And it was up to her to get them all back.

***

SHUT THE DOOR. LOCK IT. KEYS IN THE BOWL. POUR a drink. Lay down on the couch and try not to think.

Sometimes Charlie fell asleep. A half an hour, an hour, any little bit of sleep he could sneak in before the dreams started.

Sometimes music helped. Sometimes it made things worse. Sometimes a pill or two, sometimes a casual hookup, a nice gentleman or lady to help him forget for a night.

And some nights there was nothing to do but lay back and try to pretend that everything was fine, that he was not haunted by memories, that Mona was not dead, that he didn't live in fear of seeing, around every corner, one of those creatures that did not belong in this world.

He called them Nowhere Men, like the Beatles song, and tried not to think about the nowhere land they came from, or the world being at their command.

Because damn, that was a terrifying thought.

And maybe it was true, maybe the whole world was

controlled by those long, thin creatures with the terrible eyes and nightmare faces. Maybe that's why he saw them all the time, not just in his memories of the day they lost Mona, but now, at work, on the street, everywhere.

Or maybe he was going crazy and the whole thing was all in his head.

Or maybe he was already crazy.

Some days he didn't know which would be better, if the Nowhere Men were real or if he was out of his mind.

Charlie got home, went through his routine—door, lock, keys, drink—and decided to self-medicate with music. He played it loud, sang along with the ones he knew—and he knew them all—and let the drums pound him into forgetfulness for a while.

His phone automatically paused the music when it rang, which was annoying. But he answered anyway because it was the Professor and he always answered for the Professor.

"Hey, Charlie."

"And how are you tonight, love?"

She talked about nothing much for a while, which was par for the course on these calls. It was a kind of forgetting, letting the Professor's familiar voice wash over him, participating in the treasured personal banalities that make up any casual conversation between long-time friends, dancing around his apartment to the music that was no longer playing.

Finally she fell silent for a moment, long enough for Charlie to pour another glass, and then said "Charlie ... something's happening."

"Something's always happening somewhere, darling."

"No, I mean ... look, this is going to sound really weird, so don't laugh and don't interrupt ... something's *happening*. With the—the portal."

Charlie choked on his wine.

The Professor continued, all in a rush, as if now that she'd decided to say something she was anxious to have it done.

"I know that probably doesn't make any sense, and I can't put a finger on it, but something feels *wrong*. And there's a weird greenhouse or something where the pool house used to be, before ... and, um, I think I saw one of them. Those creatures. The Nowhere Men," she said, forcing herself to speak the name. "Do ... do you understand anything I'm talking about? Do you remember?"

"Yeah," Charlie said, and was surprised to find his eyes wet with tears. "I remember."

"But I *didn't*, Charlie. I didn't remember. How did I not remember? I was walking through lower campus, right past the ... the statue? You know ... the statue?"

"The weird founder statue that makes him look like a southern gentleman from a Warner Brothers cartoon? Yeah."

"And there was a garden behind it, with a path down to a greenhouse. Charlie, I've walked that route *hundreds* of times, and I've never noticed it. And there was ... a Nowhere Man. On the path. I felt the air ripple, and the shock of that sensory memory was so strong everything else came rushing back. I remember everything, Charlie. About what happened. About ... Mona. Charlie, how could I *forget* what happened to Mona?

"I know," Charlie said, because he couldn't think of anything else to say.

"So ... you do remember, too? For real?"

The Professor sounded pleading, desperate to have what she was feeling, seeing, validated. Charlie thought that, if he were more mean or vindictive or sober, he might pretend to not know what she was talking about. Give her a taste, just for a little bit, of what he had felt for those first few months, when it seemed like everyone was gaslighting him, before he realized that he was the only one who remembered.

But he didn't feel vindictive tonight, and mean wasn't a good look on him, and he certainly wasn't sober, so he said "Oh yes, Prof. I remember it all, too."

The Professor sighed, deeply, in relief, and gave a little laugh.

"I'm so glad," she said. "I'm so glad I'm not alone."

Charlie almost cried at the words. *Not alone.* He had been alone for fifteen years, sitting alone for *fifteen years* with the constant conflict seesawing in his mind. Sometimes he had been able to convince himself that it was all in his head, that the monsters were just lingering effects from a bad head injury in college. Sometimes his memories of the monsters, the demon dogs, that final fight, were all too real, and he knew there was no way it was imaginary.

But now Smitha had seen one. He hadn't mentioned the monsters to Smitha since that day in the hospital, hadn't mentioned them to anyone. It couldn't be her playing into his stories, it couldn't be some sort of shared delusion. She had seen a monster. The monsters did exist.

"Charlie—I don't think it's done with us. I think ... I think I need you all to come back."

"That's a no from me, babe," Charlie said immediately.

"But Charlie—"

"You know I love you, but I've got things to see! People to do! I can't run back to campus just for a—a weird feeling."

He wandered over to the window, looked out, jumped back when he saw a Nowhere Man standing under the streetlamp a few feet away.

"But you said you remembered!" the Professor said. "Then you remember what happened last time, and—"

"Of course I remember what happened, I've spent fifteen years being the only one who remembered. I've been half wishing I could tell you for *fifteen years*. Flipping back and forth between hoping one of you would wake up and remember, so I didn't have to wonder if I was going mad, and praying none of you ever remembered a damn thing, because it is a living hell to remember. So forgive me if the whole thing seems a little less urgent to me."

The Professor gave a little gasp.

"Oh ... Charlie, I didn't realize—"

She said more, but Charlie wasn't listening, because when he looked out the window again the Nowhere Man was right outside, staring at him.

This time he didn't jump back. This time he was frozen, a fabulous but terrified little bunny staring into the eyes of an apex predator.

Those eyes, ugh. They looked wet. Full of liquid. Shimmering in the dim evening lit by streetlights, rippling like the pool, like the portal—

—and the Words were in his head, the magical nonsense that had saved his life and condemned his future fifteen years ago, rising again unbidden to his lips, and he was screaming, a mix of alien syllables and good old American vulgarity, and he raised his fist to smash the window—

and when he came back to himself the Nowhere Man was gone, the night was clear, and the Professor was calling his name over the phone.

"Charlie? Charlie! Are you okay? Is everything alright?"

He let the curtain drop over the broken window, wrapped his other hand in his T-shirt to keep from bleeding all over the carpet.

"Charlie ... *what is going on?*"

A frown twisted his lips, where tiny blisters were beginning to form.

"It's starting again."

CHAPTER

THREE

*U*pon consideration of this case, upon evidence submitted as provided by law, it is the judgment of the Court that a total divorce be granted between the parties of Joseph Thomas McCrea and Rebecca Brooke Finton-McCrea in this case. It is hereby ordered that the marriage contract entered into between the parties to this case is hereby set aside from this date, and fully dissolved.*

Joe stopped after the first paragraph. It hardly mattered anyway—uncontested, clean, practically clinical. They hadn't even needed to separate their assets, as they'd never truly joined them to begin with; their shared apartment was the only testament to anything resembling joint lives. Separate bank accounts, sure, no problems there. But in retrospect, they'd kept separate everything. Effectively independent lives which overlapped for ... hell ... eighteen months? They'd been separated longer than they'd been married.

He thought about calling somebody. It'd been two years since Becca moved out, but the finality of divorce papers, the weird ceremony of the delivery man and the signed receipt—it felt important, somehow; awful, sad, but important. And he observed the importance alone, in his small office, a lukewarm takeaway cup of coffee for comfort while he stared at next month's scheduling on his computer screen. His location, a fairly large coffee shop at the corner of the insignificant business district of Allentown, Pennsylvania, had lost two baristas this month, one to grad school and one to a continuing refusal to show up on time for work, and he was having to pencil himself into coverage for a distressing number of shifts in the coming month. He hated working the floor, in part because he'd always hated the job, and in part because it cost him time elsewhere—time he would have to make up by staying late hours. And he was salaried, a 'perk' of management, so there would be no extra money in it for him. Even if he managed to hire new staff—another drain on time —there would be on-boarding and training and months of getting them up to speed. He was looking at sixty-hour weeks for the foreseeable future.

Should he call someone? There wasn't anyone to call really, was there? He had some drinking buddies, but nobody he'd consider a 'talk about it' friend, not really. He could call his mother, perhaps. But the first divorce hadn't gone over well with her, and he was not particularly interested in a replay of that conversation six years and another failed relationship later. It could wait until Thanksgiving, when she could get out all her single mom guilt in one miserable go.

"I did the best I could," she'd say, "but it was only me and you and I always worried that you didn't have a father figure."

Joe knew it wasn't her fault. He was the screw-up.

He looked at his phone. *I should call Charlie*, he thought. A second thought crowded in and tried to shove the first thought away in shame: *I don't think he even knew I was married again.* They hadn't spoken much over the years, and the rare text or email never got into anything truly personal. *I probably should have invited him to the wedding, though. But we kept it small—I really didn't invite anybody.* The second thought came round again with another haymaker of guilt: *you invited the Professor. You knew she was unlikely to make it, but at least you sent her a courtesy invite. But for some reason you couldn't be bothered to invite your best friend.*

A third thought snapped to attention on the heels of that unexpected end to the second thought. *Best friend? Haven't used those words in a while.*

He explored it, if only to ignore the bleak reality of the scheduling sheet for another few minutes. Did he have a best friend? It had always been Charlie, hadn't it? Charlie occupied the 'best friend' space in his head within the first two weeks of freshman year and had never relinquished the title. But could you still consider someone your best friend if you'd only spoken half a dozen times in a decade? Should thirty-seven-year-old men even care about such things?

It still felt right, somehow. The bond between them was forged from steel. Unbreakable, even by the relentless erosive force of time. But still ... a phone call? How would he even start? Maybe the bonds weren't broken, but somewhere along the line a thick, dark curtain had descended between them, and he wasn't sure how to go about lifting it.

He picked up his phone. Spun it around in his palm a few times, flicking it with his thumb as it turned to keep the momentum going until he lost his grip and it skittered across his desk and onto the floor. He was about to stand up to retrieve it when his door cracked open and a worried face peered through the gap.

"You in there, boss?"

"Yeah, Ganesh, come on in."

Ganesh, a smartly dressed, handsome man in his mid-twenties, slipped in the door as he always did, opening it just enough to squeeze his narrow frame through, sideways, and then quickly and quietly shutting it behind him just as his foot cleared the gap.

"I have … that is … do you have a minute?"

Ganesh, a normally composed and comfortable man, looked nervous. Joe's heart sank. He knew the look.

"Sit down, Ganesh. Plenty of time for you. What's up?"

"Well, it's just that …" Ganesh squirmed, looking around the room. "… is that your phone on the floor, boss?"

"When are you leaving, Ganesh?" Joe asked, ignoring the question.

"I … today? I mean, if that's okay? I'll finish out the shift, of course. Only I just got a call from KerryCorps and they said I can start on Monday."

"KerryCorps, eh? A proper engineering job?"

Ganesh smiled and nodded. "Yes! Can you believe it? Nine to five, weekends off, and decent benefits, too! The starting salary is …" Ganesh frowned, stopping. "I mean, it's good, that's all. More than I asked for."

Joe smiled back. "That's great, Ganesh," he answered. And he meant it. Ganesh was a good kid. Talented, hardworking, easy to get along with. And he'd been looking for a job in his field for years. "And you start Monday, do you? That's quick."

"I know. I'm very sorry. I could call them back and ask for two weeks. I bet they'd allow it. Honestly, I should have asked right up front. But I really wanted the job, you know, and I was afraid to sound anything but one hundred percent on board, right?"

Joe shook his head. "It's fine, Ganesh. I understand. I hate to lose my best shift supervisor, but I understand. You have to take care of yourself. And this is a great opportunity. I'm honestly excited for you."

"Thanks, boss!" Ganesh said. "I really do like working

here. You're a great boss. But you can't work in a coffee shop forever, can you?"

Joe took a moment to pack that last statement away somewhere where he wouldn't have to confront it for a while. "Congratulations, buddy. Tell you what—let's go out for drinks tonight after we close up, eh?"

"I ... don't really drink, boss."

"Right, yes, sorry. Can I buy you a burger then? Or a steak? Something to celebrate?"

"Not really a meat eater," said Ganesh, a hint of an un-asked-for apology in his voice.

"Okay, okay," said Joe. "Tell you what. You pick the place, I'll buy. Whenever you want."

"Thanks, boss. That'd be ... really nice. I'm just gonna pop back out to the floor for now, right? Finish up the shift?"

Joe nodded. "Sounds good. I'll be out after I finish the scheduling to help close up."

Ganesh tossed Joe's phone back on his desk as he left. Joe looked at it, reached for it, then sighed and swiveled his chair back to face his computer. He pulled up Ganesh's name and clicked the "remove all shifts" link. Next month's calendar now looked even more bleak than it had twenty minutes ago.

Was this all he had to look forward to? Filling in shifts as other people moved on? Stuck in the same job doing the same thing, never going anywhere, never doing anything... life, it seemed, was something that happened to other people.

Gray clouds gathered in Joe's mind as the day wound to a close. Ganesh begged off of dinner, saying his wife had already started cooking a celebration dinner before he told her about Joe's offer. Joe said it was no problem. He went home.

There was some leftover Chinese in the fridge, but he didn't want that. Everything seemed like it would taste of ash. Joe knew what was happening, knew he was starting to spiral, but he was so damn tired of fighting it that this time, he just let it happen.

He was raised to take care of his business so he made a list of numbers and people who should know. He called his boss and quit, glad that the call had gone to voicemail so he didn't have to come up with a lie for why he wasn't even putting in a two weeks' notice. He got his gun out of the safe.

A picture hung on the wall across from his chair. Charlie and Joe, arm in arm, dressed to the nines, posing by the tree in front of their college apartment building. It was from Charlie's wedding day. They had asked a passing student to take a few pictures. Surrounded by a dark frame, he and Charlie grinned like goofballs, happy in life and confident about the future as only kids could be.

We were so young, Joe thought. Ignorant of what the future held. Ignorant of all the pain and loss and failure that they would face.

He looked down at the gun in his hand.

The phone rang.

Caller ID showed an unknown number, but he recognized the area code. He answered.

"Joe here. Who's this?"

"What do you mean, who's this? Joe, it's me."

It was Smitha. Her voice hit him hard, a splash of cold water in his face. He swore and stood, the gun clattering from his lap to the floor.

"Hello?"

"... Professor?" he asked.

"Hi, Joe," she said. "It's been a long time."

"Yeeeah, sorry about that. I meant to call you over the holidays, but you know how it is. Sorry," he concluded a bit helplessly. "I know I'm not much of a friend."

"No more your fault than mine," Smitha said. "Listen, Joe —I want to get everyone together. Back here, on campus."

"Why?" Joe must have realized how he sounded because he followed up too quickly with "Not that I wouldn't love to see you guys, it's just that we haven't really kept in touch. I mean, when's the last time we saw each other? The girls' wedding?"

"I believe so," Smitha said, "and Inez and Alice have been married for ten years now."

"Yeah, that's right. So, what could make you want to get us all together now?" His voice lowered. "Smitha—did someone die? Are you dying?"

"I ... no. It's not that." She hesitated. "Joe, I'm really worried that something is wrong with Charlie. I'm having him over next weekend, to try to figure out if he needs help."

"Like, an intervention?"

"Yes. I guess. And I need you to be there, Joe. He's your best friend."

Is he? Joe wondered. Whether he still was or not, he had been, at one time, one of the most important people in Joe's life. If Charlie needed him, he'd show up.

"Yeah," Joe said. "Okay. I'll be there. And hey—Smitha? I'm glad you called. Really. It's good to talk to you."

"You too, Joe. I'm looking forward to seeing you."

The call ended. Joe turned on a light, unloaded the gun, locked it up in the safe. He heated up some leftover Chinese and ate it in front of the TV. Maybe he'd call his boss back, let him know he could do one more week. Just until it was time to go back. Until someone needed him.

Charlie sat in his office and stared blankly ahead. Ostensibly he was reading the computer screen directly in front of him. A close observer would have noted, however, that he didn't blink, that his eyes didn't move from left to right, that whatever he was thinking about was not in this realm.

The small elderly lady who watched him from the doorway eventually decided to interrupt his reverie. She went back down the hallway, banged her cane against an open door, and began calling his name as if looking for him. By the time she reached the door again, Charlie seemed well out of the odd trance. He poked his head into the hallway and smiled at her.

"What brings you up here, Mrs. Fletcher?" Charlie asked.

"Looking for you," she answered. "Faith told me where you were."

"Oh? You could have just asked her to call me. I would have come downstairs for my best gal."

"Hogwash," she said, waving her hand. "If I'm your best gal, you need to get out more."

"How can I help you, Mrs. Fletcher?" asked Charlie, grinning.

"I have jury duty," she said, producing a letter. "Just got the summons."

"Oh, no problem," Charlie answered, reaching for the envelope. "That happens from time to time. I'll give them a call and get you out of it."

"You'll do no such thing," she commanded. "I want to go."

"Mrs. Fletcher, nobody wants to go to jury duty."

"I do. It'd be nice to get out for a bit and have some entertainment other than the same three dozen books I keep reading over and over. Anyway, I'm able bodied, aren't I? And I'm still pretty clear headed, thank the good Lord, although I do lose my glasses more than I used to. It's my duty. Right there in the name, isn't it? Jury duty."

"When you're right, you're right, Mrs. Fletcher. Let me talk to Lauren," Charlie said. "I'll see if I can arrange to take you myself."

THE DRIVE TO THE COURTHOUSE WAS A DELIGHT. Mrs. Fletcher had lived her entire life in Pittsburgh and spent the thirty-minute trip acting as an eager tour guide and historian for her chauffeur. After seeing her to the right room, Charlie went back to work. A monster walked past the window in the middle of a staff meeting. He stared at his binder and fidgeted with a pen so hard part of the cap cracked.

A few hours later Charlie drove back to the courthouse to pick up his charge. A security guard escorted her out to the car. She thanked him by name and patted his cheek before settling into the passenger seat. Mrs. Fletcher had not been selected to serve, but she'd had a wonderful day in jury selection, made several new friends, and couldn't stop talking about how kind everyone had been to her.

"The judge was such a nice man," she said for the second or third time. "He gave me a little cushion for my seat—those wooden benches were very uncomfortable. He said I'm the oldest person they've had show up all year."

Charlie smiled at her. "Good for you, Mrs. Fletcher!"

"And a lovely young girl next to me saw the book in my purse, and it turns out her mom reads the same author. Jan Karon. She said her mom has tried to get her to read them too, but she's just not much of a reader."

Charlie nodded. "Some folks aren't."

"So do you know what I told her? I told her about the books on tape that you can get on your phone now. Faith was telling us all about them. She said all you need is a library card and you can get books on tape right to your phone. I haven't done it yet, but it sounds very interesting. I'm sure they have Jan Karon books, she's quite popular. She's nearly my age, you know. And still writing. If she can write books, I can certainly go to jury duty."

They were nearing the end of the drive and Charlie found himself wishing it could go on. He was in a difficult mood, and the cheerful Mrs. Fletcher was good for him. He'd never heard her quite so energized. On a whim, he drove right past Hickory Glen.

"You missed our turn, Charlie," said Mrs. Fletcher, pointing as they drove past.

"Mrs. Fletcher, I am in the mood for ice cream, and I thought you might like to join me. What do you say—can we sneak off for dessert before our dinner? There's an ice cream shop just a few blocks away."

She turned a keen eye on him. "That sounds wonderful, Charlie. And it will give us a little more time to talk."

It turned out that Mrs. Fletcher knew the lady behind the counter. They chatted for ten minutes before she got them settled at their best table with two bowls of ice cream.

"Sally's mother was the nicest girl," Mrs. Fletcher said, waving at the serving lady with her spoon. "She went to school with my daughter Beth. Now, you seem like you've got something on your mind. Care to tell me about it?"

"Mrs. Fletcher," Charlie said, "I made a big mistake."

Mrs. Fletcher nodded sagely.

"I'm not surprised," she said. "Want to tell me about it?"

Charlie poked a spoon into his ice cream and looked around. The little ice cream shop was pretty quiet.

"Why the hell not?" he said.

"Language."

"Sorry, Mrs. Fletcher."

Mrs. Fletcher patted his hand. She was in a good mood today on the heels of her successful trip to the courthouse. It had brought out the best in her, igniting her with a bit of fire. She was as sharp as Charlie had ever seen her and appeared to be waiting for him to unburden himself.

"I'm out with a handsome young man on an ice cream date," she said. "Tell me your story and take as much time as you need. I did plenty of talking on the drive, now it's your turn."

For a moment, Charlie nearly lost it and almost told her the whole thing, start to finish, monsters and portals and all. He watched her wrinkled hand lift a spoonful of buttered rum to her pruning mouth and wondered how she'd react. Honestly, she might not bat an eye. Mrs. Fletcher seemed like she'd seen some things in her day.

But no, he couldn't do that. Telling someone else, someone who hadn't been there—it just didn't seem right. Not for the first time, Charlie wondered if that was why Smitha hadn't gotten serious with Beau yet. She clearly liked him, and from everything he could gather it seemed like Beau was pretty into her. Knowing Smitha, it would be impossible for her to get close to someone without telling them about Mona and the pool house. Even if she didn't remember, somewhere part of her knew it had happened. Maybe that part was keeping her from getting close.

So no, Charlie, don't be a fool. Don't tell the truth.

"It's not that big of a deal," he said. "I told a friend I would come visit but it turns out I really don't want to. She's going to be really disappointed when I tell her I'm not coming."

Mrs. Fletcher hmmmed.

"And why don't you want to go?"

Charlie's fears crowded his brain, a clamor of thoughts he couldn't bring himself to say. *Because going back means confronting a truth that I'm dying to be true. That I'm not sure I want to accept. It means a final reckoning for my sanity. It means opening up that door I've kept closed for so long. It means talking to Joe. Looking him in the eye and watching him decide how far around the bend I've gone. It means pity. Or fear. Or both.*

Charlie swallowed a mouthful of ice cream quickly, letting the cold sweetness grab the words and pull them back down his throat.

"Because," he said, opting for a simpler truth, "there was a friend of ours that was in an accident. A really bad accident, a long time ago. Our friend—she died. And the other friend, the one who wants me to visit, lives in the same town where that happened."

"Was it your friend's fault the accident happened? The first friend, not the one who died."

It was mine, it was my fault, it was all my fault. Those words Charlie could never push away, could never stop their endless cycle in his thoughts.

"No," he said. "It wasn't her fault."

"And you want to see her, this friend?"

"Yes. I really do."

Mrs. Fletcher pointed her spoon at Charlie.

"Then you go," she said emphatically. "Charlie, I've lost too many friends over the years. Too many. What I wouldn't give to see them again ... And you think there weren't any bad memories with them? Of course there were! Any good friendship will have bad memories. My girlfriends and I used to say we were friends sour and sweet. It meant we'd be there for each other no matter what. And we were, too! You think driving Cheryl home from the hospital after her husband passed was sweet? Or when Ruthie's boy was killed in that accident, and we took her to identify the body? Or when Krista got diagnosed with cancer for the third time? I tell you, it would have been easier to just send a sympathy card and pray it never happened to us and get on with our own lives. But that's not sour and sweet friendship."

Mrs. Fletcher put down the spoon and took Charlie's hand.

"You're young," she said. "Oh, I know you think you're old, but believe me—you're young. And you will have more bad in your life, Charlie. Maybe more bad than good, I'm sorry to say. Sometimes life is like that. But there will be sweet moments, too. And they're worth the sour."

Charlie swallowed hard. The lingering sweetness of the ice cream turned his mouth bitter. Her words had cut him. What kind of a friend was he? He'd go back. He would.

"Mrs. Fletcher," he said, "you are wise."

She made a psh sound.

"I'm just old. You'll seem wise, too, when you're my age."

I am going to go back. I am. Charlie repeated the refrain to himself as he saw Mrs. Fletcher safely back to her room and promised to sneak her out for another ice cream date soon. *I am going to go back. I am.*

He was almost home when his phone rang. It was the Professor.

"Charlie, hi! This a good time?"

"Sure, Prof. What's up?"

"I'm planning meals for next weekend and I need some help. What do you want to eat?"

"Well, I—"

He swung the car into the parking lot behind his building and stopped cold. There were monsters waiting for him. Three of them, just standing, watching him with their fishbowl eyes in their nightmare hatchet faces. A demon dog prowled at their feet, hungry slavering jaws open wide in a miserable parody of a grin.

"I—"

The monsters approached, lurching together in sickening synchrony. They would attack him all at once, damn it. It was going to be like it was before, with Inez in the pool house, with their grabbing arms and the black hole inevitability of their gaping rib bone mouths. He could already feel the fear start to settle around him.

He had avoided it this long, but this was it. He was going to die in his crappy car surrounded by drive-through garbage.

"Charlie?"

The Professor's voice snapped him out of the near fugue.

"Charlie, are you okay?"

All his emotions got shoved to the side and a stone wall shot up around them. He threw the gear shift into reverse and backed out of the lot, then slammed into drive and rocketed down the alley that led back to the main street.

"I'm not coming, Professor. I'm sorry."

"But—"

"Yeah, I've got a work thing. And I think I'm coming down with something, probably picked up a death plague from one of the residents, don't want to spread that around.

And my car's on the fritz and yeah, you guys'll do fine, you don't even need me."

"I think we do ..."

"Nah. Look, say hi to Joe and the pups for me. Maybe I'll find time to come visit another weekend."

"Charlie, I really think—"

"Hey, I've got to hang up, the cops are really strict on this stretch of road. I'll talk to you later, Prof."

He hung up before she could get out anything more than his name.

The closest bar was called Hurry Sundown. Charlie started a tab and drank for an hour until the stone wall came down and he had to pay up and go outside so no one would see him break down in tears.

"I'm a coward," he told a piece of cartoon graffiti on the sidewalk. "An utter coward. And a bad friend. I don't deserve them as friends, you know? They're so damn good and I'm such a screw up. I'm a mess."

He threw up, considerately missing the sympathetic graffiti. Then Charlie called a cab and went home to fall into oblivion for the rest of the night.

CHAPTER

FIVE

The light bulb in the hallway was out again. It wasn't a big deal by itself, but to Alice, arriving home to an empty apartment after a long day of minor annoyances, it was the proverbial last straw. She asked—demanded, if she was being honest—that Inez fix it as soon as the other woman walked through the door. Inez, attacked by the sudden demand, told Alice to do it herself.

"You know I can't reach up there!"

Alice tried to keep the frustration out of her voice, but it was hard when Inez was doing that face she hated.

"That's why we have step stools," Inez pointed out.

"They don't help!" Alice shot back.

Inez rolled her eyes—a move she knew Alice found irritating—and huffed over to pull the step stool out of the closet. She grabbed the replacement bulb out of Alice's hand.

"I'm going to get the mail," Alice announced, and spent the time in the elevator going to the ground floor trying to calm down. She took a few deep breaths, watched the traffic pass on the street outside, and patted the lobby dog before going back upstairs.

Inez sat on the couch angrily reading a magazine. The hallway light bulb shone brightly. Alice put the mail in the kitchen and sat on the far end of the couch.

"I'm sorry," she said.

Inez turned the page.

"I shouldn't have snapped at you," Alice continued. "It was a long day. And I hate that I can't do it for myself and have to bother you about it. And I had nightmares again last night and—ugh, but that doesn't matter, that's not an excuse for me to be a jerk to you, and I'm sorry."

Inez shut the magazine.

"I'm sorry, too," she said. "Come here."

They snuggled together, Inez stroking Alice's hair. A glint shone on Inez's wrist and Alice reached down to play with the charm that read *forever* in silver script; a gift from Alice long, long ago. Alice's fingers on the silver word softened Inez's hard shell of annoyance.

"It was a bad day for me, too," Inez said. "That meeting in the morning didn't go as well as I had hoped and, uh, I had an episode."

Alice looked up at her wife, concern writ large on her expressive face.

"Oh, Inez."

"In the breakroom, yeah. It was short. Jeff was there and he's dealt with that before, he knew to keep calling my name and stuff, but I just keep thinking, what if it had been in the middle of the meeting? Or when I was driving home? Or what if I had been alone? What if there hadn't been anyone to ... bring me back ...?"

Alice sat up and took Inez's face in her hands.

"Hey. Babe. I will always bring you back. Always."

Inez kissed her.

"I know, Alice. I know."

"Are you going to tell Dr. Stadler?" Alice asked. Inez made

a face. Their therapist was fine but had never really been able to get to the root of Inez's waking nightmares.

"I don't know," she began. Alice interrupted her.

"'Nez, that's what she's there for."

"I know, but how many times can I say 'I feel like I stop existing' before she comes up with something more useful than 'pinch yourself'?"

"You know she's done more than that," Alice chided.

"I know, I know. But none of it has helped."

"I know."

They kissed again, lingering this time. Physical touch helped Inez stay grounded and Alice was more than happy to provide.

Alice's cell phone rang. She looked at Inez.

"Go ahead," Inez said, sitting up and straightening her shirt. She didn't look angry, or disappointed. She didn't look much of anything. Alice frowned but answered the phone.

"Hello?"

"Alice? This is Smitha. How are you?"

"Professor?"

Inez cocked her head in surprise. Alice put the phone on speaker.

"Yeah, hi! This isn't a bad time, is it?"

"No, no, this is fine," Alice said. "It's great to hear from you. How have you been?"

The conversation was awkward, stilted, the joints of it still there but crusted with rust. They creaked their way through the pleasantries until Smitha said "So listen. The reason I called."

Finally, Inez mouthed. Alice threw a pillow at her.

"It's Charlie," Smitha continued. "I'm worried about him."

"Haven't you been worried about him for the last fifteen years?" Alice asked, teasing.

"Oh, longer than that." Smitha chuckled but didn't sound amused. "Next weekend is Homecoming, on campus, you know, and I thought it'd be good for him to come visit."

"Sure," Inez agreed.

"I don't know if he'd make the trip just for me, though. You girls always had him wrapped around your fingers. Maybe if he knew you would be here, too ..."

Alice looked at Inez. Inez shrugged and frowned. Alice shrugged back. Inez shook her head a little. Alice turned away and said "Sure, Smitha, we'll come out. It'll be nice to see everyone. Should we meet on campus, or at a restaurant, or a hotel or something?"

"Well, I had hoped maybe everyone would stay with me. At my house. It's close enough to walk to campus, and I have plenty of room, and it's free ..."

Free was good, Alice agreed. Smitha gave her the address and they set the arrival time for the next weekend, Friday evening, before dinner.

"We'll have to take the day off work, to make it for dinner," Inez pointed out after Alice hung up.

"Yeah. But we have the time."

"We've been saving it for a vacation," Inez protested.

"This is kind of like a vacation," Alice said. "Anyway, what vacation? You never want to go anywhere."

They bickered on and off until bedtime.

***

Marv's Cones opened on the first day of Ravencrest's fall semester and closed the day after graduation. For twenty years Marvin and a string of young employees had served sweet treats to college students; sundaes and waffle cones and ice cream sandwiches on sunny days, rainy days, and snowy ones, too. When the weather was good the kids sat outside at the worn picnic tables or perched on the stone wall separating the stand from the 7-11 behind it. In snow or rain they packed inside, squabbling for the few chairs and complaining in chorus every time the door opened.

"Another hour and we'll close," Marvin declared. The rain outside was building up into a real storm and he wanted to get home before the worst arrived. There were three people in one of the booths, highschoolers, it looked like; their heads close together over their milkshakes in teenage confidence. The rest of the store was empty.

Anthony, working the register, shrugged. "Why not close as soon as they're gone? I doubt we get anyone else tonight."

Marvin hesitated. It wasn't so much about losing business. He knew that everyone used Marv's as a landmark, and if someone was out in the storm and needed shelter he wanted to be open for them. But Anthony was right. No one was going to be out in this.

"Sure," he said, giving in. "As soon as Betty and her friends leave, we'll shut up for the night."

Ten minutes later the kids headed out the door and Marvin locked it behind them. He flipped the sign to "Closed" and helped Anthony wipe down tables, zero out the cash register, and take out the trash.

"Need a ride back to the dorm?" Marvin asked as Anthony shrugged on a raincoat.

"Nah, I'm fine. It's out of the way for you."

"I don't mind."

"I know you don't. Go ahead on home."

Marvin smiled and patted Anthony on the shoulder. He was a good kid.

The taillights of Marvin's car headed toward town and Anthony headed toward campus. The rain was heavier now, slapping against his big black Ravencrest branded umbrella. He could have used the ride, but Marvin wasn't getting any younger and Anthony knew driving in bad weather made his boss nervous. It was nice, anyway, walking down the deserted sidewalk. Everything was quiet.

A shape formed out of the dark just ahead of him. Assuming it to be someone walking the opposite way, Anthony pulled his hand out of his pocket in preparation for a wave. Ravencrest University—Ravencrest the town, too—was small. If it was a student or professor, he probably knew them. If it was a townie, well, they deserved a wave of camaraderie for their rainy walk.

It wasn't any of those.

It took Anthony a moment to realize what he was seeing. By the time his brain realized that in front of him was a monster, a real live monster with jutting rib bones and slavering jaws, it was too late. Fear had frozen him to the spot.

The monster drew him forward and Anthony felt himself start to flow away. It was cold. The bright yellow-white light from the streetlamp filled his vision until everything was white. The boy faded.

The next morning, after Marvin left the home he kept by himself and opened up Marv's Cones, he put a Help Wanted sign in the window. His last assistant had graduated the spring before and with the beginning of the semester always so busy, it would be nice to have someone else in the shop.

***

Charlie danced by himself, ignoring the rest of the club and letting the deep beat of the music pound away unwelcome thoughts. It was Friday night, and he wasn't where he was supposed to be.

He silenced his phone so he couldn't hear Smitha's calls, every hour on the hour regularly, pleading in their sheer number. The messages she left might be pleading, too, he didn't know. He hadn't listened to any.

He could guess the general content of the messages, though. He should be there, at Smitha's house, having a council of war with his old friends. They needed him to fight the monsters. They couldn't do it without him. Please.

A fool's errand, he thought. No point in ganging up against the monsters. They'd tried before and lost. They'd—he'd—lost everything.

Was it the end of the world? If so, he might as well spend it here, with drink and song and good-looking strangers like the man who approached him and asked, "Want to dance?"

They swayed together to the pulsing music from a band Charlie had never heard of. The man introduced himself as Judah and Charlie flirted with him from habit, distracted and sad and papering it over with fake frivolity and charm.

Judah leaned over and whispered in Charlie's ear, his carefully cultivated stubble scratching Charlie's cheek, "You don't seem too into this scene. Do you want to go somewhere else?"

Charlie blinked.

"Actually, yes," he said. "Do you want to go for a walk?"

After the heat and noise of the club the cool night was a shock. The clouds shone above, and the soft whoosh of cars passing threw Charlie back to walks he'd taken with his friends. His family.

"I used to walk like this all the time," he began.

Judah listened as Charlie told him everything—the real everything, about monsters and magic words and Mona. Everything about the portal and the pool house and his friends who were, if Smitha had been successful, even now gathered to try to do it all over again.

"I don't even know why I'm telling you," Charlie finished

lamely, "except that I had to tell someone or my brain would have burst."

"I guess I'm that lucky someone," Judah said.

"You're the one who asked to dance," said Charlie, cavalier, although he snuck a look over to see how his companion was reacting. Judah seemed nonplussed, taking it all in stride. At first Charlie was surprised, until he realized that Judah probably thought he, Charlie, was on drugs.

"Sorry," he muttered.

"For what, man? You tell a good story."

A story. If Charlie could think of it as a story, something that happened once upon a time in a kingdom far away, maybe he could get through this.

Charlie wished he was on drugs. It couldn't have made his brain any more messed up than it was.

Judah stopped walking and took Charlie's hand.

"Hey," he said, "I'm sorry about all that stuff that happened. But how about this. I'm going to kiss you now and make you forget about your monsters for tonight, okay?"

"Okay," Charlie agreed. Judah was attractive, and his voice was gentle, and his hands as he put them on either side of Charlie's face were soft and warm.

They kissed in the cold night. Judah's hands slipped behind Charlie's neck. Charlie pulled him closer, pouring as much as he could offer into the kiss.

A car passed, the driver honking, the passengers cheering out the window. Charlie and Judah drew apart.

"Well okay," Judah said. "That is what I'm talking about."

"Not bad," Charlie admitted.

"Not bad! It was damn good and you know it."

"Yeah, okay." The indignant look on Judah's face made him smile faintly.

They turned around and started walking back toward the bar, holding hands, talking of unimportant things.

"Look, man," Judah said during a break in the conversation. "Not to dredge up, like, painful mental stuff, but—why aren't you going back? You know, to your college."

"Well ..." Charlie muttered.

"Yeah, that's what I thought. You're scared, I get that. But isn't it kind of, well, shitty, pardon, to not go?"

Charlie stopped walking and turned to Judah. The other man seemed to be in earnest. Maybe Charlie had misjudged him. Maybe he believed in Charlie's story after all.

"I'm just saying," Judah went on. "These monster things, right? They like, eat people out of reality? And your best friend saw one? And you're not going to help her?" He shook his head. "Like I said, kind of shitty. Pardon my language."

Echoed in Judah's words, Charlie heard Mrs. Fletcher. "Sour and sweet," she had said.

"Give me a minute," Charlie mumbled. He shivered with a sudden cold chill and walked away from Judah, hands in his pockets, to stay warm. His right hand bumped against his phone. Charlie pulled it out and checked the notifications while he was walking—a bunch of missed calls, all from Smitha. The sudden reality of what he was doing hit him like a brick wall. Monsters were back on campus, and he was leaving the Professor to deal with it on her own? Without him? Without the Words?

"What a shitty thing to do," Charlie told himself. He began walking quickly back to where he had parked. His idle walk, as always, had brought some clarity. Walks were always better with someone else, but even alone this one had helped.

Soon he could see his car parked on the street in front of the bar. Once he was back home, he could pack up quick and be on the road within the hour.

A thick, mucousy growling began in the alley to his left. Charlie turned his head.

"Charlie. Please call back."

Smitha hung up the phone and turned back to the three pairs of eyes watching her.

"Still nothing?" Alice asked.

"I'm afraid not."

Joe scowled. The expression sat lopsided on his open face.

"I came here for him and he couldn't even be bothered to show up."

Alice and Inez sat on the same couch, but with too much distance between them. The drive to campus had been long and tense.

"Well, at least we can enjoy Homecoming, right?" Alice attempted.

"Um," Smitha said.

"Homecoming? What? Is this weekend Homecoming?"

"What did you think we were here for?" Inez snarked.

"An intervention!" Joe said. "For Charlie. That's what Smitha said."

"Um," Smitha said again.

A demon dog stepped into the street.

In his memories and nightmares, the dog monsters were huge. Shadow creatures the size of horses hunted him with shark rows of sharp teeth and flames of Hell red eyes. The real thing was not much better. It was not horse size, but it did look like it'd reach Charlie's waist. There was a stench of rotting meat and dusty old potatoes. Its eyes really were red.

"Good doggie," Charlie rasped.

The monster dropped low to the ground, snarled, and bolted forward.

Charlie flinched back but reached out his hand to the monster.

"Evna," he began. "No, wait, damn, *ehan.*"

The word spit from his lips. Tiny sparks of fire fizzled and died on his tongue. The dog thing whimpered, shied to the side. Charlie's brief thrill of victory shriveled as the creature changed course and broke back toward him.

Charlie stepped forward and met the demon dog. As the monster's jaws closed around his arm, the magic Words flamed. Charlie and the monster burned.

CHAPTER

SIX

"No. That's absurd."

Joe stood abruptly and started pacing.

"I know it sounds that way," Smitha said, "and if I hadn't seen one of those things and remembered, I would have thought so too."

"That's a hell of a thing to forget," Inez pointed out. "A portal to another world? Monsters that what, eat people? There's no way that's real."

"I don't know," Alice said. Inez and Joe looked at her, surprised.

"Do you remember something?" Smitha asked.

"Not for sure. But maybe ... I mean, in nightmares and stuff. And Inez, think about your attacks. What if that's like our brains trying to make us remember?"

"There's nothing to remember!" Joe said. "None of that happened! There were no monsters, no portals."

"But Joe—" Smitha began.

"Don't you think we'd remember how Mona died?"

Joe stood from the table, his knee banging against the underside and creating a small shockwave which sent Alice's phone clattering to the floor.

"I'm going to make dinner," he announced with a growl.

"Joe, wait—" Inez started.

Smitha hurried to stand up as well. "It's my house, you are my guests, I'll make dinner."

Alice frowned at the word *guest*.

"I'm going to make dinner," Joe repeated and stomped off through the dining room, his purposeful stride somewhat offset by his unfamiliarity with the house. A moment later the remaining three at the table heard cabinets clattering open.

"Professor, when was the last time you talked to Joe?" Inez asked, fishing Alice's phone from the floor near her feet and sliding it into her wife's lap.

"Wednesday," Smitha said. "When I called to invite him."

"To guilt him," Alice corrected.

"To lie to him," Inez followed, earning another frown from Alice.

"It wasn't a lie, not entirely," Smitha started.

"Tell Joe, not us," Alice answered. "No, tell all of us. But not until Joe is back."

"I already told you all—"

"Not about the portals and monsters. Still not sure how I feel about *that*, by the way. Tell us why you thought you had to lie to us to get us here."

"I just—"

"Not until Joe is back," Alice reminded her.

"A different question, Professor," Inez asked. "When was the last time you talked to Joe *before* Wednesday?"

"It's been ... a little while," Smitha allowed.

"Three years ago in March," Alice said. "For me. I checked my phone. A few texts or emails in between, but the last time I *talked* to him was almost three years ago. Inez said it's about the same for her."

Inez nodded. "We were talking about it on the way up. We

talk with you sometimes, and Charlie calls every now and then—"

"Usually at two in the morning, when he's drunk," Alice said.

"Still, he calls. Sometimes. And we call him on his birthday, don't we? But we haven't talked to Joe in ages."

"He doesn't like the phone," Smitha pointed out.

"Yeah, I know," Inez answered. "'Joe doesn't like the phone.' That's what we always say to forgive ourselves for not talking to him."

"He could call us," Smitha said.

"Of course he could," Inez snapped. "But he doesn't, does he? And we don't call him. It's been three years since we've talked. Longer since I've seen him in person."

"Professor?" Joe yelled from the kitchen. "Where do you keep the vegetable oil?"

"Cabinet above the stove," she yelled back. "Do you need me to—"

"No!"

The three women looked at each other. Smitha's phone rang, startling them all as it rattled on the tabletop in front of them. She shrugged and retrieved it, but just stared at it while the ringtone played on.

"Is it Charlie?" Alice asked.

"No ..."

"You can get that if it's important," Inez said.

"It's not—I mean, it's just Beau," Smitha said as the noise stopped. "He'll leave a voicemail."

Alice picked up on the hint of a smile that rolled across her friend's face.

"Beau? Who's Beau?"

"That sounds like a fake name," Inez said.

"He's just a friend," Smitha said quickly. Her phone dinged to indicate a voicemail had indeed been left. Smitha couldn't help but glance down at the transcript. She smiled again, a bit fuller.

"Just a friend?" Alice asked with a laugh.

Smitha nodded, but nobody believed her.

They sat in silence for a time, listening to the sounds of Joe clattering around in the kitchen. The cooking batter smell was homey and comforting, even in the chill that surrounded the three women.

"So," Alice tried after a few minutes, "how are things with the college?"

"Fine," Smitha said. "Fine. Enrollment is really high right now, so I've got full classes. I like that."

"Are they anything like we were?" Alice asked. "I don't really hang out with eighteen-year-olds very often."

Smitha shook her head.

"After fifteen years of teaching, they all just seem so young. I know we were, but I don't remember us being that young."

Joe reentered the room, carrying a stack of empty plates in one hand and a serving dish stacked high with pancakes in the other. He disappeared to the kitchen again and emerged with four mugs of coffee, two per hand, in a precarious but well-practiced balancing act. Each mug, handed out, was made just the way they had each liked it two decades ago. Inez enjoyed hers darker these days. She drank it anyway.

Joe made one final trip to the kitchen, ignoring Smitha's protests that they could have helped him carry things out, and came back with an arm full of extras, naming them as he dropped them on the table.

"Syrup. Butter." He grimaced. "Peanut butter."

"You remembered!" Alice clapped her hands together with a grin.

Joe watched her slather butter and peanut butter on the pancakes with only partially exaggerated disgust.

"You haven't broken her of that yet?" he asked Inez, who was drowning her plate in syrup.

"I pick my battles," she said.

"Pancakes were an inspired choice," Smitha said. "A proper family meal."

"Not a *guest* meal?" Alice quizzed. Inez kicked her under the table.

Joe frowned. They ate, the food becoming an easy excuse for the uncomfortable silence between them.

When Smitha finished, she began collecting dirty dishes. As she picked up Joe's plate, she forced herself to speak.

"Thanks," she said. "For cooking. It's been a long time since somebody has cooked for me. I usually do it myself. Or order in," she added. "Probably more the latter than the former, if I'm honest."

"You haven't cooked for Beau yet?" Alice teased.

Joe, who had been avoiding eye contact, sat up.

"Beau? Who's Beau? That sounds like a fake name."

"That's what *I* said!" Inez chimed in. Joe grinned at her.

"He's just a friend," Smitha said quickly.

"A friend she wants to kiss," Alice clarified. Joe grinned again.

Smitha scowled at her. "I do not. I don't. Well, I don't *not* want to kiss him. Okay, yes. I do. I do want to kiss him. But I don't think he wants to kiss me. Or at least, I'm not sure yet."

"Have you asked him?" Joe replied.

"*No.*"

"Maybe you should consider it," he said, his eyes twinkling.

"Maybe *you* should consider staying out of my business," Smitha snarled, rallying her anger to override her embarrassment at hearing her own self-excoriations coming out of her old friend's mouth. Immediately she flushed and clapped a hand to her own mouth. "Oh, Joe, I'm sorry," she said. "It's a tough situation and I ..."

"No, you're right," said Joe, standing up. "It is not my business. It's late. I think I'll just turn in."

"Joe—"

"The pancakes were delicious," Inez cut in, trying to stall any further conflict. "Thank you."

Joe grunted.

"So ... I guess we should get to bed, too," Alice added. She stood and stretched, faking a yawn that soon turned into a real one.

"If you'd like," Smitha said, her voice small. "Let me show you to your room."

"That's okay," Inez said. "We saw it when we brought our luggage in."

Smitha waited until she heard the bedroom doors close before allowing herself to cry.

PART TWO
FIFTEEN YEARS AGO

CHAPTER

SEVEN

The green door banged open. It ricocheted off the wall and swung back. Its painted panels were out for vengeance but were foiled by the rubber toe of a canvas shoe jammed forward to stop its advance. This sent it careening back on a return trip into the wall that was too much for the old door. It cracked along its top hinge, swinging to an ignoble stop at a cockeyed angle, hanging limp and crooked. A lanky young man in black skinny jeans and a faux western shirt with white embroidered pockets and pearl snaps slipped past it and into the room, depositing a long, green duffle on the floor with a thud. He tossed his blond hair out of his eyes with a twist of his neck and grinned.

"Am I the last one to the party?" he asked. A wiffle ball whistled across the room and bounced off his head.

"I knew you were gonna break the door one of these days, Charlie." A tall, broad-shouldered man unfolded himself from a couch on the far wall and stepped toward the newcomer. He wore a Ravencrest College T-shirt and athletic shorts that had seen better days.

"Never liked that ugly green color anyway," Charlie

answered, meeting his friend in the center of the room as they wrapped each other in an enormous hug. "Good to see you again, Joe. I've missed you."

"I just saw you two weeks ago, goofball. You met me and Dad at the Planet of the Apes marathon at The Arthur, remember? And you painted that door sophomore year when we moved in."

"No wonder all mankind thirsted for my blood," Charlie mused.

Before they could separate, another body slammed into them as a small woman with a giant braid ducked beneath the akimbo door.

"Joe! Charlie!" she exclaimed as the hug expanded to include her. "Oh, I love you boys so much. What happened to the door?"

"I see you've brought the female of your species," answered Charlie.

Smitha looked at Joe.

"He's doing a Planet of the Apes thing," Joe offered by way of explanation. He laughed and rolled his eyes as he tried to disentangle himself from his friends. "We've missed you, too, Professor."

"Can someone get the door?"

Standing at the top of the staircase which led to the apartment that occupied the entire top floor of the small building was their fourth and final roommate. Their family was complete.

"Mona!" Smitha exclaimed. "Your hair! I love it!"

Mona winked beneath her purple tipped bangs.

"Aw, am I the last one?" she asked. "Guess I'm buying dinner. If I can ever get inside."

"I've got it," Joe said, stepping over to lift the crooked door. He tried to line it up enough to swing it the rest of the way open, but the second hinge gave way when he lifted and the top of the door cracked off his head.

"Joe!" Mona yelped, skipping into the room as Joe grunted and leaned the door against an interior wall. "You're bleeding!"

Joe reached a hand up to his temple. It was slick with blood.

"He bleeds!" crowed Charlie. "The Lawgiver bleeds!"

"Professor?" asked Mona.

"It's a movie thing, I think," Smitha answered. "Ask Joe."

Joe waved a bloody hand in a vague motion. "Planet of the Apes," he said. "Did anybody pack any band-aids? Or ... bigger band-aids? Or stitches and a doctor who knows how to do stitches?"

"The Professor's mom is a doctor," Mona said. "Professor, did you pack your mom this year?"

"No, I did not pack my mother to bring to college," Smitha laughed. "Although she'd probably come if I asked. She hates when summer's over."

"Here, I've got this," said Charlie, unbuttoning and shrugging out of his shirt so he could pull off the t-shirt underneath. He wrapped it around Joe's head like a bandana, tying it in the back to hold it in place.

"Gross," Joe said. "Smells like sweat. This can't be hygienic."

"First of all, I don't sweat; I glisten. Second, I smell like your next, best boyfriend."

"Nah, man," Joe laughed. "You're way out of my league."

"I don't mind slumming for you," Charlie replied, and blew his friend a kiss.

"Uh, hey. Hi. I think I have some hydrogen peroxide," said a voice from the doorway. A young woman was peering in through the empty door frame from underneath swooping black bangs dyed blue at the tips.

"Who's the kid?" asked Mona.

"Dunno, darling. I've never seen her before," said Charlie, pulling his faux-western shirt back on but leaving the snaps hanging open. "Professor? Lawgiver?"

Joe shrugged; Smitha shook her head.

"Great hair, kid," Mona said. "Who are you?"

"Alice Martin."

"Hello, Alice Martin," Smitha said. "Not that we don't like meeting new friends, but... why are you at our door?"

"Looked open?" suggested Alice, unable to hide a grin.

Charlie laughed.

"Listen," she continued, "I have some hydrogen peroxide downstairs, if you want me to get it."

"Oh, you must be the new neighbor," Smitha said. Alice nodded.

"I'm in 1A."

"What happened to Tibbs?" asked Charlie.

"Tibbs is in 1B," Mona answered. "He's already here, I saw that beat up Blues Brothers poster hanging on his door. He comes early for band camp."

"1B? Really?"

"Yeah, he moved across the hall last year. Remember? You taped extra paper around the number on his door so it said 'T1Bbs.' "

"Right. Who is in 1A, then?"

"Uh, me?" interjected the new girl.

Charlie waved a hand. "I meant who *was* in 1A."

"Freddy Ernst," Smitha supplied.

"The handsome Dutch fella, right!" Charlie said, snapping his fingers. "What happened to handsome Freddy?"

"Graduated. Summer courses," said Joe, still pushing Charlie's shirt against the wound in his head. "What's hydrogen peroxide?"

"Ugh, graduated? Really? I'm going to miss that boy," Charlie lamented.

"We lived in the same building for three years and you never spoke to him," said Smitha.

"But he was always doing those soccer workouts in the yard. Didn't need to talk to him, I just liked watching." Charlie turned to Alice hopefully. "You don't happen to play soccer, do you, 1A?"

"What? Uh ... no?"

"Field hockey? Volleyball?"

"No?"

Charlie sighed. "I do love a body in uniform." Mona slapped him on the arm.

"Hydrogen peroxide is an antiseptic, Joe," said Smitha.

"Thanks, Professor. You have some, Alice?"

"Aww, look at her," Mona teased. "Charlie, you're scaring the new girl."

"No, he isn't," said Alice. "And yes, I do. Have some, that is. Hydrogen peroxide. That is, if you were talking to me. Things are a little hard to follow around here."

Charlie threw back his head and laughed from deep within his chest. When truly amused, Charlie's laugh could break through clouds like a summer sun. "1A, you have no idea."

"Why do you have hydrogen peroxide?" asked Mona. "Not that I'm complaining."

"I think my mom packed an entire pharmacy," Alice explained. "I've not really been away from home before, and she's convinced I'm going to die at college."

"Wait, you're a freshman?" Charlie frowned. "I didn't think freshmen were allowed to live off campus."

Alice nodded. "Usually, yeah. I was waitlisted. I only found out I got in this week, and there are no rooms left in the freshman dorms."

"Guys, she's a freshman," said Charlie. "I was flirting with a freshman."

"You'll flirt with anyone, Charlie," Mona pointed out.

"Not freshmen," Charlie protested.

"Since when?" asked Mona. "You flirted with me when I was a freshman."

"I was a freshman, too! I'm a senior now," answered Charlie. "Sorry, freshman. No offense."

Alice laughed. "Flirt away, old man. But you should probably know that boys are not my thing."

"Old man. Old man? You wound me."

"Speaking of wounds," interjected Joe, a hint of impatience in his voice. "Remember me? The guy bleeding from his head? Maybe we can get on with the hydroplane whatever it is? And get your stinking sweat out of the actual wound on my head?"

"Let's go down to my place," Alice suggested.

Felix Tibbs marched down the sidewalk, unconsciously staying in step with the cadence in his head. A few hours of marching band practice had drilled the beat into his head. His curly red hair bounced in time. All around him parents and students were rushing to and from cars, arms piled high with boxes and pillows. Old friends greeted each other loudly, new friends smiled shyly as they passed, and the campus, so quiet all summer, exploded with life.

Tibbs had been in town for band camp for the past week, so he mostly ignored the hubbub of move-in day. The chaos grew less as he headed off campus. Still humming the cadence, he stepped off the well-maintained college sidewalk and, unknowingly, into a nightmare.

Tibbs passed into a part of the road where several old

trees towered over the path, their mature canopies blocking out much of the bright early autumn sun. Among their gently swaying shadows hid one that was sharper, deadlier. It followed Tibbs, who shivered at the sudden cold and thought it was the shadows that had lowered the temperature.

"Buh bum bah dum," Tibbs sang, the music finally breaking out.

Just ahead the canopy opened up and he could see, in the resumed sunlight, the side street that led to the house.

Tibbs heard a sound behind him and glanced back, ready to make way for a jogger or a reunited couple seeking a little privacy. His feet stopped short, not of their own volition, as a freezing cold fear seeped into him. Steps behind, a monster reached out with sharp, grasping ribs.

"What—" Tibbs managed. The only answer was intense fear and a sharp tug as the monster began to feed. There was loss, and absence, and darkness, and then, finally, nothing.

WHEN ALICE UNLOCKED HER OWN DOOR, SHE turned around to see all four of her neighbors waiting in the stairwell behind her.

"Oh. Okay? Everybody is coming, then? Okay. Come on in, I guess? There's ... one chair. And a bed."

"Dibs on the bed," said Charlie, plopping down. Mona dropped into his lap, burying her hand in his hair.

Charlie leaned down to kiss Mona. He missed the glances that passed between Smitha and Joe.

"That's new," Joe whispered.

"Not really," Smitha whispered back. "It was brewing all last spring. I guess it finally boiled over this summer."

"Um, I can't get in my room," Alice said from behind them.

"Ope! Sorry!" Smitha walked all the way into the room and settled herself in the broad easy chair.

Joe and Alice were still standing in the common hallway leading to the stairs when the exterior door opened and another young woman walked in. Her dark eyes flashed and her thumb traced a smile across her lower lip as she took in the scene before her. She glanced briefly at Joe before lingering for a long moment on Alice, eyes running from the blue tips of her hair to the frayed cuffs of her too-long jeans, worn thin from being walked on.

"So this is college, is it? Beautiful women and dudes bleeding from their heads? Seems about right." She stuck a hand out, pulling Alice into a firm handshake. She traced the tips of her fingers along Alice's palm as they disconnected. Alice bit her lip. "My name is Inez Garcia. I'm in 1B. Freshman. Wait list."

"I'm 1A!" Alice squeaked. She cleared her throat and continued. "I'm Alice. Also a waitlisted freshman. And this is Joe. He and the rest of them live upstairs."

"Howdy," said Joe, nodding. "We were just heading in."

"The rest of them?

"There's kind of a lot."

"Can I come in?" Inez asked. "It'd be nice to meet the neighbors."

Alice shrugged helplessly. "Might as well. Everyone else has." She pushed Joe's shoulder to guide him into the apartment. Inez followed a step later, admiring the broad sway of Alice's hips as she led the way.

"Hey guys," said Joe, waving. "We found 1B in the hall."

"Admin finally opened up 1B, huh?" asked Mona. "It's been closed as long as we've lived here. The last guys trashed it so hard it took that long to remodel."

"Do you play any sports, 1B?" called Charlie.

"She's a freshman, Charlie," said Alice.

"Damn it all!" said Charlie. "Two new neighbors this year and they're both freshmen?"

"I play soccer," offered Inez. "If that helps."

Charlie whimpered. "You're killing me, freshman," he muttered. Then he noticed Inez's eyes locked on Alice as she leaned down to rustle through a hard-shelled suitcase at the foot of her bed, and grinned. He bent forward and whispered into Mona's ear.

"Ten dollars says they're sharing an apartment by fall break."

Mona pinched his leg. "Hush, you," she murmured. "Leave the pups alone."

Alice straightened up, a nondescript brown bottle clutched in her left hand. "Found it," she said.

She ran into her small bathroom and reemerged with a wash rag, dumping some of the contents of the bottle onto the rag and handing it to Joe. Joe pulled the makeshift bandana-shirt off his head and chucked it into Charlie's chest. He raised the rag to his wound and yelped.

"Baaaaaaargh! That stings!"

"Here, let me," said Smitha, taking the rag and wiping away the rest of the blood with slow, careful strokes. Alice was back shortly with another rag, which she gave to Joe to hold against his head until the blood clotted up.

"Thanks, kid," said Joe. "Welcome to college."

Mona hopped up from Charlie's lap. "You pups want to join us for dinner?" she offered. "We'll be getting food from Sun Garden, the most mediocre Chinese takeout north of Pittsburgh. My treat. Family tradition says the last one to get home on the first day buys."

"Your parents make you buy dinner?" asked Alice.

"No," said Mona, shaking her head and waving at Joe, Charlie, and Smitha. "My family."

"Come on, Alice," urged Inez, draping an arm around the shorter girl's shoulders. "Let's do it!"

Alice smiled. "Okay, I'm in."

"Wonderful," Smitha beamed.

"I like the new neighbors," said Mona. "Let's go see if there's still a menu on top of the fridge. Who wants to call in the order?"

"I can do it," Alice volunteered, eager to make a contribution.

"I like the enthusiasm, 1A" Charlie nodded. "But there's a trick to ordering from Sun Garden—you gotta ask for Vic himself; he'll throw in extra when he recognizes our address."

"Vic?" asked Inez.

"Come on, freshmen. I've got so much to teach you," said Charlie, turning for the stairs.

Joe cornered Charlie as Mona rummaged for the menu.

"So what's going on with you and Mona?" he hissed.

"What isn't going on with us?" answered Charlie.

"Is it serious?"

"Hey there, big fella, you're just jumping right into this conversation, aren't you?"

Joe nodded.

"I've known you for three years now, Charlie. I've learned that if I don't drive straight to the point, you'll dance around making jokes for hours."

"So what is the point?"

Joe put a hand on Charlie's arm.

"Just ... I'm happy for you. Both of you."

Charlie slung his arm around Joe's shoulder and hugged him tight.

"I love you too, man."

CHAPTER

EIGHT

Alice glanced around the room, marveling at how quickly the upstairs apartment had come to feel like home in just two months. She barely spent any time in her own apartment these days. It had mostly become a place to study when the distraction level in the big apartment grew too high.

The boys were gone for the weekend. Joe, who worked part-time at a big box store in town, had volunteered to pick up some extra shifts. Charlie was back home, helping his dad with something. Mona had declared the girls would turn the weekend into an extended movie marathon, overruling Smitha's protestations about a mounting pile of homework and Inez's concerns about soccer conditioning. Alice offered no objections.

Alice glanced sideways at the beautiful Latina girl sitting next to her on the couch. They'd been inseparable since their first meeting. They spent nearly every free minute together, much of it here in the common room of the upstairs apartment. They were ... close. Very close. Inez regularly had an arm around Alice's shoulders, they sat pressed against each other when they watched TV, they found all manner of reasons to be in physical contact. It was innocent enough to be ascribed to a libertine friendship but brazen enough to feel like something more.

Once, when helping change a power outlet in her bedroom at home, Alice had accidentally touched the tip of her screwdriver to an open wire and sent a jolt of electricity through her arm that rattled her teeth. That was how she felt when Inez touched her, like a living energy was firing through her, so intense that it was almost painful. She lived for it, but was scared to put it in the open, scared to address it, for fear that it might go away. They'd fallen asleep together on the couch a few days ago and Alice had woken up with Inez's arms wrapped around her. She'd never felt more terrified or more alive.

"We can turn up the heat if you girls are too cold," Smitha offered, noting the thick quilt Alice and Inez were huddled under.

"Maybe they just don't want us to see them holding hands," said Mona, emerging from the closet in triumph, a battered set of DVDs in her hand.

Alice felt a blush rising up her neck. Her hand was resting on her thigh, and Inez's hand was wrapped around it, her thumb tracing a casual, repeated pattern from Alice's knuckle to the base of her thumb. The heat of the flush made her hands sweaty. She was immediately self-conscious about how Inez would react to holding a sweaty hand, so she pulled back, slipping her hands on top of the sheet and opening them to cool in the air.

"I'm going to make tea before the movie starts," announced Smitha. "Does anyone want tea?"

"I thought you drank coffee," Inez said.

"I drink coffee because I need it. I drink tea because I like it."

"Make a cup of that mint stuff for me, would you?" asked Mona.

"That sounds good," said Alice.

"I don't like tea." Inez shook her head. "Too bitter."

"Oh, girl, you have to try the mint, trust me. A little milk and sugar and it tastes like drinking a dessert," Mona promised.

"Okay," said Inez, happy to please the older girl. "Why not. I'll try some mint tea."

The tea was distributed a few minutes later. The milk Smitha added took just enough off the heat that they were able to start drinking it right away. Inez gave the cup a distrusting look, but followed Alice's lead and took a sip. Then a second and third.

"Okay," she said, nodding. "I like tea."

"Told you!" said Mona.

After the cups were emptied and made their way to the sink, Mona pushed *The Producers* into the DVD player. Inez leaned back against Alice, pulling Alice's arm around her. Alice froze, not in panic or fear, but in a sudden desire to press the moment deep into her memory.

She looked at her arm—her very own arm—falling over the girl's shoulder, her hand resting lightly on Inez's stomach. Inez's chin was tucked over Alice's arm where it crossed her chest, and both of Inez's arms were wrapped around her own in a—Alice dared herself to use the word cuddle. They'd spent a lot of time together, and shared a lot of touch, but this was different. This was intimate. Inez—tall, strong, beautiful Inez —was in her lap, hugging her arm.

She was startled from her reverie when Inez poked her again.

"Breathe," Inez said.

"Huh?" asked Alice, before realizing she'd been holding her breath. "Oh, right. Yeah."

She flushed and her hand grew sweaty again. She tried to pull away, but Inez held on, shaking her head.

"Mine," she whispered playfully over the fanfare of the movie's opening credits.

Alice spent most of the first two movies barely paying attention to the screen, the entirety of her being focused on the girl beside her. She read every moment, felt every shift, trying to decide exactly what was happening between them and what it meant. Was Inez just being ... Inez? Was this how she connected? Alice certainly never saw her like this with Mona or Smitha. She repeatedly told herself to stop analyzing the moment and instead enjoy it for whatever it was, but she refused to take her own advice. Her heart was thumping, and she knew Inez, pressed against her chest for the better part of three hours, had to feel it. How could she not? It was like a tiny sledgehammer beating against her ribs. She checked more than once to see if she could see Inez's head bobbing with the beat of her own heart.

After *Blazing Saddles*, Smitha stood and declared that it was too late to start another movie.

Mona gaped at her. "It's not even midnight! We could easily sneak in at least one more. There's no class tomorrow."

"We've got all day tomorrow to watch the rest of them," Smitha answered. "And Sunday, too."

Smitha locked eyes with Mona and cast an intentional look to the two younger women on the couch, who did not appear to process the conversation. Mona nodded.

"Sounds good," she said. "We can stop here and pick up with *Young Frankenstein* after breakfast. I think I'll head out for a bit, though. I'm not quite tired enough to sleep. Maybe I'll hit Blue Isaac's for some late-night breakfast and get a start on that sociology project. You girls want to come?" she couldn't help teasing.

"Huh? Oh," said Inez, looking over at Alice and smiling.

"No thanks, I think we'll stay here. Maybe watch another movie, if that's okay with you guys?"

"Sure, as long as it's not a Mel Brooks. Those have to wait until we're all here. Once we start a marathon together, we have to finish it together. Family rule. Smitha, you want to join?"

"I promised I'd call Ryan before bed," Smitha said.

"Ryan? Ryan from our gen ed literature class last year?" Mona asked.

Smitha shrugged.

"Yeah. He's ... well, he and I have been ... talking."

"Well, you enjoy your talk, hot stuff," Mona said, and sauntered off with a knowing nod of farewell.

Inez stood and stretched. Alice kept her eyes locked on her, noting how cool it got when Inez peeled away and wishing the girl were still against her.

"What should we watch?" asked Inez.

"Hm? Oh, this is good," said Alice, not hearing the question.

Inez smiled. "You're welcome to watch me any time you want," she said.

"What?" Alice played the conversation back in her head and realized what she'd said. "Oh, that's not what I meant, I mean, I do like ... it's not that, uh ... how about *The Princess Bride*?" she tailed off.

"We just watched that on Wednesday," Inez said.

"I know," said Alice. "I've watched it dozens of times. It's the sort of movie that I can watch and barely pay attention to, because I know it so well."

Inez raised an eyebrow again. "What are you going to be paying attention to, then?" she asked, raising onto her tiptoes to stretch again.

Alice watched her, helpless. "I ... what?"

Inez grinned and trotted over to the DVD player to pop in

the much-loved film. She returned to the couch and dropped down beside Alice, not leaning against her this time, but sitting directly beside her, an arm over her shoulder.

They watched together as Fred Savage, sick in bed, talked to his mother, played an old video game, and welcomed his grandpa into his room. Grandpa started to read, and when young Fred Savage got to his first objection, Inez leaned over and whispered into Alice's ear.

"Is this a kissing movie?"

Alice's heart raced. She offered the smallest of nods, and felt Inez's hand connect with her cheek, turning her until they were face to face.

"Hi," she said, lamely, and kicked herself for not coming up with anything more romantic.

"Hi," Inez answered. And then she kissed her, and the world exploded.

They separated a minute later, and Alice reeled. Inez, typically the very essence of surety, looked at her with a tentative, almost worried expression.

"That was ... good," Alice said, and kicked herself again. "I mean, that was great. That was incredible. Could we ... maybe do that again?"

This time Inez nodded slightly, and Alice, her hand somehow on Inez's neck, pulled her forward. The thinner girl pressed her arms together and allowed herself to fall forward into Alice, who locked her hands together at the base of Inez's back. The next kiss lasted a bit longer; the third probably could have set a world record. There was no more ambiguity. No more wondering what things meant, no more interpreting words and touches, no more second guessing. There was now, simply, Alice and Inez.

"Go, baby, go!" shouted Alice, rising from her seat and clenching her fists in the air.

Inez broke free from midfield and dashed toward the goal. She split two defenders just as a lobbed pass dropped at her feet. She collected the ball without breaking stride, tipping it from the instep of her left foot a few feet ahead of herself, keeping her body positioned to prevent an attack from the defender. There was only open grass between her and the goal, and Alice saw her girlfriend's eyes flash.

A shrill whistle from the referee brought the action to a halt just before Inez put her toe to the ball for a shot. She pulled up, tapping the ball instead to the nearby line judge and retreating towards midfield.

"Why did they stop?" asked Alice, indignant. "She was going to score!"

"She was offsides," said Smitha with a shrug.

"But that's the side the goal is on," said Alice, sitting back down.

"She got in front of the defense before her teammate touched off the pass," Smitha explained.

"Isn't that what you're supposed to do?" asked Alice. "I still do not understand this game."

"Do you want me to explain again?"

"Not really. I won't remember even if you do. Sports don't stay in my brain."

Charlie leaned over and tapped her on the shoulder.

"If it makes you feel better, I don't understand it either."

"Joe and his dad have tried to teach you about sports for three years," Mona pointed out.

"I'm proud to say it still hasn't taken," Charlie replied.

On the field a longer whistle blew, signifying the end of the half. Inez and her teammates jogged back to the home sideline. Inez caught Alice's eye as she went and blew her a kiss.

"What was that about?" asked Jessie, a speedy sophomore who often played on Inez's left wing.

"What was what about?" asked Katy, the junior midfielder who had chipped the offsides pass a few moments earlier.

"The freshman is flirting with somebody in the crowd," Jessie answered. "Blowing kisses."

Inez smiled and deflected. "Can you believe they blew that pass offsides? I thought I had it measured. Must have been just a step ahead."

"Who's the boy?" asked Jessie, glancing into the gathered crowd.

Ravencrest was a small campus, and their sports programs were neither big nor successful, so assembled spectators were mostly parents, friends, a smattering of dedicated student fans, and any assorted student who wandered past the field on lower campus that day with nothing better to do than stop and watch a game.

"Alice," said Inez, nodding to her girl with a smile.

"Oh, your weird roommate?" asked Katy, rolling her eyes. "She comes to all our games, and obviously has no idea how soccer works. Is she that hard up for friends?"

"Aw, lay off the kid," said Jessie. "Alice is alright. It's nice that she comes to watch us. I wish more people did."

"Alice is great," said Inez, defensively. "She doesn't care about soccer at all, but she shows up to support me. And she's incredibly smart, you know? She has this way to sort of ... sort out what everybody in a room is thinking, and thread a conversation that pulls them all together, and ..."

"So, it's just your roommate," said Jessie, disappointed.

"... and she's really pretty, you know? She hides it beneath baggy clothes, and she slouches a lot because she doesn't want people to look at her. But she's gorgeous, really, when you look."

"Her?" said Katy flatly.

"Yeah, listen, you can be your roommate's wing-woman sometime when there are dudes around, okay?" said Jessie. "I'm sure she's great and all, but I was hoping you were crushing on someone. Not just saying hi to your roommate."

Inez blushed.

"You are," said Jessie, pointing a finger into Inez's chest. "You are crushing on someone! Who is it? And don't pretend you were just waving to your friends over there, I can tell. You're blushing!"

"It's Alice," said Inez.

"Come on, man, stop dodging."

"She's my girlfriend," answered Inez.

"Oh. Like your ... girlfriend girlfriend?" Jessie asked, startled.

"Mmhmm."

"Like you ..." Jessie waved her hands. "You ... like, you are dating?"

A growing crowd of teammates had given up on feigning disinterest and were actively listening to the discussion.

Inez nodded again.

"Gross," muttered someone. Inez flinched and fought the urge to throw a middle finger in the direction of the voice she was pretty sure belonged to Gracie, a trim junior who thought she was in line for team captain.

"Oh. Well ... okay. That's cool, I guess." said Jessie. "But you're ... roommates. I mean ...?"

"We have separate apartments," said Inez, clarifying. "Not that I've slept in mine for a while."

"You moved in together?" squealed Shannon.

"Not exactly,' Inez said, growing increasingly uncomfortable with the questioning. "We both tend to sleep upstairs, in our friends' apartment. It's ... big," she tailed off.

"Oh, is that the gang of freaks that sometimes comes to

the game with your roommate?" asked Gracie from the back. There were a few giggles.

"My girlfriend," Inez corrected.

"Right, sorry, your girlfriend," Gracie sneered. More titters. She gestured over to the stands. Even at that distance it was obvious that Alice, in typical baggy hoodie and jeans, was looking at Inez with shining eyes. Smitha at least wore a Ravencrest sweater but had taken the break in action as an opportunity to bury her head in her textbook. Charlie took up three rows of bleachers, his long legs stretching to the seat below him and his hands gesturing above his head as he talked about something animatedly. He must have gotten cold; Mona's black feathery coat was draped over his retro striped shirt and thrift store pinstripe pants. Mona, all punk black and buffalo plaid, sat between him and Smitha, eating a soft pretzel. Even Inez had to admit that they looked out of place, a Breakfast Club-type group of misfits come to life.

"So, this is who you want to be friends with? The nerdy little Indian girl and the pouty glam freak and his insane girlfriend with platinum lipstick?"

"Back off," snarled Inez, and grabbed her water bottle so she wouldn't be as tempted to throttle the other girl.

"Not cool, Gracie," snapped Jessie. "I don't see any of your friends coming to our games."

"That would require her to have friends," said Frances.

Katy peered across the field.

"Didn't you hook up with that guy last fall at a party?" she asked Gracie. "The pouty glam freak?"

Inez nearly choked on her water.

"Wait, what?" she sputtered.

"I'm so jealous," said Shannon, the only other freshman on the squad. "I wish I found somebody already. You're lucky."

Inez smiled, thankful for the support. "Yeah, I am."

The game ended, and after the perfunctory handshakes with the other team, Inez headed straight for Alice.

Alice wrapped her up in a hug.

"I'm sweaty," Inez insisted.

"Don't care. You did great! You scored!"

Inez grinned. "I did."

"Sixth goal this year!"

"You're counting?"

"It was a good game," chimed in Smitha.

"Thanks, Professor," said Inez.

"Not that I'm complaining, but usually you head straight to the locker rooms. Do you need something?" asked Alice.

"A kiss?" said Inez, suddenly shy. The crowd, not large to begin with, had thinned out considerably, but a number of her teammates were still lingering around, finding excuses to delay the locker room trip while they watched Inez and Alice from the periphery.

Alice laughed and tugged Inez toward her. Inez's eyes fluttered as she breathed in the smell of Alice's strawberry lip gloss. Alice had been wearing it almost exclusively since the weekend prior, when Inez had commented on how much she liked the taste.

They lingered for a minute, one short kiss turning into a few longer ones. Charlie and Mona whooped. Inez pulled back, still in Alice's arms, and smiled.

"Thanks," she said.

"Any time," Alice answered, "but—"

"Don't worry about it. I just like being seen with you," Inez teased, waggling an eyebrow. "Raises my status."

"Get out of here," said Alice, laughing. She planted a hand on Inez's butt and shoved her down the path that led to the sports building. "Come back when you're clean."

While Inez was in the shower, she could hear Gracie still talking loudly about "the freshman and her freak friends." But the taste of strawberry lingered on her lips, and that—plus Shannon's equally loud "SHUT UP, Gracie!"—were enough to keep her from charging out of the shower and committing a deliberate foul on her teammate.

Barely, but enough.

GRACIE WAS THE LAST TO LEAVE THE LOCKER ROOM. She was stewing, everything wrong circling over itself in her mind, cutting her bad mood more deeply. She had missed a shot on goal in the second half. *Cut.* The hot water had run out near the end of her shower and now she was cold. *Cut.* That freak freshman was turning the team against her. *Cut cut cut.*

She toweled off her hair viciously, threw on her clothes, gathered up her things in her gym bag. The zipper stuck. *Cut.*

Something clattered behind her and she spun around, glaring.

"Who's there?" she demanded.

She received no answer but the gaping maw of a monster, drawing her into nothingness.

Cut.

As the end of the semester drew near, no one in the house was particularly looking forward to Christmas break. Inez and Alice were eager to go home again, as freshmen often are, but did not relish the thought of being separated for so long. The other four, as seniors, were already starting to cut ties with home, some in a more gradual way— Smitha talking to her mom about where she was going for graduate school, Joe and his parents looking for possible apartments—and others more abruptly.

"I can't ever go home again," Charlie moaned.

He paced the living room, shaking his head.

"Come on, man. I know your dad. It can't be that bad."

Charlie moaned again in Joe's general direction.

"You don't know what he said to me. You don't know what I said to him!"

"I mean, you've told me three times, so I kind of feel like I do." Joe hopped up and took Charlie by the shoulders, stopping him. "Look. You're both the kind of guys who say what they're thinking, yeah? You've had this kind of blow-up before. What about over the summer when you had that fight about the car? You made up in what, like, a day?"

Charlie shook his head.

"Not this time, man."

Joe bumped Charlie with his shoulder.

"It'll work out okay. You'll see."

"What'll work out?" Smitha asked, coming into the living room.

"Charlie had a fight with his dad," Joe explained. Smitha made a face and gave Charlie a quick hug.

"Family is hard," she said. "Do you need somewhere to go for break?"

"You can come with me," Joe offered. "Dad loves you."

Charlie collapsed into a chair, shoulders slumping as a big rush of air escaped him.

"No," he said. "I'll go home. Joe's right. I need to call and apologize. Maybe tomorrow morning."

"Call him in the afternoon," Joe said. "Remember, tomorrow is our Christmas morning. Last day we're all together before break, yeah?"

Charlie brightened up.

"Oh yeah!"

"And today is your Chem final, isn't it?" Smitha reminded him. He deflated again.

"Oh yeah." Charlie sighed, stood, and headed for his room to study.

THE NEXT MORNING CHARLIE STUMBLED OUT OF HIS room wearing only an open blue bathrobe and a festive pair of boxer briefs. A light was on—not the main overhead light, but a small corner lamp next to the rickety, bowl-shaped chair where Smitha sat perched like a bird in a nest, wrapped in blankets and reading a book. Joe was in the tiny kitchenette cooking over a plug-in grill, the smell of breakfast sausage having roused Charlie from his slumber. He kicked the couch and, when nobody moved, sat heavily on top of the two young women who had fallen asleep there the night before. Inez groaned and bucked him off, only to land on top of him on the floor a moment later when Alice gave her a shove.

"Go brush your teeth," Alice said. "Your breath smells like stale coffee and rotten pumpkin."

"I ... what?" Inez asked. "Rotten *pumpkin?*"

"Yeah, have you ever smelled rotten pumpkin? It's putrid."

"Love you too, baby."

"Love may be blind, but it is not anosmic. Brush your teeth and then come kiss me good morning."

"What's anosmic?" asked Charlie. "Is that when you can't stop bleeding?"

"It means not having a sense of smell," said Smitha, not looking up from her book. Alice nodded.

"Like ... being blind in the nose?" asked Joe, walking in with a plate of eggs and sausage. Alice rolled her eyes.

"Sausage!" said Charlie, plucking one from the plate.

"Meatless sausages are on the other side of the egg barrier," Joe explained, gesturing at the plate, where two stacks of sausages piled perilously high were separated by a Great Wall of Egg.

"You don't need to tell us, mate," said Charlie. "The color gives it away."

"Toast and potatoes are in the kitchen. I'll be right back," Joe continued. He twirled around Inez, who was just emerging from the bathroom as she beelined back for the couch and sat on Alice's lap so they were face to face.

"Merry Christmas, baby," she said, drawing her in for a long kiss.

"Argh, gross," said Inez as she pulled away. "Your tongue is *fuzzy*. Why did I have to brush my teeth first, and you didn't?"

"Woman's prerogative?" hazarded Alice.

"I think that's about changing your mind," said Smitha, turning a page.

"And *I have it too*," said Inez. "Now go brush your teeth, heathen."

Alice lifted herself from the couch, and Inez turned to watch, as she did nearly every time Alice left a room. Charlie laughed.

"Your tongue's hanging out, darling," he said, shoving Inez.

"I'm just trying to scrape the fuzz off."

"Here's the rest of breakfast," Joe said, coming back with a second plate. "Whole wheat to the left, white bread to the right, potatoes are fried in tons of butter and the remains of the sausage grease."

"The boy clearly thinks we're color blind," said Charlie. "He's telling me which toast is which, like I can't observe evil whole wheat from fifty paces."

"Is color blind like being anosmic in the eyes?" asked Smitha, her eyes still on her book.

"I didn't realize you were reading a joke book," Charlie retorted. He reached out for a sausage, but Joe batted him away.

"Wait for everyone, you bottomless pit."

"I do have a bottom and it's fantastic."

"Just go see if Mona's awake," Inez demanded. "And hurry up or we'll start without you."

Mona was sprawled in Charlie's bed, wearing one of his shirts and an old ratty pair of gym shorts. He thought she looked beautiful.

Charlie slid in next to her and pushed a lock of hair away from her face. He draped one arm around her waist, lightly, so as not to wake her. Then he closed his eyes, breathed deep, and just let himself be. This was one perfect moment, and he wanted to soak it in and keep it close as long as possible.

When he opened his eyes again Mona was smiling at him.

"Hey there, sleeping beauty," she said.

"I think that's my line."

"Wake up earlier next time."

He kissed her.

"I love you."

"I love you too, Charlie. Do I smell sausage?"

Even if the table hadn't been covered with wrapped presents, there wasn't enough room for them all to sit comfortably so they had gotten used to eating wherever. Inez and Alice stayed on the couch—having claimed the most comfortable seat early, they were not about to give it up. Mona made a plate up for Smitha, who had finally relinquished her book, and then sat on the floor at her feet with her own plate. Charlie constructed a sausage, egg, and toast sandwich, ate it in three bites, then started on the dishes.

When Charlie returned from the kitchen, he jerked a thumb toward the laden table.

"Youngest one distributes the presents," he explained. "Family rule. Always been my job, but guess who finally gets to sit around and be waited on this year?"

Inez looked at Alice. "Do you ever get the feeling they make up these 'family rules' just to get us to do stuff for them?"

"Mmm. I think you're onto something." Alice stood, stretched, and crossed to the table, where a haphazard but impressively large pile of gifts waited for her to sort and assign.

She picked up the presents she had purchased first, their shiny blue wrapping making them easy to spot. A quick tour around the room and they were dropped in everyone's laps or at their feet. She repeated the process several more times, through the Professor's immaculately wrapped gifts with hand-tied bows, Mona's functional but over-taped packages, Joe's gift bags and Charlie's platinum silver paper that nearly blinded her when it reflected the light. Finally, there were only Inez's gifts on the table, each one wrapped in thick brown paper with thoughtful, hand-written notes in her neat script scrawled across the tops.

The last gift she picked up was Inez's gift to her. The small box was wrapped firmly in the brown paper, with a small red bow adorning the corner. She read the note.

Mi Novia, mi amor, mi corazón.

You are all I need. You are beautiful and strong and charming. You'll always be my 1A. I love you. Merry Christmas.
Nez

"Hey, stop crying and sit down so we can start opening!" Charlie demanded. He waved at Inez. "Make your girlfriend stop crying."

Inez grabbed Alice by the hand and pulled her onto the couch. She kissed Alice's eyes, but somehow that only served to make the tears flow harder.

"I tried," she said with a shrug.

"Don't try any harder," Joe pleaded.

Mona looked behind her. "Well, Professor?"

Smitha looked around the room, beaming at her gathered family.

"Go ahead," she said, and the present massacre began. By the end of it, bows and wrapping paper were scattered everywhere. Charlie and Joe were loading up the Nerf guns Inez had gotten them. ("If I get shot in the head I'm confiscating them," Smitha warned sternly.) Mona, aghast that

Alice had never heard of Alkaline Trio or My Chemical Romance, was singing snippets of songs to her very loudly while waving around the concert tickets that Charlie had gifted her. And Inez, smiling broadly, was admiring the bracelet from Alice, a simple silver chain with the word "forever" in script dangling toward her wrist.

Charlie glanced out the small window and did a comedic double-take.

"It's snowing!" he announced. "Someone come make a snowman with me."

"Put some clothes on first," the Professor said.

A few minutes later most of the group had clattered out the door, bundled up and laughing. Smitha stayed behind to pick up wrapping paper, getting a large black trash bag and stuffing in handfuls.

"Did you forget something?" she called when she heard the door open again a minute later.

Charlie, clumps of snow from his shoes dropping on the floor, walked over to her and bent down.

"Yep," he said, and kissed the top of her head. "Merry Christmas, Professor."

And he was gone again, out the door, humming a carol to himself.

LATER THAT DAY, AS THE SNOW SLOWED TO A FEW light flakes, Charlie slammed the door to his bedroom and flung himself onto the shabby couch next to Smitha's chair. Smitha, who had heard the yelling, kept reading her new book from Inez and said nothing.

After a minute of no one paying attention to him, Charlie sat up and huffed loudly. Smitha ignored him. He flung himself down again, facing Smitha. She ignored him.

"Oh, come on, Prof," he exploded finally, jumping up and standing directly in front of her.

Smitha put down the book calmly.

"Yes?"

"I know you heard that."

"Well, I didn't hear all of your dad's side."

"Am I being unreasonable?" Charlie asked.

"I really don't want to get in the middle of it."

Charlie swore.

"That means it is my fault."

Smitha smiled at him and gave an apologetic little shrug.

"Ugh, fine. Fine. Should I call again now?"

"I wouldn't. Let him cool off first before you apologize."

Charlie nodded.

"You're a good counselor."

"I have many skills."

Charlie returned her grin.

"I guess I'd better figure out something to do, then. Do you want to go watch a movie or something?"

Smitha smiled but shook her head.

"No thanks, Charlie. I'm going out with Ryan later."

"Oooh, Ryan!" Charlie fluttered his eyes and fanned himself. "When are we going to meet this big hunk of all right?"

"Go away, Charlie," Smitha said, laughing.

"Fine, fine. I know when I'm not wanted." He blew her a kiss on his way out the door.

<hr>

THERE WAS A ROAD THAT LED OUT OF TOWN, toward the outlet malls and the highway and the rest of civilization, that was well enough traveled to merit a few low-cost advertising billboards but not so well traveled that it saw much traffic after about 11 PM. This meant that if someone was so inclined, they could take a late-night trip down the road, scale the small ladder at the back of one of the two billboards, and find total privacy hiding on a narrow bench behind a giant road sign that was currently advertising the legal services of Jenty, Thomason, and Cho, attorneys at law.

Maybe not total privacy—it was only about eight feet off the ground, so if someone walked over with a flashlight and looked up at just the right angle, they would see you. But the billboard blocked line of sight from one side of the road and the bench was high enough to be above headlight level from the other.

Ryan's shoulders hit the bench with just a bit of force, and he arched his back in anticipation as Smitha sat on his lap, one hand to either side of his head. Her unbraided hair draped around them.

Smitha's head dropped down and their lips met, the warmth of excitement temporarily driving away the chill of the night air. Ryan wrapped a hand in Smitha's long black hair and pulled her tighter.

"How'd you find this place?" Ryan asked, parting from Smitha for a moment to look into her eyes. "It's perfect."

"We do a lot of walking."

"We?" Ryan kissed Smitha on her nose. "Anyone I should worry about?"

"Not at all. Just Joe, Mona ... the family."

"It's so cute that you call yourselves a family," said Ryan.

"You think I'm cute?" answered Smitha, closing her eyes and tilting her chin down in a clear invitation that Ryan was quick to accept.

It was a good night. They talked and laughed and flirted and kissed until Ryan reluctantly said he had to get back to campus in time to at least get a few hours of sleep.

Ryan went down the ladder first, reaching up to help

Smitha down the last few rungs. Her feet had barely hit the ground when he swept her up in another kiss.

"You like doing that," Smitha said when they parted.

"I do," he confirmed.

"So do I." She gave him a hug, snuggling into his chest to keep warm. "The family wants to meet you soon. Do you want to have lunch with us all tomorrow?"

Ryan wrapped his arms around her and held her closer.

"They're intimidating! What if they don't like me?"

"They'll like you."

"But what if they don't?"

Smitha pulled away and held Ryan at arm's length.

"Ryan. They will. How could they not?"

She shivered abruptly and shoved her hands in the pockets of her red jacket.

"Is it just me," she said, "or did it get even colder somehow in the last couple of minutes?"

CHARLIE AMBLED DOWN THE ROAD, FINGERS wrapped around a bottle in the deep recesses of a pocket in his jeans. The movie theater in town had only one screen and they were playing some comedy that looked insultingly unfunny. Charlie wasn't in a comedy mood, so he started walking.

It was a good walking night. It was chilly but as long as he kept moving it was bracing, clarifying, more than freezing. He talked to himself as he walked, replaying the argument with his dad. He knew he'd have to apologize—he wanted to apologize, and in retrospect he really had been wrong—so he tried out different openings, different phrasings, any way to make what was coming out of his mouth sound right.

It didn't help that he was drunk.

"Sorry is," he tried out, and chuckled. "Sorry seems to be. Seems to me. Sorry seems ..."

"Charlie? Is that you?"

Under a looming billboard were two figures. They came into focus as he drew closer—Smitha, and a tall dark-haired boy. He fished for the name.

"Prof! And—Ryan? Oh damn, did I disturb a do not disturb situation?"

"Oh, I've wanted you two to meet!" Smitha said. "Charlie, this is Ryan. Ryan, this is Charlie, who lives in the house?"

Charlie noticed, with some mix of amusement and annoyance, that Ryan stood straighter and was maybe even puffing out his chest a little. Humans are such animals, he thought.

"You're gorgeous," he said out loud, which wasn't exactly what he was intending but oh well, it wasn't wrong, either.

"And I think you're drunk," Ryan replied.

"Probably!" Charlie said cheerily. "I may need a designated walker—any takers?"

Smitha gave him a little frown.

"We were just leaving," she said.

"I'll chaperone, then!"

"We don't need a chaperone," Ryan said. "You should probably go."

"Are you jealous of me?" Charlie looked at Smitha with mock wonder. "Some red-blooded male is jealous of me?"

"Charlie ..."

He caught the warning note in her voice and knew that he was annoying her, but he was finding it hard to stop. He didn't like Ryan's tone; one he had encountered all too often in his little podunk hometown from football players who thought with their muscles and didn't know anything of the world outside the turnpike exit. One that he had, more recently, heard from his father during their arguments.

"Think I'm going to take your girl?" He threw an arm around Smitha sloppily. She shrugged it off with a deeper frown. He transferred the attention to Ryan, giving him a wink. "Or maybe you're afraid I'll take you from her?"

"I don't have anything to worry about from you," Ryan said harshly.

Smitha crossed her arms.

"Charlie, you're being mean. I'm going home. I'll see you at the house and I expect an apology."

She turned and left, her red jacket fading down the road.

"Aren't you going after her?" Charlie asked Ryan. "It's not gentlemanly to let a girl walk home by herself."

Ryan looked like he was going to retort, then shook his head and let out a big breath, visibly calming himself down.

"Look man," he said, "I don't know what I did to you, but I don't want to take it any further. You're special to Smitha and she's special to me. I am going to go walk her home, and next time we meet, let's try to pretend it's the first time and hopefully it'll go better."

Charlie cocked his head.

"Huh," he said. "Smitha wasn't lying. You're the whole package."

"Did she say that?" Ryan glanced over to where Smitha had gone and smiled. "Tell you what—why don't you walk home with us?"

"Yeah, ok," Charlie agreed after a pause. "Thanks. Just, uh, let me go ahead for a minute? I should apologize."

Ryan nodded.

"I'll be right behind you."

Charlie nodded back and jogged off. Ryan jiggled his hands in his pockets against the chill and started counting to 100 by Mississippi's. He was at 30 Mississippi's when a car went by.

Its headlights played against the empty space leading up to

the billboard and illuminated, for just an instant, the face of a nightmare. Ryan saw it and stiffened. In the light, the creature also saw him.

The headlights were gone, casting the world back into darkness.

Fear hit as the creature arrived. Ryan froze, the fear forcing him to retreat from himself as the creature reached out with non-existent arms and grabbed the boy by the ears. It sucked in a breath filled with Ryan's essence.

Its arms were solid now. Its shoulders, too. It was coming into being, its discordant presence insisting it had the right to occupy a piece of reality. The boy was fading, nearly transparent, and the creature pulled him into its spiked ribs, impaling the evaporating remains of Ryan's existence on the barbed ends as a half dozen tongues lolled out of its mouth in pleasure. It drew out the last of the boy's essence. The creature stretched, shivered, fitting itself into reality and its new corporeal form. Sated and real, it slipped back into the night.

Further up the road, Charlie nearly passed Smitha before he recognized her.

"Hey!" he greeted her, slowing down to match her pace. "Out for a walk?"

"Yes, I needed some fresh air. That apartment can get so stuffy in the winter. You?"

"Jogging off a bender, I'm afraid. Probably not the best idea; I feel like I'm going to throw up."

"Oh, Charlie."

"I know, I know. Want to walk me home?"

"Always. Let's go."

CHAPTER

TEN

Charlie was up early, dressed to the nines and singing along with the spring birds when Smitha, pulling her robe around her, entered the living room.

"Good morning, Charlie," she greeted him with a smile.

"The best morning, Prof," he replied, picking her up in a huge hug. "I'm so nervous I feel like I'm going to throw up my kidney."

"You won't," Smitha said. "You'll be fine."

"Nope, I'm going to die of nerves," Charlie declared. "I might as well make breakfast before I am deceased."

"Tea first, please," Smitha said, and headed back into her room to get dressed.

When she returned, Charlie had tea and toast, eggs and oatmeal laid out on the table, and the cooking smells had woken the pups up from their shared sofa.

"Mmm, breakfast," Alice mumbled, stumbling over to the table and gratefully taking the cup of tea that Smitha handed her.

"You look nice," Inez said, noting Smitha's carefully coiffed hair and rich blue and red paneled lehenga. "Charlie, you too. What's the occasion?"

Charlie draped a loose bowtie around his neck and gave a Cheshire grin. He fiddled with it unsuccessfully, finally leaving it tied in a lopsided, floppy bow.

"Class presentation?" Alice guessed.

"On a Saturday?" Inez teased her.

"Whatever. Maybe a job interview?"

"For both of them?" Inez sipped her mint tea and studied her two friends. "Senior recognition? I know Smitha has a scholarship recognition banquet coming up, maybe Charlie's escorting her?"

There was a knock at the door. Joe, wandering out of his bedroom, snagged a piece of toast.

"I'll get it," he said and chewing, walked to the door and opened it.

"Hey there, Mr. McCrea!" Charlie called. "I'll start some coffee for you."

"Dad?" Joe said in surprise.

"Thanks, Charlie, I'd love some. You look great. You too, Smitha." Joe's dad closed the door behind him and gave his son a comfortable hug. "Good morning, son."

"Dad, what are you doing here? I mean, I'm happy to see you, but why are you here? Where's Mom?"

Mr. McCrea exchanged a look with Charlie.

"Your mom wanted to stay at home today," he told Joe. "She wasn't, uh, interested in the festivities."

"Festivities?" Joe asked.

"A funeral?" Inez guessed. "A wedding?"

"Got it in like, eight," Charlie laughed.

"Ooh, whose wedding?"

Mona opened the door to her bedroom and left them all momentarily speechless.

She wore a white skater dress with mod blue accents slashing out from the waist. Two braids were twisted back at the crown of her head to meet and spill down her back with the rest of her long, curled hair. Tiny star hairpins nestled, glimmering, in the waves.

Charlie nearly floated over to her. He put one arm around her waist and gently touched the stars with the other.

"Hey Lisa," he said. "Marry me. Today."

Mona brushed the light stubble on his cheek and smiled.

"OK, Lover Boy. I think I will."

Alice gasped.

"Wait, is this for real?"

"Is what for real?" Inez asked.

"As real as houses," Charlie said, proudly holding Mona close.

"That's not the saying," Smitha said, smiling.

"Wait wait wait," Joe said. "Wait. Wait."

He marched up to Charlie and looked him full in the face, frowning a little.

"I'm waiting, Joey," Charlie said, but leaned back slightly.

Joe transferred his searching gaze to Mona. Then suddenly he threw his arms around both of his friends and squeezed them tightly.

"You goobers," he said over their shoulders, his voice husky with welling tears. "You absolute dolts. Why didn't you tell me before?"

"Surprise?" Charlie offered, and patted Joe's broad back.

The pups crowded around as well but Smitha soon shooed everyone away with warnings not to mess up Mona's hair and makeup.

"So, this is happening? Today?" Joe asked, still a bit in shock.

"Today," Charlie confirmed. "Smitha has been helping us get all the paperwork in order. We're heading down to the courthouse as soon as everyone's ready. It's go time, baby."

Joe looked over at his dad, who was shaking his head in the slightly bemused way he often did at Charlie's antics.

"And you're here because ...?"

Charlie cleared his throat.

"I asked your dad to come. I kind of ... I don't know. I wanted a dad here? And I'm not talking to mine ... And, uh ... I knew he'd show up."

Mr. McCrea took off Charlie's bowtie and re-tied it correctly around Charlie's neck.

"Charlie, I am honored to be here," he said earnestly. "Your dad, Mona's parents ... they're missing out on something beautiful, and that's their fault, not yours."

Charlie screwed up his face in the way that instantly told everyone he was trying to hide that he was about to cry.

"Go get dressed, girls," Mona said gently, herding Alice and Inez towards the stairs down to their rooms. "You too, Joe. Let's jam."

THE JUDGE'S NAME WAS TOM, HE HAD A BEARD AND mutton chops so magnificent they made Charlie want to start growing out his own, and he was gruffly delighted to perform the ceremony.

Joe and Inez stood at Charlie's side—Smitha and Alice at Mona's. Joe's dad looked on, beaming, as the judge began.

"Today we have come together," he said, "to witness the joining of these two lives. For them, out of the routine of ordinary life, the extraordinary has happened. They have fallen in love."

Joe swiped surreptitiously at his eyes.

"A good marriage must be created," Judge Tom continued. "It is remembering to say 'I love you' every day. It is never being too old to hold hands. It is putting the needs of the unit before the desires of the individual."

Charlie's hands, held loosely in Mona's, were trembling. Mona squeezed them and mouthed *I love you*. Charlie squeezed back, mouthed *I know*.

"And now for the vows."

As Mona and Charlie repeated after Judge Tom, Smitha passed Alice a tissue and used another to dab at her own eyes.

"... my partner in life and my one true love," Mona finished. "I will love you today, tomorrow, and forever."

Judge Tom looked at Joe.

"Do you have the rings?"

Joe reached into the pocket of his khakis and pulled out two rings that Charlie had given him only a few minutes before. He handed them to Judge Tom.

"The ring is an ancient symbol of eternity; it has no beginning and no end. A visible symbol of an eternal promise of love," Judge Tom said.

Charlie had found the rings in an antique jewelry store downtown. They were simple bands, old but kept shiny, etched with a repeating circle pattern. Mona's had a tiny pearl on top.

Charlie's smile, when he slipped the ring onto her finger, was so bright it almost outshone the sun.

When it was over, after Joe and Smitha had signed the marriage certificate as witnesses, after Judge Tom had declined their somewhat delirious offer of lunch, the family went back to the house. Joe's dad used Smitha's camera to take a few photos of the group, the spindly tree in the front yard and the cracked concrete steps that led to the building making a somehow perfect backdrop for impromptu wedding photos. He gave the camera back to Joe and sat on the concrete steps to wait for everyone else to change.

It was a warm day, for the end of April, and surprisingly

there was no rain. Mr. McCrea leaned back on the steps and let the warm sun soak into his skin. He hated that those kids didn't have their own parents here for their wedding day. Maybe he'd call up Charlie's dad later, have a talk with the guy. Nothing mean, just let him know that Charlie was a good kid, that Mona was his perfect match, and that he was sure, absolutely sure, that they would be very happy together. He'd speak to his wife, too. She should have been there.

A shadow fell over Mr. McCrea's face and a chill took away all the warmth he had collected.

"Maybe I'll go inside to wait," he muttered and, opening his eyes, began to sit up from the stairs.

The monster reached out its spindly arms, grasped his face as it rose, and lifted him up, up, up to its hellish mouth. It drank of him deeply. And then he was gone.

Upstairs, Joe paused in the act of taking off his suit jacket and shuddered at a quick chill that ran through him and was just as soon gone.

"We have to celebrate!" Alice gushed once they were all back in comfortable clothes and lounging in their usual spots in the living room.

"Want to go get something to eat?" Joe suggested.

"Joseph," Inez scolded. "Your best friends just got married and you're asking about food?"

"I'm hungry," said Joe with a shrug. "We can make it a celebration lunch."

Charlie nodded his head. "Listen, I'm famished. I am all for food. Any food. Good food, bad food, whatever. Just put it in my mouth."

"Fine," Alice conceded, "but then what?"

"We could go to a movie?"

"We always do that, Prof. Plus I don't think anything good is out right now. What else?"

Inez snapped her fingers at a sudden idea.

"Isn't church doing that carnival thing today?" she asked Alice.

Inez had promised her mother she'd attend a church while at college, and Alice often went with her to a large, nondenominational congregation within walking distance of campus.

"Right! The spring fling carnival thing," Alice said. "That could be fun!"

"Why not!" Charlie said. "Carnivals are fun. But food first, definitely. We must have food, before Joe and I wither away to nothing."

After a large lunch at a nearby restaurant—not too fancy but not fast food, since it was a special occasion—the family walked over to the church and paid five dollars each for bracelets which would let them ride all day. Smitha halfheartedly protested, saying that at fifty cents a ticket, the maximum value she would get out of her bracelet was perhaps three dollars, and only then if she rode the little carousel twice. She was not a fan of rickety, lurching carnival rides and despite Charlie and Mona's best efforts, could not be begged or threatened onto the Scrambler, the Tilt-a-Whirl, or the admittedly small and busted looking bouncy house. Alice and Inez spent some time in the bouncy house and reported back that it was not worth the time it took to take off their shoes.

Charlie and Mona pressed their bracelets to the limit, looping through lines several times in a row. Joe typically joined for the first ride and then stood with Smitha, talking and laughing as Charlie and Mona tilted, whirled, and tea-cupped past them.

Even Joe drew the line at the run-down funhouse, though.

"I hate those things," he said. "I really hate being scared."

"Let's go get something to drink," Smitha suggested. "Pups?"

"I like being scared," Inez said. Alice, cuddled up to her side, nodded enthusiastically.

"It's not scary!" Charlie protested. "It's just goofy mirrors and uneven floors."

"You know Joe's a lightweight," said Mona.

"It's true," Joe said. "We'll catch up with you later." He and Smitha walked off in search of pop.

Charlie, Mona, and the pups walked through the entrance, a large dark opening designed to look like a gaping clown's mouth.

"Don't let it eat me!" Mona grabbed Charlie's arm and laughed.

Inside they stumbled over rocking planks and squealed as air jets blew down their neck. Around a corner a raggedy scarecrow clown loomed from the ceiling. A suddenly dark room gave Inez and Alice a chance to steal a kiss. Charlie and Mona did, too.

But Charlie's heart wasn't really in it, and Mona could tell. She held him back in the next room, letting the pups run ahead making silly faces in warped mirrors.

"You ok, Lover Boy?" she asked.

Charlie started to lie flippantly, then abruptly changed his tune.

"Actually, Lisa, this place is starting to creep me out."

Mona looked at his paler-than-normal face and grabbed his hand.

"Come on," she said. "I'm getting you out of here."

Charlie nodded but stayed where he was, glancing from side to side at the mirrors.

"I see something," he whispered.

"Only your goofy face," Mona teased, trying to draw him forward.

"No—don't you see them? They're like shadows. With

teeth. I can't pin them down. And it's cold. Something's wrong."

Mona tugged his hand again.

"Charlie, let's go. Come on, babe."

This time he let her pull him through the hall of mirrors. Charlie saw, in the edges of the mirrors as he passed, a spiny dark thing, jaws gaping, claws reaching. He closed his eyes and walked faster, not stopping until he felt the open air around him and heard the loud noises of the carnival instead of the tinny *Entry of the Gladiators*.

A few minutes after the family was settled at a rickety picnic table, eating hot dogs and letting the fizzy pop tickle down their throats, two girls entered the funhouse. They did not come back out. No one ever remembered they had existed.

Later in the evening, once the crowds had made line looping impossible, the group of six strolled through the long alley of carnival games, eating tall snow cones from melting paper cups, when a prize hanging from the interior ceiling of the Bowler Roller game caught Joe's eye. It was an enormous, inflatable Tyrannosaurus Rex which stood almost four feet high and was wearing an inexplicable beret perched on top of its monstrously large head. Joe started giggling.

"What's gotten into you?" Smitha asked.

Joe pointed at the dinosaur and the others looked up, confused. The baffled looks on their faces only set Joe deeper into hysteric giggles as he tried to explain.

"Look at the hat," he said between gasping laughs. "It looks so fancy. That dinosaur thinks he's a sophisticated French gentleman."

Joe erupted in giggles again as he finished his sentence. The idea was absurd, but his laughter was infectious. Watching Joe lose his mind over an inflatable dinosaur was too much for Charlie, and he dissolved into laughter as well.

"I bet he plays the violin," Charlie giggled.

"And attends the theater," said Joe, snickering.

"He doesn't own a television," added Alice, getting into the spirit "because he thinks it rots people's brains."

"Dinosaurs had tiny brains," Smitha pointed out.

"That's why he needs to take care of it!" Mona yelped, giving way to the laughter that was now consuming their entire group.

"He probably has a list of his favorite wines, and talks about what cheeses pair best with them," said Inez.

"He's a connoisseur," said Charlie, pinching the bridge of his nose.

"He's a Connoisseurus Rex!" Smitha said, and the group fell to several long minutes of laughter. When they finally recovered, Joe waved to the plastic dinosaur.

"See you later, Connoisseurus Rex," he said.

"Not on my life," Charlie answered. "That thing is coming with us. He needs to live in your room."

"Aw, you're going to win me a prize?" Joe said, fluttering his eyelashes and holding a hand to his cheek.

"Anything for my guy," said Charlie with a wink. "Now, watch me work. I'm good at this game."

The dinosaur was ticketed as a "jumbo" prize. A regular win—shoving the bowling ball up the metal rails just hard enough that it would crest the second hill but not so hard that it would maintain enough momentum to roll back over the hills and return to you—netted a "small" prize. Per the chart on the wall beneath the dinosaur, four small prizes could be exchanged for a medium prize, three mediums for a large, and two larges for a jumbo. This meant twenty-four wins would be required to take home Connoisseurus Rex; at a quarter per chance, that worked out to a minimum of six dollars on a perfect run of wins.

"Are you sure about this, Charlie?" Mona asked, pulling on the edge of his sleeveless tank. "That's a lot of wins."

"You're just jealous that I'm winning it for Joe and not for you," he teased.

Mona rolled her eyes. "Sure, I absolutely am jealous that my silly husband is going to waste a bunch of money not winning a plastic, inflatable dinosaur for my other silly friend. That's definitely what this is about."

Charlie beamed a little at the word "husband" but still went to get some money exchanged for coins.

"Aren't these games all rigged?" Inez asked.

"You don't have any faith in me," Charlie moaned, holding a hand to his wounded heart. "Just trust me. Joe will be sleeping with that dinosaur tonight."

"There is no scenario in which that statement is true," said Joe. "I don't care if you do win it, it won't be coming to bed with me. I'm not that lonely."

"But he is a dinosaur of refined tastes," Charlie pointed out. "I'm sure he is a gentle and generous lover."

"Let's go," said Joe, taking a few steps away.

Mona grabbed his arm and pulled him back.

"I need to see how this plays out," she explained.

"You mean you need to see Charlie waste a bunch of quarters on a bowling ball game?" Smitha asked.

"They will not be wasted!" Charlie insisted. "I am sure that dinosaur is coming home with us tonight."

"How sure?" asked Joe.

Charlie looked at the quarters in his hand—one full roll and one partial. He dumped out the contents of the partial roll, counting up six dollars and seventy-five cents.

"Twenty-seven quarters sure," he said.

True to his word, Charlie was excellent at The Bowler Roller. Few quarters were wasted as he racked up wins, a growing stack of stuffed animals piling up before him. Four finger puppet farm animals became a stuffed shark. Four more became a cow and another four a kangaroo. Together, the shark, cow, and kangaroo were exchanged for a large stuffed ostrich, and the cycle began anew. Soon, the ostrich was joined by a stuffed robot and the two of them were solemnly handed over to the bemused teenager working the booth.

"Fare thee well, Oliver and Joebot Three Thousand," Charlie said as he traded them in. "Our acquaintance was brief, but your service was noble. You have done well in aiding my quest to unite our dear Joe with his one true love, the Connoisseurus Rex."

"You named the robot after me?" Joe asked.

"Don't get too excited," said Charlie. "Here." He handed across the flat cardboard box the carnival worker had handed him in exchange for Oliver and Joebot. "Here is your long lost love. Er, he may need a bit of a ..."

"Nope!" said Joe, loudly. "There are several ways I can think of in which that sentence might end, and I do not want to hear any of them."

They walked home in the soft glowing night. The pups ran ahead, playing with their shadows in the orange-tinted streetlights. Joe and Smitha followed, talking about their plans for after graduation. Charlie and Mona followed slowly, his arm draped over her shoulder, her head nestled against him.

Smitha glanced behind her and smiled.

"Joe," she said, and gestured behind her. Joe looked back and nodded. He called over to Inez and Alice. "Hey pups! Movie night in 1B! Last one there has to pay for pizza if we get hungry!"

He took off down the street, Connoisseurus Rex's box under his arm. The girls followed, Inez's long legs flying. Smitha followed more slowly but still keeping ahead of Mona and Charlie. She was content to pay for pizza if it meant a little more time to enjoy the warm glow inside her. It had been a perfect day.

CHAPTER

ELEVEN

The nearest town of any size was almost half an hour away depending on traffic and weather. If the students of Ravencrest wanted to go on a special date or do some substantial shopping, and if they had a car on campus, they went there. Charlie had a truck. It wasn't in great shape, and he really didn't love the whole truck aesthetic, but it had been cheap, and he needed a way to get around.

Charlie and Mona pulled into the student parking lot and sat with the radio on for a moment, singing along until "Folsom Prison Blues" finished. Mona hated country music and it was the only station around campus, but one thing being with Charlie taught her was that there was always some good to find in everything. Cheesy as it sounded, he was right more often than not. Johnny Cash was the good in country.

They took their time walking back from the parking lot. Ravencrest College wasn't large and Charlie was social, so they stopped several times to chat with people. A girl was sitting outside, studying for finals and optimistically trying to get a tan in the early May sun while playing a best of the '80s CD. Charlie yelled at her to turn it up and grabbed

104

Mona by the waist, swinging her down the sidewalk and serenading her. He sang as he twirled, his voice and his hair golden in the afternoon light. Mona laughed and sang along.

Arms around each other's waists, they went down the sidewalk until Charlie stopped them at the bronze statue of the college's founder.

"Hey," he said. "I've got something to show you."

"I've seen it," Mona said archly.

Charlie feigned shock.

"There are children around!" he said. "Save that sort of talk for later."

"Promise?"

Charlie waggled his eyebrows comically, then stood to attention and swept his hand up, presenting a tall, overgrown hedge. Mona looked unimpressed.

"Plants?"

"My dear, you cannot see the forest for the hedge. On the other side of the hedge."

Mona thought she'd explored every corner of the campus in the last three years, and she'd never noticed a hedge here before. Despite herself, she was interested.

"Go on, Lover Boy," she said. "Tell me."

"No, no!" Charlie said. "It's better seen."

Charlie looked around ostentatiously, a spy willing the world to catch him. Then he winked at Mona, let go of her hand, and plunged into the hedge.

Mona crossed her arms and waited. She knew it wouldn't be long. Sure enough, a few seconds later Charlie popped his head back out of the bush.

"Well? Are you coming?"

"You know how I feel about nature, Charlie. You'd better give me a damn good reason to follow you in there."

He grabbed her hand and pulled her forward until their

faces were so close they were sharing breath. He paused a second, then closed the gap between them.

Charlie kissed like he lived—mercurial, deliberate, and full of passion. Mona, almost always slightly angry at the world, gave as good as she got. When Charlie started to pull away, she grabbed his hair and kissed him again before letting him go.

Charlie arched an eyebrow and said smugly "So? Good enough?"

She pursed her lips.

"For now. I'll need a second installment later."

Mona took Charlie's outstretched hand and let him draw her forward, through the tangle of branches.

They were in a clearing, a strange open space in the middle of this strange grove. Trees arced overhead, a skeletal ribcage closing off the clearing from the rest of the world. A few broken pillars cast short, jagged shadows on the mossy floor.

"See?" Charlie said proudly. "Isn't it great?"

"Very," Mona agreed, examining one of the pillars. "It's weird we never found this place before, though, isn't it?"

Charlie shrugged.

"Here, this is the best part!"

He grabbed her hand again and led her past a few columns and some twisted trees to a building, long and low, that hunkered in the shadows of the clearing. It was covered with old vines and new fallen leaves.

"What is it?" Mona asked, trying to clear off a window and peer through.

"I don't know! Isn't that great?" Charlie crouched down, fiddling with the doorknob. "I think, if I get some of the rust off of this—"

The knob turned. Charlie looked up at Mona and grinned.

"Let's go see what's inside."

The only light to see by came filtering through the vine-and-dust covered ceiling and windows. It was dim and orange and painted everything in wavy bars. Abandoned exercise equipment was piled everywhere. Busted treadmills were shoved to one side.

They spent some time exploring the room. Everything was coated with a thin layer of dust, which made Mona sneeze. There wasn't that much to see and Charlie soon got bored. He poked around in a few of the piles, making his way eventually to the back of the long room.

"Hey, look at this!"

Mona glanced up from the old pair of roller-skates she was playing with to where Charlie stood past a handful of forgotten pool tables.

"I found a staircase!" Charlie said.

Mona stood, dusted off her hands and joined him. An open doorway led to a wooden staircase that disappeared into darkness. She shivered and rubbed her arms. It wasn't cold, exactly, but there was something ...

Charlie wrapped his arms around her from behind.

"You okay?" he asked.

"Yeah. Just a chill." Mona laughed. "Someone walked over my grave, I guess."

"No one would dare. You'd haunt them."

"It's true."

"My beautiful ghost." Charlie spun her around and kissed her. She reached up and laced her fingers behind his neck. They stood, pressed together in the semi-darkness, fully absorbed in each other.

When they drew apart, she cupped her hand gently on Charlie's cheek and smiled up at him.

"Don't worry," she said. "I wouldn't haunt you."

Charlie laughed and pulled her in for a quick hug.

"Fine, don't haunt me, then. See if I care." He kissed her

again, a quick peck on her lips. "Now, let's see what's down here."

The dark staircase led down to an echoing, empty room. A huge pool, Olympic size and looking very deep without any water, took up most of the room.

"I wish I had a skateboard," Charlie said, his voice bouncing off the concrete shell.

"You don't skate," Mona pointed out.

"I could learn."

"Anyway, it wouldn't be a clean run. There's something down there."

Charlie walked closer to the edge of the pool and peered toward where Mona pointed. A large pedestal rose from the center of the pool. Two steps led up to the top of the pedestal.

"What is that?"

Mona shrugged. "Part of the pool cleaning equipment?"

Charlie shook his head.

"No way. I've cleaned enough pools. I've never seen anything like that."

"Wait a minute." Mona held up one hand. "You were a pool boy?"

"For one delicious summer, yes."

"Huh. I didn't think that was a real thing."

"In a rich enough neighborhood, sure. There was a gated community about twenty minutes from my dad's. Those people were loaded."

"Rich or drunk?"

Charlie smirked.

"Yes."

He crouched down and gripped the edge of the pool.

"I'm getting a closer look."

After he jumped down, he reached up and caught Mona as she pushed off from the edge. Their footsteps across the cracked pool floor echoed back and forth around them. As they got closer, something on top of the pedestal began to flicker into view.

"What is that?" Charlie said again.

Mona felt a chill up her spine as she looked at the glimmering form above the pedestal. It shimmered and sparked, green and yellow and purple. Trying to focus on the rough translucent rectangle made her feel sick.

"Charlie," she said, "let's go home."

Charlie had drawn ahead of her and was now at the pedestal, one foot on the bottom stair.

"Sure," he said, but his eyes were on the flickering lights. Mona wasn't sure he'd actually heard her. She licked her lips.

"Charlie, please. I don't like this. It's—wrong."

"Trust me, babe," Charlie said, and reached out his hand.

"Charlie—no!"

His fingers touched the shimmer.

IT STARTED WITH A SONG. IT WAS A MASSIVE SONG, swelling and crashing over Charlie and dragging him under until he had to come up for air, but he couldn't, there was no air, there was only music. As he listened, as he drowned in it, it began resolving into smaller songs. It was every song Charlie had ever heard, every lullaby and music box and storefront doorbell and "I love you" and-hymn-and-thesoundofrainandlovesongandwhisperthunderrock-songchurchbellbirdsongsilence-

Charlie slammed his hands over his ears but the song, drilling into him, did not stop. It did not stop, but it began to change, to resolve into individual words, languages that burned in Charlie's mind. And with the words came knowledge.

He knew, suddenly, that his world was only one world of

many, all different by large and small degrees. He knew that there was a world where humans had died out long ago, and a world where music was magic, and a world so near to his own that the only difference was that the college had a different name. And he knew that all the worlds were connected through one place, one central landing, with portals like the one he touched. Like the one that touched him.

The words were coming fast now, the knowledge faster. There were threats to his world, and they were coming through the portal. The unmakers. The hollow eaters. They were through the portal already, and it needed to be closed. He had to close it. They had to close it.

And if he didn't—

He stumbled back, crying out. A thousand memories which were not his own invaded the front of his mind, pushing everything else to the back. There were too many of them; he couldn't focus. He couldn't think.

"Charlie, are you okay? What's happening, baby? It's okay. You're okay."

Who was that? What language was it in? He thought he should remember, but there were so many things to remember now and he couldn't sort them out. He was awash in memories, they cascaded over him in waves, threatening to drown him. Something was touching him. Something warm around his shoulders.

"Come on, Charlie. Talk to me, tell me what's going on."

The familiar voice was harder to hear as he slid deeper under the sea of the other lives which were suddenly his. The other voices were louder. The languages he couldn't understand had coalesced into a single, multi-throated intonation. There were Words in his head, and they wanted out. The portal had to be closed, and the Words would close it. He knew which ones. It was his job to do it. He was born for this, had spent a lifetime—maybe many lifetimes—training for this. The Words demanded release; they beat against the inside of his skull like desperate prisoners. It hurt like hell.

"Charlie! I'm here, baby. I'm right here. Snap out of it."

The small voice weaved through the Words and got swallowed by the cacophony. The Words demanded to be spoken, but he resisted. There was something else. Something important. The Words would close the portal, but something else had to happen. He knew, but he couldn't remember. He flailed around in the expanse of imagery, but it wasn't there. Or rather, it was there but he had no idea how to find it. There were too many of them and they were so alien.

The pain was immense. He screamed a pitchless, wordless howl which he hoped would release some of the pressure threatening to explode within his skull. It didn't. He was dying. He said a Word. Lightning raced from him, energy flowing from his head to his fingertips and leaping at the portal. His mouth was on fire. He realized the Word had burned him on its way out. He felt hollow and knew, remembered, that the Words drew their strength from him. He snapped his jaw shut before the next Word could escape. He felt the power building and was afraid if he didn't stop them the Words might kill him. Then again, he was dying anyway.

He drifted away into the memories, trying to escape the fear by disconnecting from his body. It worked, after a fashion. As time passed, he managed to force the pain into the background; to sublimate it beneath his own will. It was his pain, and he could control it, with effort. He told the Words to shut up. But with the pain managed, he realized he'd drifted so far away from his body that he couldn't remember who he was. He had memories of so many lives, each of them simultaneously intimate and foreign. Who was he? He had no way to know, adrift in an endless ocean of selves. He needed a foothold, an anchor. An element of his true self from which he could reconstruct the rest. But he didn't even know where to look. Every memory felt as real as the next and he was too tired to sort through them. It was easier to just let go.

"Please, baby. I need you to come back to me. I'm here, baby. I'm here. I'm here for you."

You.

A small voice. He knew that voice. He knew those words. He understood them. Not as pictures or memories or impressions or interpretations. That voice was real. He belonged to that voice. He grasped it and wrapped it around himself, a drowning man clinging to a life raft that hit him just as he was slipping beneath the waves. He let it pull him home.

His eyes fluttered. Tears splashed onto them from a face above his own. A face he knew. A name ...

"You're Mona," he said.

She laughed and nodded and cried harder.

"You're Mona, and I'm ... Charlie?"

She nodded again, beaming at him through the tears.

"That's right, baby, that's right," she said, running a hand through his hair.

"What happened?" he asked.

She just shook her head, still crying. Charlie was content to lay still for a minute longer, letting her cool hands on his face ground him in this world until he felt steady enough to sit up. Then it was his turn to soothe Mona, to reassure her that he was back, that he was, at least mostly, okay.

"What happened?" he asked again when her tears and the whirling in his head both subsided.

"Well, a hole in the universe opened up and you spit lightning at it. I think," Mona answered.

"Thought so," he said. "Is it still there?"

She nodded.

"Yeah, I think I missed a piece of the instructions. Or several."

"Instructions?"

"I don't know. Maybe. It's all a jumble and I need to not think about it right now or I might ... go away again."

"Don't you ever leave me again," she said, and leaned over and kissed him.

Charlie winced.

"Burnt my tongue," he explained. "All that lightning spitting. I won't leave again."

"Promise?"

"As long as you're here to remind me of who I am."

She nodded. "That seems fair. I am an expert in the subject, after all. Do you think you're up to walking? I'd like to get out of here. Away from that ... thing." She waved at the portal.

"Me too. Let's go." He still hurt, but he was already learning now to shift the Words into the back of his brain where he could try to ignore them, and that helped a great deal.

They left the cavern, arms so tight around each other it was impossible to know who was supporting whom. The portal sparked in the gloom they left behind.

TWELVE

Charlie walked through endless worlds, each a heartbeat away from his own. He saw worlds that were covered in ice, worlds where small islands rode a sea of lava. He saw tiny villages inside mountains and tremendously huge cities under the sea.

They were all abandoned, all deserted by their inhabitants. Stone stairs for giants to walk down, tiny boulevards where mice could promenade, human structures on Earthly worlds, all empty of life.

But the monsters were there. Sharp faces poked out of windows, bulging eyes gleamed wetly from shadows. Tall, spectral fiends walked bone-lined streets while squat, bulky monsters, dog-like muzzles dripping gore, galloped at their side. In every world, every dusty forgotten realm, the monsters ruled.

In Charlie's dream, his world was overrun by monsters. People, fuzzy faceless dream people, were trying to evacuate through the portal but Charlie was trying to keep them from going. He grabbed people and told them on the other side of the portal was death, but they pulled away and kept going through. His family came, Joe and Inez and Alice and Smitha and Mona, and he tried to stop them. They listened to him politely.

"But Charlie," Smitha said when he finished, "we don't believe you. You're lying."

And they walked into the portal without him.

Charlie tasted blood and ash in his mouth. The portal closed with lightning bolts of green. And he was alone.

He ran toward the portal, beating on the cracked cement pool floor until his fists bled. He cried for them to come back, that he'd rather face death with them than be left alone. The portal stayed closed.

"CHARLIE! CHARLIE, BABY, WAKE UP!"

His eyes fluttered open. Mona leaned over him, her worried eyes searching his face. Sunlight from the window lit up her hair, making the red strands among the purple burn like fire. Charlie's mouth was dry—he realized he had been calling out in his sleep.

"That must have been quite the nightmare," she said.

"It was ... bad." Already the memory of the dream was fading in the morning air. He could remember only flashes of images. Something about the family, losing the family, the family leaving him. He shivered.

"Poor baby." Mona settled down next to him. She put her head on his chest and slung one arm across his body. Charlie could feel the warmth of her breath through his thin cotton undershirt.

He slipped an arm around her and pulled her tighter.

"Want to talk about it?" she asked.

"No."

Her hair smelled like warm vanilla sugar. There were better shampoos, but Mona knew that Charlie loved the scent.

"Want me to talk?"

"Sure. Distract me with banality, love."

"How is finals week going?"

Charlie groaned.

"Oh, don't remind me. I'll pass, but Mukherjee's final is the last one I have left and it's going to kill me."

"Then study."

"We're seniors, Lisa. I've been studying for three years. Surely that's enough."

Charlie followed the curve of her back with his hand, lightly running his fingers up and down. Her presence, the simple conversation, helped him shake off the last wisps of fugue from the nightmare. She was the sun burning the fog away.

"You have bewitched me," he said suddenly, "body and soul, and I love ... I love ... I love you."

Mona propped herself up on her elbow and looked down at her husband.

"Where did that come from?" she asked.

"Nowhere in particular. You just look really beautiful right now."

Mona, in a ragged T-shirt and old pair of gym shorts, flushed.

"So, beautiful," Charlie continued, "let's kiss until our faces fall off."

Mona laughed. She grabbed a pillow and smacked him in the face with it. Charlie stopped another hit by reaching up and kissing her. She melted down into him, reciprocating the kiss. His hand grazed the small hairs on the nape of her neck, and she wiggled in delight. Morning stubble gently scratched her chin. Charlie's mouth, beneath hers, formed into a smile.

Sunlight filtered through the small window, dappling the

room with warm buttery overtones. Someone, probably Smitha, had made coffee and the smell seeped around the bedroom door. A low murmur of voices, a muffled laugh, came from the kitchen.

Mona drew away. She sighed contentedly.

"That's a nice way to start the day."

"I can think of something nicer."

"Absolutely not. I have my final meeting with my supervising teacher in an hour, and you're supposed to meet up with Smitha and the pups to study for your last finals."

"But I'm hungry," Charlie complained, nipping playfully at her shoulder.

"You're always hungry." Mona kissed him again and stood from the bed. "Go eat some cereal while I take a shower."

Charlie lay in bed after she left, hands behind his head, watching the sunbeams play on the ceiling. In a few minutes he would get dressed and go to the kitchen, but for now he enjoyed the comfort and quiet. He considered that lingering in bed on a warm spring morning was one of the truest pleasures in life.

He fell into that half-sleep that is so disconcertingly pleasurable, the feeling of not quite connection with a world not quite real. His eyes dropped. The voices from the kitchen ran together, a low rumble that began to coalesce into something just barely intelligible.

"Ehan," he whispered, giving the word form.

A spark flickered between his teeth, the small electric shock waking him up completely. He sat up and rubbed his mouth. Had he accidentally bitten his lip? Had he dreamed the word, the small spark? It hadn't burned his tongue like it did when he screamed it in the empty pool. Charlie shied away from examining it any further. He was worried about falling into contemplation of other worlds, green fire from the portal on campus, monsters. He remembered all too well the feeling of losing himself, of his edges softening and running away into memories and worlds that weren't his.

He left the bedroom and joined the family for breakfast, letting the familiar voices, familiar words, familiar tastes, ground him in this reality. Charlie knew he was going to tell the family everything, about the portal and everything. But not yet. Not over breakfast. The heavy weight in his heart told him that everything was going to change, had already started changing. Let them have this meal, this shared sunny morning and sunny eggs and sunny faces. Let them— let *him*—feel the sun now, against the dark that he felt sure was coming.

"BUT I DON'T WANT TO STUDY ANYMORE," JOE whined. He threw down the notecards he had been studying. "This test doesn't matter. It literally doesn't matter."

"Every test matters," Smitha said, lacking enthusiasm.

"This one doesn't," Joe insisted. "I did the math. I could bomb this test, I could get a zero, and I would still pass."

"Passing isn't succeeding," Smitha retorted.

"It is when it's your last final of your senior year, *Mom*," Joe replied.

Smitha smiled at that and laid down her own cards.

"I think Charlie agrees with you," she said, and gestured across to where her friend sat staring blankly into space. His study sheets lay untouched on the table; his left hand, hanging down, drummed a frantic beat in the air. "Right, Charlie?"

No response.

"Charlie?"

Mona just shook her head and got to her feet, stretching.

"He's zoned out. I need a snack. Joe, come with?"

"Yes!"

"Smitha?"

Clearly torn, Smitha glanced down at her notecards and grimaced.

"I shouldn't ..."

Inez put one hand on her hips and shook a finger at Smitha.

"Young lady, too much schoolwork is going to break your brain."

Joe opened his hands wide as if to say "See?"

Smitha laughed and stood from the table.

"Well, when you put it that way."

The three seniors walked away in the direction of the student union.

Alice scooted closer to Charlie and put a hand on his arm.

"Charlie? Are you okay?"

He started at the touch, swung backward in an almost comically exaggerated manner. But in the moments before he could arrange his face, Alice saw his look of pure terror.

"Yeah sure," he said absently.

"Charlie."

Alice firm and insistent was a rare thing, rare enough that the steel in her voice took Charlie aback.

"Actually," he said, "no. No, I'm not okay."

"Do you want to talk about it?" Inez asked.

"I do. But not yet. Something happened to me, to me and Mona, and I want her here to talk about it. And I want Smitha and Joe here, to hear it."

Alice and Inez exchanged worried glances. Serious Charlie was more rare than resolute Alice.

"Well, okay. Do you, I don't know, want to take a walk or something? Until they come back?"

Five minutes later they were at the entrance to campus, but instead of turning left and onto the sidewalk that would lead them toward the dormitories they veered to the right, down a mostly unused walking path which ran roughly parallel to a small creek that threaded through a lightly wooded area just outside of town proper. Charlie stayed uncharacteristically quiet, leaving the pups to try to carry the conversation.

Up ahead, the path spilled out into a public park. It was nothing as fancy as the kind with a playground and ball fields: just an open area with a few benches and picnic tables that was kept reasonably manicured by the town. A few weeks ago Charlie had mentioned it to them, describing it as "one of the best after-hours make-out spots in town" with a wink. He wasn't wrong. Alice blushed in the general direction of a nearby bench.

A single pavilion stood at the edge of the park. Charlie squinted at it. A figure stood almost indistinguishable from the corner post.

"Looks like we're not the only ones here." He winced, reaching for his head. "Boy, I'm getting one hell of a headache."

Alice tried to tell herself the chill she felt was just a cold spring wind making one last attempt at a storm, but she knew she was lying. Her skin had turned to ice. She was cold to the bone. To the soul. She looked at Inez and saw that her jaw was set and her eyes panicky.

"Let's go home," said Alice, suddenly gripping Inez's arm tight. "Please, let's go?"

The figure standing at the post moved. The air bent, rippled around him as he went. His movement was somewhere between a stagger and run, as though he were being dragged through space by a rope attached to his sternum. Seconds later he stood in front of them.

Charlie fell to his knees, clutching his head and moaning. The man stood between Alice and Inez, his hatchet shaped face pivoting between them as though weighing them against each other. Through the terror, Alice thought: *That's not a man.*

This was difficult because it required her brain to rewrite reality. A human mind will, in the end, always try to fit what it is seeing into an accepted paradigm. The creature staring at her out of its watery eyes, with a slitted nose and long mouth, was so far beyond the framework of the human paradigm that it nearly emerged out the other side, so far removed from reality it defied acceptance or definition. Despite the wave of freezing terror washing over her, Alice had to fight to believe the thing in front of her existed.

A grinding noise at her feet ripped Alice's attention away from the apparition in front of her, and she looked down to see Charlie gritting his teeth so hard sparks were flying from them. Another thing that defied reality. Teeth don't fire green sparks, no matter how intense the grinding. In a moment of hilarious terror, Alice wondered if he had been eating wintergreen mints.

The hatchet-faced monster opened robes Alice hadn't realized it was wearing with arms Alice wasn't sure she could see. How was it gripping the frayed black edges of the previously unseen robes? Were there fingers? It seemed it was more the idea of motion than motion itself, the suggestion of arms pulling at the space in reality where a robe would be, if the creature were a man and his vestments were a robe.

Alice could feel her fear washing over her face in relentless, invisible waves. The chill in her bones magnified past the point of pain and into blissful disassociation as it immobilized her. She could only watch from the back of her mind as the creature moved toward Inez.

Beneath the open robes was a jagged set of ribs, cracked open and pointed out in sharp barbs, as though the organs inside had burst out and left the gates swinging open behind them. They weren't ribs, probably, and who knew if they had ever guarded organs. But they looked bony and occupied the space where ribs should be, so Alice's mind filled in the gaps with something familiar.

Inez, rooted to the ground beside Alice and paralyzed in the same way, couldn't even whimper as it took hold of her head behind her ears, dragging her forward toward the jagged, iron maiden rib cage.

Describing what happened next would prove to be impossible for Alice, like describing the fading remnants of a nightmare whose structure did not make sense even while it was happening, and slipped away upon attempts to reconstruct it, leaving behind only a sense of empty horror and surety that one would never be whole again.

Inez unbecame. Her place within the universe shrank. Alice fought to remember her name, struggled to understand why the empty space beside her felt a bit like the memory of an old friend. Meanwhile the arms of the creature became real, no longer the suggestion of arms but fully visible limbs, frightfully thick and knotted in sinuous masses of flesh.

The watery eyes gleamed and the long mouth twisted and bent in a feral grin, splitting across the hatchet face and revealing a mouth full of teeth and leathery tongues. With its new arms of flesh, it pulled ... someone .. forward again, until they were mere centimeters from the barbed tips of its ribs.

Charlie staggered to his feet and shook his head madly in an attempt to scatter away the visions he did not understand, the dreams which were not his. Finally, relenting to a memory which did not belong to him from a time eons before his birth, he opened his mouth and let the Words escape.

"Ehan evna thae!" he screamed, the Words tearing from his throat with fury. He felt his lips burn, felt the skin near his mouth char and split. A tooth somewhere chipped and tiny pieces of tooth-bone tore several deep cuts into the roof of his burnt mouth. Too powerful; he needed to learn to control

them. More Words tried to follow, but Charlie placed the palms of both hands on his jaw and forced it closed. That was enough.

The Words struck the creature like a physical blow, sweeping through its not-quite-yet-form and driving it backwards. Green fire smacked against its face, the force of the strike cutting deep below its right eye. A large divot of skin at its jaw was torn away, revealing its giant, writhing tongues. The creeping reality faded from its arms and back to its source. Inez collapsed to the ground, unconscious. The creature glared at Charlie from its watery eyes before turning and retreating into the woods on the far side of the park. As it fled, the air stilled. Alice fought off the cloud of terror that had forced her inside of herself.

"Inez!"

Alice looked around wildly, eyes full of fear and barely restrained madness as she hunted for the half of herself which had almost been written out of her memory. She spotted Inez's limp form on the ground beside her and fell on her in a heap. She wrapped her arms around Inez's waist and sobbed.

Charlie drew himself up, his face a mess of blood. He wheezed through his dry throat. Out of breath and overwhelmed by the knowledge of what he'd just done, he couldn't shape any words, but he drew Alice to her feet and slung Inez's limp body over his shoulder. Even once he thought he could talk again, Charlie kept quiet. He was thinking.

Once they made it back to the apartments, Charlie gestured toward the door of 1A.

"Your place?"

Alice shook her head, eyes wide, and pointed up the stairs.

"Please?"

Charlie nodded, secured his grip on Inez, and forced himself up the fifteen steps, counting each one with a groan.

At the top of the stairs Alice darted around him and sat on the couch. This time it was Charlie who shook his head. He turned to the room he shared with Mona, pushed in the door with his hip, and deposited Inez carefully on the bed.

"Are you sure?" Alice asked anxiously. Charlie stretched out his back, prodded the burned places inside his mouth with his tongue, and nodded.

"I know the two of you love that horrifying couch but take the bed. Please. You need to take care of your girl."

"Charlie, the couch will be fine for Inez. I need to watch her in case... in case she needs me."

"No arguing today, pup," said Charlie with a slight smile. "Just listen to your brother, okay? You can watch her in there just as well."

Alice bit her lip, looked down at Inez, and gave in. Charlie nodded and turned toward the door.

"Charlie?" came Alice's small voice from behind him. He turned back around.

"Yeah, kiddo?"

"What was that thing?"

"I'm not sure. But I have ... sort of an idea. A memory."

Charlie braced himself for the questions that would follow the slip of the tongue, but Alice let it slide.

"What did it do to 'Nez?"

"Not sure on that, either. But she'll be fine. We'll talk about it all later, when everyone is back and Inez is awake."

"Okay. Charlie?"

"Yeah?"

"What if it comes back?"

"I'll be waiting."

THIRTEEN

Inez didn't wake up the rest of the day. She stirred a few times, muttered and whimpered, but otherwise slept. As the day drained into night, Charlie found the noise in his head increasing. Every time he tried to think about what happened—Inez, the Words, the monster—the memories in his mind chimed in, tried to help, but he still hadn't learned how to interpret or control them. It all left him with a furious headache and a sense of paranoia.

The others returned, asking question after question. Alice, at Inez's side, stayed silent, leaving Charlie to face the onslaught alone.

"What do you mean, you got attacked? By like a bully or something?" Joe started pacing angrily. "I bet it was that Michael Lafferty. That guy's had a big mouth on him about you since sophomore year."

"It wasn't—" Charlie began, then frowned. "Wait, he has? What has he said? No, never mind, that's not important. It wasn't a bully. It was a ... hell, I don't even know how to describe it. It was a monster."

"Charlie, this isn't the time to fool around," Smitha admonished him.

"I'm not fooling, Prof, honest. It was, like ... I don't even know. It was, like, man-shaped. And ... empty. And it tried to, like, eat Inez? But sort of like suck her out of existence?"

Now Joe looked worried.

"Charlie, are you having a stroke? This doesn't make any sense."

"It doesn't," Alice said from the doorway. She supported Inez, groggy and pinch-faced, to their spot on the couch. "It doesn't make any sense at all, but he's not lying. It's true."

"Charlie, tell them about the pool house," Mona urged.

Smitha stood.

"No one say anything yet," she commanded. "We need tea."

The apartment filled up with uncharacteristic silence, a thick, heavy fog that stuffed Charlie's lungs with cottony anxiety. Once they each gripped their favorite mugs, inhaling the scent of their favorite tea, Smitha settled herself back in her chair and looked at Charlie.

"Now," she said.

Charlie swallowed hard. He was never at a loss for words, but it was, perhaps unsurprisingly, difficult to tell the others about a glowing cosmic oval.

"Okay," he began. "Okay. Okay."

He stopped and frowned.

"Okay?" Mona asked, putting her hand reassuringly on his leg.

Charlie nodded.

"Okay. So. Yesterday, Mona and I went down to that statue on lower campus. There's this building there. It looks like it's been abandoned for a long time. We've never seen it before. I think it was hiding? Somehow? There's this big empty pool inside. And, uh, there's a portal."

Joe frowned.

"The building was hiding?" Joe asked.

The Professor cocked an eyebrow.

"A portal?" she asked.

"Yeah, like ... like a door? To other places?"

"Okay ..."

"Like Gozer's temple in Dana's fridge. Like a Stargate. Like the wardrobe to Narnia." Charlie sighed. "I'm running out of examples, guys."

"I think I get the idea," the Professor said. "It sounds pretty unbelievable, though."

"Are you sure you guys weren't—" Joe mimed drinking a bottle.

"Not at the time," Mona said, offended. "It sounds unbelievable, but you'd better believe it. I saw it, too. Charlie stuck his hand in it."

Charlie nodded.

"What was it like?" Joe asked.

"Not great," Charlie admitted. "It felt like sticking a finger into an electrified soap bubble. I was kind of afraid it would close and my arm was going to get cut off. Or that something over there was going to grab me."

Alice gasped abruptly.

"Something like that monster that almost ate Inez?"

Smitha turned to the pups.

"You two," she said. "Your turn. Explain."

Charlie let Inez and Alice tell about their encounter with the monster in the park. Hearing another two people talk about it made him feel saner. It helped, hearing someone else confirm that it wasn't all in his head. And hopefully it would make Joe and the Professor more likely to believe his story, too. He needed that boost—he hadn't even told them the weirdest part yet.

"—and Charlie said something I didn't understand, and it

made the monster let Inez go and we brought her back home," Alice concluded. "You know the rest."

And there it was.

Smitha turned to Charlie.

"Explain," she repeated in a strained voice.

"The soap bubble gave me powers," he said.

Joe, who had been taking everything in quietly, burst out laughing.

Smitha shushed him, annoyed.

"I'm sorry," Joe said, "but do you know how weird that sounds? And how much weirder it would sound coming from anyone but Charlie?"

Charlie grinned over at his friend.

"You're right," he said. "You're absolutely right."

"He is right," Smitha said, "but I'm still waiting for my explanation."

"Sorry, Prof," Charlie apologized. "I don't have much more of an explanation, I'm afraid. When I stuck my hand in the portal, something happened and somehow, I got these, like, memories in my head. Old memories, of things I never knew before. And words in a different language that I'm pretty sure isn't from anywhere on Earth. Powerful words."

"That's what you said to the monster?" Alice asked.

Charlie nodded.

"Some of them, anyway. Some of the words are more powerful than others. Some drive away the monsters and some —" He paused, then shook his head again. "I don't know what they do yet. Something else. They have some other power. It's just—it's just not clear in my head yet."

"How can we help?" Joe asked.

"Hang on," said Smitha. "I need help understanding this better."

"You and me both, darling," answered Charlie.

"You ... what do you mean when you say 'power'? I

understand that you've got memories you don't recognize. I can sort of understand that there are words in your head which you can't translate but feel compelled to say. But I just can't find a framework to understand what you mean when you describe the words as a power. Do you mean they have ... like, a deep meaning, or something? A heavy impact?"

"No, it's just power. Raw power. It's like a bunch of pent-up energy inside my skull, and when I let it out it draws energy from my entire body."

"It's like there's lightning in his teeth," offered Alice. "I saw it when Inez was ... when Charlie saved Inez. And then it shot out of his entire body."

"Like the Emperor?" asked Joe.

"What Emperor?"

Alice rolled her eyes at Inez. "Palpatine. Star Wars, baby."

"Oh, the wrinkly guy in the black robe."

"We're going to watch those movies again sometime, and you are going to pay attention."

"Do I have to?"

"It's not a bad point of reference, though," said Charlie. "I mean, the Emperor definitely wasn't crawling around on the ground clutching his head and screaming, but ... maybe? Sorta like that?"

"I'm sorry," said Smitha. "I still can't get it. I just don't understand how that can be inside your head."

Charlie made a decision and knelt in front of Smitha. He reached out.

"Here, Professor. Give me your hand."

She did, with no questions. Charlie looked her in the eye for a moment, then winced in anticipation and screwed his eyes closed.

The Words were there. He wasn't sure what they all did yet, or how to use them. But he was starting to see the patterns, starting to learn. He reached out to the Words, summoning them, calling them to him for the first time instead of being called by them. They were waiting and leapt when he called. He whimpered as the pain slammed into him, but it was a different pain. He was in control this time—the Words weren't trying to break out, they were waiting for his order.

This was the clearest and most easy to understand memory in Charlie's head: summoning and controlling the power. He *knew* how to do it. He *remembered*, even though he'd never done it before. He just had to trust the memory. He knew everyone was looking at him, he could feel it even with his eyes closed, but he had to press on.

"*Ehan evna thae*," he whispered, as quietly as he could. He felt the Words slip through his teeth and summoned all his will to shape them as they escaped. Even letting the tiniest bit of power slip still dried out his lips a bit—he could feel them chapping. But he was in control. Joe yelped in surprise. It was the first time he had seen or heard Charlie using the Words.

Step one accomplished. Now for the riskier part. He almost gave in at this point; what he'd already done was risky enough. But Smitha needed to understand. He needed her to get it. It was ... it was important that the Professor believed him. And he had to start learning to control it at some point. Might as well be now.

There was another memory lurking, another piece of the instructions that built toward something he had yet to understand. But he'd seen it in there and so he searched for it, like he was trying to recall a critical chapter in a textbook during a test. He found it. He remembered.

Charlie whispered the Words again, but this time he shifted the power draw, moved it around so it was coming from his guts instead of his teeth. He opened his mind, stretched it out until he could feel every inch of his body, finding the energy in every cell, carefully selecting the ones he needed and letting the power flow from them.

Success number two. Joe yelled again, and Alice gasped. Mona tried to wrap an arm around him, but he shook his pain-addled head. He couldn't have another body touch his right now. He needed to concentrate on the Professor.

And now, Charlie thought, *for my final trick ...*

He opened up his mind again, stretching out to find himself, and followed the ends of his fingers to where they interlocked with the Professor's. He pushed. She squealed, twisted in her seat, but let him in. He felt her as though she were an extension of himself. He tugged on the power again, summoned the Words, and let them flow down his arm and through his fingers, guiding them into her body. It was astounding. He felt her energy, burning even brighter than his, and knew that if he wanted to he could pull it out and add it to the Words, multiply the power through his connection to her.

Her fingers were clenched in a death grip around his own. He risked cracking open one eye and saw her face distorted in a mask of pain, her mouth cocked open. Flecks of green lightning leapt between her teeth.

He could push the Words out through her. He remembered how. But he tugged on the reins, calling them back. Biting down on the power, bringing it to bay, was not a fun experience. The Words wanted out. But he was learning. The Professor's grip relaxed, and he let her go. Mona threw herself into his lap, pulling his head to her chest and stroking his hair.

Smitha turned to him, eyes wide. "How do you stand it?"

"That's only a tiny piece, darling," he said. "I was keeping it on a leash."

The Professor gasped. "Charlie—how awful."

He shrugged and let Mona stroke his hair, eyes closed. He

was afraid to see their faces, afraid that Joe and Inez and Smitha would be looking at him like he was a freak. Or maybe they wouldn't be able to look at him at all, maybe they would leave him, leave him all alone—

"Damn," Joe said. "That looked awesome."

Charlie opened his eyes.

"It didn't feel awesome," Smitha said. "It hurt."

"You guys had fireworks in your hair. I bet it hurt. You looked like wizards or something. Is it bad that I kinda want to see it again?"

"Focus, Joe," Charlie said.

Joe ran his fingers through his own hair.

"Right," he said. "So. There are monsters that—eat people? And a portal to another world. And Charlie has Force lightning and Inez almost got eaten. Am I missing anything?"

"There's one more thing," Charlie said. "We, um ... we have to do something about it."

"We have to what now?" Joe asked.

"I know, I know," Charlie said. "But it's part of my memories, from the portal. As long as the portal is open, those monsters are able to come through. Our whole world is in danger from them. They're like locusts. They'll eat everyone. I remember other worlds, worlds where they weren't stopped. Desolate, empty worlds ..."

Charlie trailed off, staring down at his hands. Then he shook himself and looked up.

"Sorry. Just—yeah. It's bad. It will be bad, here, too, if we don't stop it."

Alice shivered at the shadow in his voice. Inez drew her closer.

"How?" Inez asked. "How are we supposed to stop this?"

"I don't really know?" Charlie sounded lost. "I think we have to close it somehow."

"Close the—portal?" Smitha asked.

Charlie nodded.

"Close the mystical portal that leads to a hell world and that is disgorging monsters that eat people out of existence?" she continued.

Charlie nodded again.

"So ... how?" Inez repeated.

Charlie shook his head.

"I don't know. I have some ideas, some stuff from my memories, but nothing real solid. I just don't know."

Mona, who had been keeping quiet while Charlie tried to explain himself, threaded her fingers through his and shuffled closer to him.

"How can we help?" she asked, her voice soft.

"Just be here," Charlie said, almost inaudible as he stared at the floor. "For now, just be here with me."

"I'm here, baby," Mona said. She put her head on his shoulder.

"I'm here," Joe said immediately after, coming over to sit on Charlie's other side.

Smitha, Inez, and Alice each echoed "I'm here" in turn. When Charlie lifted his head again, his eyes were bright with tears, but his usual smile was back on his face.

"I love you guys," he said. "I really do. Can I have some more tea?"

FOURTEEN

The tea was warm and soothing and only burned a little on Charlie's freshly chapped lips. He set down the cup and looked up at his friends' waiting faces, trying to pull together his scattered thoughts and unwanted memories.

"So. I told you there's a portal, right?"

"In the abandoned pool house," Mona offered.

"Right. So that portal, that's where the Nowhere Men are coming from."

"Nowhere Men?" interjected Joe. "Like, from the song?"

"What song?" asked Smitha.

"The Beatles," answered Alice.

"Why are we talking about the Beatles?" asked Inez.

"It's just what I call them," said Charlie with a shrug. "Anyway, there's this portal, and we've got to close it, or they'll keep coming. I think. And I sort of maybe kind of know how to close it, because I remember doing it before. Except I never have, and the memories don't really make sense, and when I tried to focus on them, I lost track of who I am and Mona had to pull me back. So that's where we are, I guess."

There was a general round of confused nodding as everyone tried to follow along.

"I think I'm with you," Joe said. "Or at least, as with you as I can be. Any idea how we go about closing this portal thing?"

"Nope. Okay, yes. Maybe. From what I can tell, it's connected to how I can push power in and out of you guys."

Smitha's shoulders twitched in memory of their recent pain.

"Right, so," Charlie continued, "the Words need power to work, and they take it from me. From us, probably, if I was connected to you. I think we need a LOT of power to do this. It's like ... like daisy chaining a bunch of batteries."

"We're batteries?" Inez asked.

"Basically, yeah. Sorry. I can just about taste the shape of the Words I'll need to use, and even thinking about them right now makes me feel like I'm going to die."

"That bad?" Joe asked with a frown.

"Worse," said Charlie. "I don't know how to describe it, exactly, but it feels like the Words are draining you and damaging you at the same time. Like you're being sucked dry, and then lit on fire."

"Which is why we all need to be a part of this," Mona chimed in. "You will kill yourself if you do it alone. You need us."

"All of us, I think," Charlie agreed. "Six is important. There were six last time. And the time before that. There are always six."

"Last time?" asked Alice, pursing her lips.

Charlie waved a hand vaguely, fluttering it through the air. "Other memories. Keep up. I think we need six to make sure we have enough juice to do it without killing anybody."

"So can you just, you know, power up before rolling down there?" Inez asked.

"I don't think I can store it up like that. I think I have to be touching you when it happens."

"You've only got two hands, pal," said Joe. "How are you going to touch all five of us at the same time?"

"I've got more than hands, buddy." Charlie winked outrageously. Mona gently knocked him on the side of the head.

"Down, boy," she said.

"Maybe we could all touch you?" Smitha suggested. "And do not turn that into a dirty joke."

Charlie looked dubious.

"One big group hug? Maybe. The Words sorta need to ... flow, or something?"

"So, what if we all just stood in a big line?" asked Joe. "Like the world's weirdest conga dance?"

"Can you do it if we're all connected to each other?" Alice added. "Or do you need to be touching each of us directly?"

"That's ... I don't know. That's a good question. Let's find out!"

Charlie stood and pulled Mona up after him. He grabbed Mona by the shoulders and Mona, in turn, helped Smitha up and put her hands around the other girl's waist.

"*Ehan evna thae,*" said Charlie quietly, trying to let just the tiniest bit of power flow into the Words. He pushed them forward into Mona, reaching into her and finding her alight with brilliant strength. He stole a bit of it and wrapped it around his own. Then, crossing his fingers on Mona's shoulders, he pushed the power forward. He felt the Professor, saw her startle a bit at the tug of power. He let the Words slip away and they all relaxed.

"Well?" asked Joe.

"It worked," Mona confirmed. "Really buzzed my teeth there."

"Sorry," said Charlie. "I was trying to keep it as small as possible."

"It did work, though," Smitha said. "I could tell it was going through me. I could feel you and Mona, and something connecting all three of us."

"Is there a finite amount of power?" Alice mused. Charlie shook his head.

"I don't think so. I think the only limit is how much I—we, I guess—can physically stand."

Joe leaned back against a chair and steepled his fingers together.

"Okay. Let me make sure I've got this straight. We go to this place that isn't really there, we form a line by holding hands or whatever, and then you, Charlie, at the back, say your ethan-whatever words and push power through us, and the portal closes?"

"Sort of? I don't know. And I think there are different words to close the portal; the ethan-whatever is for hurting the monsters."

Joe groaned.

"I'm never going to keep all this straight."

"You don't have to," Mona pointed out. "All we have to do is go down to that portal so Charlie can use us as batteries."

Charlie walked over to the window. He looked out at the steady campus lights for a moment, then turned back to his friends.

"You don't have to. Come with, that is. It's going to hurt. Probably a lot. And the monsters might be there and ... I can't just volunteer you for that. And I don't want you to say yes without thinking about it. Really thinking about it. And if you don't want to commit to that, it's fine. It really is."

"I'm in," Mona said instantly.

"Geeze, Lisa, I said think about it."

In response Mona held up her left hand and pointed to her wedding ring with her right.

"I still don't understand it," Joe said. "But if you're in trouble, I'm there."

"Me too," said Smitha. "I couldn't bear to know you were taking such a risk by yourself. Not when I could help."

"You two should probably stay behind," said Charlie, turning to the pups. "It's going to be—"

"We can't," Inez said. "If ... if those things are coming back, we have to stop them. I'm terrified of going down there, but I'm more terrified of you going down and not coming back, and then having to live in a world with those monsters and no way to fight them."

Alice nodded.

"There's really no choice, is there?" she said. "We've seen what they do. We'd just spend the rest of our lives hiding in fear and jumping at shadows."

"Living shadows," said Inez with a shiver. Alice grabbed her hand and squeezed it.

"Well," said Charlie, "I can't say I'm not glad."

He didn't look glad. He looked sick, and worried, and more nervous than Smitha had ever seen him, even on his wedding day. He also looked, to Smitha's eyes, older and more mature, as if he had aged ten years in a day. She could see the tension in him, taut and twanging his psyche. He wouldn't last long in that state, he couldn't. She stood.

"So," she said, "when do we go? Now?"

Charlie glanced at the clock. It was nearly midnight.

"Not yet," he said reluctantly. "There will still be people around and I don't want anyone else to get roped into this mess. Let's wait until the night crowd thins out. Say, 2 a.m.?"

"What are we supposed to do for two hours?" Joe grumped.

Charlie saw the heads swing toward him and he wiggled

his eyebrows suggestively because he knew they expected it. His heart wasn't really in it, though. His heart was too busy pounding like a jackhammer.

Mona slipped her hand into his.

"Let's take a walk," she suggested.

FIFTEEN

"2 a.m.," murmured Alice, looking down at her watch.

"How have I never noticed it before?" asked Joe as the six of them stood gazing down the path behind the founder's statue. The dilapidated structure, while tucked back on an unused area of lower campus, was clearly visible. "We walk past here all the time."

"Charlie said the portal hides it," answered Smitha.

"Not exactly hides it, per se," said Charlie. "I mean, it's a giant building. But it ... I don't know, it diminishes it. Washes it out of your memory. Makes it fade into the background."

"Yeah, I understand the words you are saying," Joe said. "I just don't understand how it works. It's so hard to believe."

Charlie tried to explain again, but he wasn't particularly clear on the point himself. The memories were hard to wade through, and it hadn't seemed like the most important bit to concentrate on solving.

"It's some sort of high-tech defense system, I think," he said. "Like a built-in camouflage. It changes the landscape around it to something unnoticeable, but it also messes with the memory of anyone who tries to look at it. You forget as soon as you look away."

"Still doesn't make sense," Joe grumped.

"Ancient alien space magic," offered Charlie.

"Good enough," Joe answered. He shouldered his baseball bat and pushed open the gate. "Keep up, I don't want to do this alone.

"I still can't believe you brought a baseball bat," huffed Charlie, right at his heels. "What are you gonna do, hit it in its not-body?"

"I can try," Joe grunted. "Just having it in my hands makes me feel better."

"Where'd you even get a bat?" asked Charlie. "You haven't played school baseball since freshman year."

"Trunk of my car," Joe said. "I play work league ball sometimes."

The brief exchange took them to the far end of the path, right up to the battered front door of the old rec hall nobody seemed to remember.

"This is it, eh?" asked Joe.

"This is it," Mona answered. "The place where I kissed Charlie and his entire world changed."

"Since the invention of the kiss, there have only been five kisses that were rated the most passionate, the most pure," Charlie began, in the intonation of Peter Falk's grandfather voice. Mona dug an elbow into his ribs, but he continued. "This one opened a portal to a world full of demons."

"You never opened a portal to a hell dimension for me," Inez said to Alice.

"Not yet," Alice said. "Give me time."

They fell into formation without thinking. Charlie and Mona were at the front, hands clasped tightly together, leading their little family. Alice and Inez walked behind them, Alice holding her girlfriend's forearm clutched between both hands, her nose just topping Inez's shoulder as she drew as close as possible. Inez's silver bracelet bounced against Alice's fingers. Joe and Smitha fell into place behind, shepherding the flock. Smitha grabbed Joe's hand as they walked and he squeezed it, drawing comfort from her nearness.

Charlie fished the flashlight they'd found from his pocket and shined it around the large room, illuminating what appeared to be a ramshackle combination of game room and workout room. Ancient exercise bikes, rowing machines, and weight benches occupied three quarters of the expansive space, and the back corner was home to a dilapidated selection of pool tables.

"This is weird," said Alice. Her voice bounced around the high ceilings and cement walls of the place, echoing in a sequence of bizarre fragments as snatches of sound waves were absorbed by dark corners and old furniture.

Joe prowled around, checking out the old equipment.

"Man, this place looks like it used to be awesome," he said from deep within a row of rusting exercise machines. "It's a shame it got so old and broken down."

"Joe, it wasn't ever new or useful, remember? This is just a ... a disguise the portal is wearing," Smitha said.

"Oh. Yeah," Joe said. "I still don't really understand that very well."

"I can't stand this place," Smitha continued. "Let's keep moving. Which way to the portal?"

"Staircase back by the pool tables," answered Charlie.

They crowded around the low staircase, three pairs of children staring into a dim walkway leading to the doom of the world.

Charlie looked around at the gathered faces of the five people who meant the most to him. His best friends, Joe and Smitha. The pups, who had become sisters to him in such a short time. And Mona. His best girl. His wife, he remembered with a smile.

"What're you smiling at, weirdo?" asked Mona.

"I love you guys," he said. "You are all here because of me. Because I'm going crazy and have magic Words inside my head and because I'm afraid of what will happen to me if I don't do what they say."

"We're here to close the portal," Smitha said. "You know, to save the world and all that."

"Yeah, but only because you believe me. I went insane, and instead of throwing me out or turning me over to someone, you listened. You just ... you believed me."

Alice nodded. "We've seen a lot. Plenty to back up what you're telling us."

"But that doesn't matter, does it?" asked Charlie. "You would have come on my word alone."

"Yes," said Joe and Smitha together. The others nodded in agreement.

"And now we're here, and there's nothing left to do but go down those stairs and do our best to end this thing."

"I'm scared," Inez whispered.

"Me too," said Charlie. "Terrified."

"Ready?" asked Mona.

"Let's go," he answered.

They fell back into their formation, Charlie and Mona leading the way down the broad stairwell, standing shoulder to shoulder. Inez was quivering, her skin slick and cold with fear. Alice held her, feeding her with the confidence and surety of unconditional love. Neither could have moved alone, but together they found a way, following a step behind. Joe, reciting the 23rd Psalm under his breath, looked at Smitha and saw her lips moving as she uttered nearly silent prayers in Hindi. He smiled at her and shrugged. She held out an arm and he took it, leaning in close to let the words of their prayers wash together.

The staircase opened at the bottom into a vacant, underground pool room. An Olympic sized pool, empty, cracked, but still somehow majestic, occupied the majority of the space, and at the bottom of the pool ...

The shape was hard to pin down. It was most like a stone pedestal, with the hazy notion of a door above it. A barely there portal to another elsewhere, ringed edges periodically crackling in sparks of yellow, purple, and green.

A wave of bone searing cold washed over the six. They weren't alone. Half a dozen Nowhere Men haunted the long-drained pool, pitched and terrifying howls ripping from their hatchet faces as they noticed their new company. The air seethed and rippled in multiple directions, a still pool of water upset by a fistful of rocks thrown from every angle. It was dizzying.

They'd prepared, though. Charlie had passed the Words through all of them before they left the apartment, and they no longer seized up in fear, retreating into their own minds when confronted with the breached and impossible hole in reality created by the monsters. Charlie looked at his friends and nodded. Alice reached out her hand and he grabbed it, pulling energy from her and mingling it with his own. His heart surged as he reached into her and surrounded himself with her nervous but willing strength.

He fought down the pain in his head and found the Words waiting like dogs tethered to the end of a leash. Alice gasped as the heat and pain surged through her, but she gritted her teeth and held on, feeding her energy into Charlie as he wrapped it around the Words and let them fly.

"*Ehan evna thae!*" he cried, cutting off the link as the Words escaped him. It hurt, but he was learning to manage it, learning to pull only what he needed to prevent the draw of power from immediately eating him alive.

The Nowhere Men were in the bottom of the pool, gliding around the portal and watching the humans to see what they might do. Charlie made good use of his first shot, lightning tearing through the nearest Nowhere Man and unmaking it, like a pillar of ash needing only to be touched for it to collapse. A vital but fleeting first victory was scored. Alice cheered, her face ashen but proud.

Mona slid into place as Inez pulled Alice away. She grabbed Charlie's right hand and planted a kiss on his cheek. He reached for her, dove into her, wrapped himself in her potent and furious strength, delighting in how it felt mixed with his own. It was more intimate than anything they had shared.

He had just begun to summon the Words again when the counterattack came. The five remaining Nowhere Men leapt from the basin, yanked through the air in their weird, jerking movement as though they were being dragged. They cleared the six-foot walls of the pool easily and landed among the little band of humans.

Joe uncorked his bat, ripping it off his shoulder with the vicious and practiced swing of an athlete. It cut a blurred line of aluminum reality through the rippling air. Joe's aim was true; the bat connected with the ribs of the nearest Nowhere Man.

The bat *should have* connected with the ribs of the nearest Nowhere Man. But the aluminum baseball bat swished through the air, through the monster's form, and followed through to Joe's opposite side without touching anything.

"Damn it," Joe swore. "Charlie?"

Charlie, busy with his own battle, absently sent a shot of power at the Nowhere Man Joe had attempted to hit. It glanced off, not enough of a direct hit to evaporate the monster, but enough to make it pause. In the moment the power hit, Joe noticed the monster shudder and ripple. It seemed, briefly, to occupy real space in a way it hadn't before. He swung again.

This time the bat connected. The Nowhere Man winced as several of its rib bones cracked. It turned its hatchet face to stare at Joe with one watery eye. It reached for him with one ethereal arm. Joe stepped back, hopping sideways and taking a third swing into the opposite side of the creature. This hit connected again, broke off a tip of bone, and the creature's howl changed from anger to pain.

Three Nowhere Men homed in on Alice and Inez, perhaps attracted by Inez's palpable fear. Alone among the family she knew what it felt like to be taken. The thought of it happening again was crippling. She froze in place and Alice pivoted in front of her, a human wall between the monsters and her beloved.

One of the three reached out for Alice, invisible hands making contact with the sides of her head. She flinched as it drew her toward itself.

"Inez," she whimpered, the single word taking all her effort.

Inez exploded into action. She wrapped her own arms around Alice's chest, hugging her from behind and pulling her backwards.

"You can't have her!" she screamed, her voice lifting over the howls of the Nowhere Men.

She pulled back on Alice as hard as she could, but the monster held tight. Charlie was spraying power indiscriminately now, flailing with the Words to try to hit as many monsters as possible. A splatter of energy hit the three Nowhere Men near the girls. Joe seized the opportunity and cracked his bat into one of the other two Nowhere Men, driving it away under a relentless assault. Joe was bleeding from several cuts on his arms, but he was a fury of calculated movement, always ducking, spinning, twisting at just the right angle to avoid the lanky reach of the monster as he beat it backwards.

The third monster evaporated in a flash of incandescent light as Charlie, his energy twined with Mona's, sent the Words flying again to aid the girls. Now there was only Alice, Inez, and the Nowhere Man in front of them.

Joe yelled wordlessly. Both of the Nowhere Men he'd attacked were rallying and his sweaty hands were cramping, losing their grip on the bat. Smitha was running from the fifth and final monster, having lost her footing and tumbled into the empty pool when they leapt up.

The first creature pressed Alice to its ribs, pulling her tight despite Inez's efforts to keep her away. Its tongues lolled as it prepared to draw in her essence and steal her place in the fabric of the world. Inez appeared over Alice's shoulder, a thin silver necklace wrapped around the knuckles of her fist, with a small silver pendant protruding between the second and third knuckle. Alice vaguely, through her terror and fear, recognized the pendant. It was her Christmas gift to Inez.

"Mine!" Inez screamed.

She rammed her fist forward with a punch that carried the weight of every shared moment she'd experienced with Alice.

The edge of the pendant drove into the Nowhere Man's left eye. It split open in a spray of puss-like white jelly. The creature barked in pain and raised its arms to its face. Inez pulled back on Alice with a mighty tug, separating them from the Nowhere Man and sending them both sprawling to the floor. Alice shivered, clinging to Inez as she began to come back to herself.

"Mine," Inez repeated in a growl. "Forever."

"Inez!" Charlie yelled, reaching out.

The girls scrabbled to their feet and ran to Charlie, who

grabbed Inez's hand. The silver locket poked his palm, but it was the smallest pain in a body filled with sharp twinges and aches. Inez's energy teemed with righteous anger and Charlie pulled it in greedily. He looked over to where Joe was dancing along the edge of the pool, clearly winded and losing steam as he fended off more Nowhere Men at the length of his flagging metal bat. Charlie focused on one, trying to line up a shot. Aiming was still tricky business, with the attack more of a blast than a bullet.

Smitha screamed.

She'd lost her footing in the bottom of the pool. The Nowhere Man that had been pacing her caught up, leaning over her as it prepared to feed. Charlie glanced back to Joe and saw him fall to one knee.

Smitha screamed again.

Charlie looked between his best friends. He could save them both, he could—but the monsters were on top of them, both of them, and the Words were fighting to be released. Charlie knew there was no time. He looked at Joe.

Joe nodded towards Smitha.

"Ehan evna thae!"

The creature above Smitha unraveled. A moment later Joe's knee buckled and he toppled down into the pool with a sickening crack and thud.

Charlie went to break for Smitha but Mona pulled him back, pushing Inez aside.

"There's no time," she hissed. "It has to be us again."

She opened herself up and Charlie dove deeper in, pulling more energy from her seemingly endless well. He'd been adding only a bit of his own to each blast, knowing he needed to conserve himself, because he was the only weapon. Now Charlie dared to pull a bit more from himself and shouted again. The Words obeyed gleefully.

"Ehan evna thae!"

One of the two remaining Nowhere Men was struck and eliminated. The second was bearing down on Joe, but Smitha had assessed the situation and sprinted for Charlie. Alice and Inez reached down to haul her up over the side of the pool and she fell into Charlie's arms, nearly knocking him over and wrapping him in a hug.

"Do it," she urged.

Charlie reached into Smitha, acting as quick as he dared, pulling energy from her and shoving it into the Words. He rushed it and put too much into it, the Words blistering his mouth as they left. He felt Smitha tense and buck as the power ripped from her, and saw her face twist in pain, but there was no taking it back.

"*Ehan evna thae!*"

The last of the Nowhere Men exploded into non-existence as silence fell over the room. It snapped a second later when Smitha yelped "Joe!" and scrambled back down into the pool.

The family followed her and gathered around Joe. His right arm bent beneath him at a very ugly angle and blood oozed from a long gash above his left ear. Inez pulled off the flannel shirt she'd been wearing and pressed it against his head.

"He's breathing," Alice announced, holding a hand in front of his mouth and nose. A bit of the tenseness evaporated.

"Do we need to get him to a doctor?" asked Mona.

Smitha nodded.

"Yeah, but not yet," Charlie interrupted. "Give him a few minutes, see if he wakes up. He'll kill us if we pull him out of here before finishing this. We'll never get another shot like this one again."

"Can we try it without him?" asked Inez.

"If we have to," Charlie answered. "But the instructions call for six. I remember there being six of us when we did this on ..." He shook his head. "Sorry. I still haven't gotten used to having other people's memories."

Mona rubbed his shoulders. "We'll try it with five if we have to. Let's give him a minute first, though. I'm ... I'm sure he'll be fine."

Smitha, eyes snapping and dark hair flying out of its bonds, faced her with uncharacteristic ferocity.

"Fine?" she demanded. "Look at his arm. He's not fine. But he might be okay. He might survive."

"You think I don't see that?" Mona countered. "I didn't mean he'd be sunshine and roses, I just meant he'd be ... fine. He has to be. We need him."

"Right, there has to be six," Charlie said.

"That's not what I meant," Mona whispered. "We just need him. We need all of us. We're a family."

Smitha sagged, her ferocity draining away.

"We do," she said. "We are."

They embraced. Alice and Inez folded them in on either side. Charlie wrapped his long arms around as much of the group as he could and rested his cheek on Mona's hair. They breathed out the tension and fear from the fight, breathed in each other's strength and love. When the cluster broke, they felt just a little bit better.

"I'm going to go check out the portal while we wait for sleeping beauty," Charlie announced, striding toward the platform in the middle of the pool. Mona followed him, catching his hand as they went.

"It's beautiful," Mona said as they circled it. "Magic. Real magic, isn't it?"

Charlie shrugged. "I guess so. It's really ancient, anyway. You can feel its age."

"I sorta want to walk through," Mona said, reaching a hand out. "Don't worry, I'm not gonna. Wherever it goes, that's where the Nowhere Men come from, and I never want to see that place. But it's so compelling."

"I know," Charlie said.

As they turned together to have a full look at the portal, the flickering green, yellow, and purple lightning suddenly shot into vibrant opalescence. A film of silver formed over the surface of the portal and split open as a Nowhere Man walked through. This was not one of the mostly empty Nowhere Men that existed largely en potentia. Its gnarled and muscled body was fully formed and fully corporeal. This was, Charlie's memories coldly told him, a monster who has already fed. Charlie yelled in horror and fell back, pulling Mona with him.

As Charlie scrambled for footing, he took in the Nowhere Man in front of him. It was so much larger than the spectral monsters they had been fighting, close to eight feet tall and thick as an oak tree. It glowered at him, watery eyes spitting malevolence. Beneath its right eye Charlie noticed a deep, open wound, just starting to heal over. A chunk of flesh was missing from eye to jaw, leaving an odd, open gap where one of its tongues spilled out. Charlie knew that face. He had made that wound. This was the Nowhere Man who had nearly taken Inez. Charlie had ripped its face open on their first encounter. Sometime between then and now it must have taken someone and made itself real. Charlie wondered who and realized, with a wave of nausea, that he wouldn't remember the person anyway.

Charlie pulled power from himself in the few seconds before the Nowhere Man lurched at him, digging deeper than he wanted to and slapping power into the Words. His mouth blistered as the Words poured out.

They ricocheted off the Nowhere Man. Charlie frowned and scrambled back a few more feet, Mona tugging at his arm. Charlie desperately pulled more power and tried again. This time the Words struck. A small cut opened on the creature's chest. Bad, but not nearly enough to cause problems. It seemed the Words didn't hold the same power against a fully formed Nowhere Man, against the well-fed creature who had become real.

He slung again. And again, the power just deflected off the monster as it kept coming. Mona threw herself on Charlie and knocked him to the ground as the Nowhere Man lunged forward. It missed, but now they were cowering at its feet.

The Nowhere Man made eye contact with Charlie and snarled a long sequence of angry alien words. Had Charlie had the time, he would have recognized a few of them. It raised a giant arm to strike them but rocked sideways and missed when a metal bat slammed into its head. Charlie and Mona clambered back to their feet and saw Joe looming behind the creature, his right arm dangling uselessly at his side and his left arm clutching his baseball bat. The monster turned on Joe, growling.

Mona slipped her hand into Charlie's and gave it a squeeze. "Let's get 'im, baby," she whispered.

Charlie had become so familiar with Mona that they were essentially a single energy source in his mind; a continuous ebb and flow of one being between two bodies, their auras perfectly paired and intertwined. He sank into the twining.

Joe swung the bat into the Nowhere Man's face, almost accidentally catching the wound Charlie's magic had the day before. The creature flinched and screeched, and thick black blood began oozing from its mouth.

"Ehan evna thae!"

A streak of lightning crashed into the creature's back, packed with as much energy as Charlie would risk. The power ripped a slight gash in the creature's shoulder and it stumbled to its knees. Charlie gasped—all that power and it barely made a scratch. Joe stepped forward and swung the bat upward, clipping the monster in the face again and drawing more blood. It used its forearm to shield off another blow and struggled back to its feet.

"Hit him again!" Mona cried.

Smitha, Alice, and Inez had run forward when the attack began, arms outstretched and already connected in a chain, reaching for him to lend their strength. Charlie grabbed Smitha's arm now, despairing at the use of more power they couldn't spare. But he had no choice. They were all going to die here if the monster wasn't stopped.

But they weren't needed.

When the Nowhere Man turned to face Charlie, it left its back exposed to Joe. Joe noticed the small wound Charlie had opened on the creature's shoulder and laid into it, flaying him with the aluminum bat. He heard its shoulder break and kept swinging, black blood splattering all over him and mixing with own. He worked his left wrist over and over, forcing his arm to swing the bat with increasing speed and unyielding fury. After the shoulder broke, he started swinging horizontally, driving his weight into the creature's collar bone until he felt it crack as well. The creature fell back, but Joe refused to relent. When the Nowhere Man stumbled, he focused again on its wounded head, thrashing and pounding until the monster, its wraithlike form leaving a broken body behind, turned and fled through the portal. Then the bat clattered to the ground as Joe finally let it slip from his grasp. The echoing thud of the bat hitting the pool floor hadn't faded before Charlie charged at Joe and hugged him.

"MVP!" he shouted.

"First and last time," Joe panted. "Everybody okay?"

"I mean, everybody but you, I think," Mona answered. "Have you looked at your arm?"

"Flesh wound," he grunted.

"It is not, Joe," Smitha protested. "You need to see a doctor."

"What was that thing?" Mona asked. "It was different —worse."

"It's what happens when Pinocchio eats all his spinach and gets his wish," Charlie said grimly. "The Nowhere Man becomes a Real Boy."

"Should we leave? Maybe come back ... later?" Inez ventured. She and Alice were holding each other tightly, and the taller girl kept casting fearful glances at the portal. Every inch of bravado was gone. Inez was terrified.

"There's no time," Charlie said. "I'm sorry, I'm really sorry, but we can't risk more of those things coming through. We need to close the portal. Now."

There was a tone of command in his voice that made them all stand up straighter and pay attention. Charlie was boisterous, enthusiastic, dramatic, persuasive, compassionate —Charlie was many things, but he was not commanding. But the rest of the family would no more have disobeyed him now than privates would a five-star general.

"This is it," Charlie continued. "We do it now."

His voice softened and he was Charlie again, winsome and cheeky and a little bit needy.

"So, gather up, cowpokes. It's time for the last charge of Wyatt Earp and his Immortals."

There was some argument, in the end, over who should stand in the final place, hands on the portal. According to Charlie's memories, he, as the caster, would stand at the end of the line, reciting the Closing Words and pushing them forward through the other five, drawing power as it went. Someone had to stand at the end, both hands on the portal's pedestal, the funnel through which Charlie would push the Words powered by their combined energies.

Joe tried first, insisting it was his right as Charlie's best friend. Smitha and Mona objected, but covered in blood and glaring defiance, he brooked no argument. This plan was scuttled when Joe's mangled right arm was unable to keep his hand stationed properly on the pedestal.

"Are you willing to listen to me now?" Mona asked. "Listen, it has to be me. Charlie and I connect like nobody else, and you know it. This is going to take everything he has, and I'm going to be here to make sure he stands his best chance, okay? Now give me your arm, Joe."

Joe squirmed and grunted but kept a stoney face as Mona pulled his right arm up onto her shoulder and tied it down with the bloody flannel. He put his left on her other shoulder and whispered *thanks*. Smitha slid in behind him, then Inez, then Alice.

Charlie walked up to the front of the line and gave Mona a long, slow kiss, his tongue tracing the ridge of her lip as they parted. "I love you, wife," he said with a wink. "Let's finish this so we can graduate and take a proper honeymoon."

"I love you too, husband. You've got this."

"We've got this," Charlie answered.

"I love you, too! All of you!" piped in Alice. A chorus of "love you toos" answered her while Charlie returned to the end of the line.

He stood behind Alice, dropping his hands heavily onto the girl's broad shoulders.

"Okay, Waltons. Everybody ready?" he called. There were various grunts of assent.

Charlie reached into himself. This one was going to hurt. He'd already spent more energy than he'd wanted to, and he was going to have to dig deep. He searched every corner of himself and flooded energy into the new sequence of Words queuing up in his mind. He felt the familiar pain as the power burn lashed his body with searing heat. He hated the thought of what was coming next, but he knew there was no other choice.

Rather than reaching into Alice to borrow her power, he

pushed the Words into her, letting them flow out his fingers through her shoulders and into her chest. They brewed there for a moment as he culled her power, pulling it to the Words, wrapping it around them. He knew it was burning her, too. He felt her flinch and distantly heard her voice cry out. When he could risk no more, he moved the Words forward again, and again, and again, taking strength from each of his dearest friends and repaying them with agonizing pain.

At last, the Words rolled into Mona. Charlie pulled deeply from her, greedily, more deeply than he had from anyone. He pulled until he found the limits of her seemingly limitless reserves. He felt her trembling, felt her pain as the Words, bound in lightning and fire, brewed in her chest and demanded release. Her knees buckled but she locked them and forced herself to remain upright. Her skin burned, blistered, and peeled.

There. He could hold no more—they could give no more. It was time.

Charlie finally unleashed the Words. He whispered them, but they flowed out from Mona, pouring into the pedestal.

"Metsa kodru rima mkaba."

The pedestal glowed from the energy, a sequence of lights and shapes leaping to life on an ancient, incomprehensible control panel. The lights surrounding the edge of the portal splashed and flickered as the portal began drawing in on itself. What was initially a ten-foot-tall oval shrank to eight feet, then six, then four. In moments it was the size of a quarter.

It wavered. It stopped.

Charlie moaned. He searched himself, drawing out a few dregs of power from the core of himself. Joints ground. Bones snapped. He struggled to stay upright, his flesh burning so fiercely he smelled it cooking. He desperately shoved the Words forward, stealing another tiny measure from Alice, who screamed in distress but kept her hands clamped on the shoulders of her girlfriend as the Words moved on. Inez had a bit more, but not much, and nearly fainted from the pain as the Words passed through her and into Smitha, whose teeth were chattering from the intense heat. He took what he could from her and wept as he pushed the Words into Joe. Joe's stalwart demeanor finally broke and he sobbed in panicked pain, his brain clinging to just enough sanity to keep his left hand anchored on Mona, his nails digging deep cuts through her t-shirt and into her shoulders.

Mona's body thrashed as the Words poured into her and Charlie asked for yet more, but her hands stayed firmly planted on the control panel. She twisted and contorted, her face locked in a savage mask of agony, but she held firm. Charlie pulled everything he dared from her and unleashed the Words again.

"*Metsa kodru rima mkaba.*"

The wedding ring on Mona's finger melted as the power passed through, fusing her temporarily to the pedestal. She held. The portal shrunk from the size of a quarter to the size of a pinprick, a single dot of purple, green, or yellow light, barely perceptible, flickering above the dais. Charlie, still weeping, tried to speak.

"We need more," he croaked. "Just a bit more. Almost there."

Smitha tried to answer, but only succeeded in spitting a mouthful of blood and bile on the floor. Inez and Alice were too far gone into pain to process his words, remaining upright only through an effort of supreme, selfless will.

Mona forced away the pain and spoke in a clear voice, ignoring several shattered teeth, her words only slightly garbled by a split tongue.

"From me. I'm here. End it."

Charlie found a single thread of energy left inside of him and split it in half. It was just enough to spark the Words again. His knee shattered with an audible pop, and he stumbled forward to the ground. Thankfully Alice was in front of him, and she was just short enough that his hand could stay locked on her shoulder even from a kneeling position. He passed the Words right through her and Inez, taking no time to linger or search. They were empty, he knew. He paused at Joe, but there was nothing left in him, either. He siphoned a fraction from Smitha, who offered up a weak flame, and shoved the Words quickly into Mona.

She was empty. She'd given him everything, and it had nearly killed her. He despaired for what he had done to his love, to his whole family. To everyone who mattered most to him in the world. A chain of helpless and broken people, thanks to him.

He almost quit, then. He almost gave up, pulled back, swallowed the power back into himself and died of its force to spare the others.

But ages of memory clamored at him that he couldn't, that it would spare them now only for them to be unmade later when Nowhere Men poured through the still open portal. No choice. No other choice. It had to be now.

"*Metsa kodru—*" he began, and stopped, holding the Words back. They were dying, they were all dying. He couldn't.

"I love you, Charlie."

Mona's voice was soft and mellow but full of conviction. Her words, as powerful in their own way as Charlie's Words, bounced off the sides of the empty pool and echoed back to him in a disjointed chorus.

I love you, Charlie. I love you. Love. Love you, Charlie. You, Charlie. Love You.

A spark kindled inside of her, a tiny mote of energy drawn to life by her love. Charlie grabbed it, pulled it, twisted it into himself and, for a final second, relished in the unsurpassable joy of her being, her essence, twined to his own. Then he wrapped Smitha's into the bundle. His best friend. His wife. Himself. A strand of three cords. It had to be enough.

"*Metsa kodru*," he grated through a failing voice as the pain crashed through his defenses and crippled him. "*Rima*," he continued, his vision fading. "*Mkaba—*"

Mona's scream ripped through his soul as he fought with the final Word. He felt it flowing from her fingers as she died. He tried to make out the flickering pinprick of the portal to see if it was still there, but his eyes failed him. The rest of his body followed.

CHAPTER

SIXTEEN

"Is it closed?"

Smitha sat up straight in the chair and looked over at the hospital bed. Charlie was moving, shifting restless against the sheets. His voice was small and hoarse, but it was the first he'd spoken in days and the sound of it made Smitha's heart glow. She reached out and gently took his bandaged hand.

"Charlie?"

"Is it closed?"

"Charlie, it's me. Smitha. It's me."

His eyes fluttered half open.

"Prof?" he whispered. His fingers twitched against hers, brushing painfully against the still-healing burns on her palm.

"It's me, Charlie. I'm here. Don't move."

He tried anyway, struggling to sit up in the reclined bed. Smitha gave up trying to keep him down and helped him, letting him use her as a brace to push upright. They were both winded by the time he was sitting.

"How do you feel?" Smitha asked when she had her breath back. "Should I call for the nurse?"

Charlie blinked in the harsh fluorescent lights, looking around the spartan room. Then he looked down at himself, at the IV in the crook of his arm and the bandages around his chest. His fingers brushed against the remote for the bed.

"That would have been easier," Smitha said, noticing.

"You know me—have to do it the hard way. Something to drink?"

There was a plastic water bottle on the stand by his bed. Smitha handed it to him and Charlie sipped through the straw, wincing at the suction and the cold water hitting the sores in his mouth.

"How is everyone else?" he asked, handing the bottle back. The skin around his mouth was tight and stretched painfully when he talked.

"You're the worst off. Joe has a broken arm. We've all got burns and cuts—they say the blast must have thrown us pretty far."

Charlie frowned.

"The blast? Did the portal explode?"

It was Smitha's turn to frown as she asked, "What portal, Charlie?"

The door opened after a brisk knock and a nurse stepped in wheeling a cart full of instruments and electronics.

"I'm sorry to interrupt, but I've got to take your vitals," she explained.

Smitha stood.

"I'll go tell the others you're awake. We've been worried."

"Smitha, wait—"

She was gone. Charlie leaned back against the pillow and meekly submitted to the nurse's tests.

"Your blood pressure is fine," she reported. "You do have a slight fever. On a scale of one to ten, how's your pain?"

Charlie had no idea how to answer that question.

"Eight?" he guessed. The nurse nodded and made some notes on her chart.

"I'm going to bring you some more pain medication. The IV is almost empty but now that you're awake you can take it by mouth. Drink as much as you can, but slowly. Hit the button if you need help getting to the bathroom. The doctor will be in to see you later."

She wheeled out her cart and shut the door behind her, leaving him all alone.

Everything hurt. Even his hair hurt, the roots irritated his scalp whenever he moved his head. His hands hurt. He took another drink from the water bottle. It hurt to swallow.

What had Smitha meant, *what portal*? Maybe she had hurt her head, gotten a concussion somehow. If there was a blast— the portal would cause an explosion, or implosion, or something when it closed, that was physics, right? If there was a blast, maybe it had given her temporary memory loss.

If only it had worked that way for him. Charlie remembered everything.

"We did it," he whispered. The salt tears stung their trails down his burnt face.

The nurse, whose badge read Marci, returned with two little pills in a small white paper cup. She handed Charlie the cup and watched as he swallowed them both.

"I'll take the IV out while I'm here," she said, and busied herself with the line and pole. "We're going to keep the fluids in, though. There will be a pretty nice bruise there. Sorry about that."

Charlie indicated the rest of his body and managed a weak grin.

"It'll be fine."

Marci smiled back.

"It's good to see you awake," she confessed. "We weren't

sure you were going to make it when they first brought you in."

"That bad?"

"I've seen worse. But it wasn't pretty. A number of deep abrasions, burns over most of your body—mostly second degree, with third degree in one or two places—plus you had head trauma, abrasions and burns in your mouth, and you were in shock."

Marci continued, rattling off his injuries and the further tests they would have to run, but the words meant nothing to Charlie. He tried to nod in acknowledgement but moving his head that much made him so dizzy he threw up. Marci cleaned him up, explaining that he was suffering some symptoms of vertigo thanks to an inner ear injury inflicted by the blast. Before he could ask her what she meant by blast, the doctor came in to inundate Charlie with more words, long sentences and syllables that all ran together. The pain medication made him drowsy, and he dozed off in the middle of a sentence about further procedures and recovery times.

In his dreams ghost monsters with open rib cages and many tongues came after him again and again. He shot green fire at them to drive them away but when they began to burn he saw that they had the faces of his family, Alice and Inez and Joe and Smitha all burning, glowing as his fire consumed them. That was bad, but worse was when he turned away from the writhing bodies. Mona was burning, too.

Green flamelets danced in her hair. Her eyes dripped tears of fire. The skin of her face was reddening, peeling. Her white wedding dress was charring, brown to black with sparks of embers glittering like rubies.

"You, Charlie," she said. Her voice was turned horrendous by shriveling vocal cords. When her mouth opened Charlie saw her tongues, split and bleeding, her teeth shattered, her lips burning away.

Mona reached, emerald fingers of flame licking hungrily down her arms toward him. The maw in her ribs was a famished void that called out for him to fill it. The tongues that protruded from her burning mouth lapped at the air. She was a monster alight with his fire.

Charlie woke screaming—at least, he thought he did. The only sound coming from his open mouth was a hoarse, grating breath that was somehow worse than a scream.

His fire. His fault. Mona was dead—he knew it, he had felt her die, but he couldn't think about that for long, not now—and everyone else was hurt and it was his fault, all his fault, his words that brought them to the portal, his fire that burned them.

He managed to draw in a shuddering breath, then another. The crawling urge to scream was fading, replaced by a pressure behind his eyes. A heavy weight settled in his throat. He felt tired, so tired in his soul.

"Knock knock?"

"You don't have to say 'knock-knock' if you actually do it."

"I don't want to disturb him if he's sleeping!"

Charlie tried to say "Come in" but nothing came out. Swallowing felt like forcing needles down his throat, but he did his best to clear away the junk and tried again, this time getting a slightly louder result. It was enough that Inez and Alice heard it and opened the door, creeping in like ballet dancers avoiding a creaky floorboard.

"Can we come in?" Alice whispered.

Charlie nodded.

The two girls sat on the uncomfortable chairs next to the bed. They wore hospital gowns with big robes over them and warm gray socks with grippy soles. They looked bad, although not, Charlie suspected, as bad as he did. Deep bruises spread over their shoulders, showing where the gowns' necklines gaped. Half-healed blisters and cuts dotted their arms and faces. Some of Alice's hair was singed in a strange pattern and one ear was shiny burn red. Charlie realized, to his horror, that it was where he had spoken the Words past her.

"How are you?" Alice whispered.

"Why are you whispering?" Inez asked in her regular tone.

Alice frowned at her. Charlie stopped the incipient argument by reaching for Alice's hand and croaking "It's fine. I'm fine."

"You don't look it," Inez observed.

"ICU chic is in this year," Charlie said. That earned him a smile from Inez and a giggle from Alice.

The water bottle near his bed had been refilled while Charlie slept. He took a drink, then said, "Hey—what happened? How'd we get here?"

Alice looked concerned but Inez nodded.

"I didn't remember at first, either," Inez said. "But campus security came to see us and said the old gas tank exploded."

"Gas tank?"

"In the grove," Alice said. "Remember how we found that huge old tank half buried in the little cluster of trees near the chapel? Their best guess is that the contents were dangerously under pressure and all our fooling around near it set it off."

That was not what Charlie remembered. He remembered monsters and a fight and a portal at the bottom of an empty swimming pool.

Alice patted his hand nervously.

"Charlie ... do you remember about ... about Mona?"

She didn't meet his eyes. Inez did, and her gaze was pitying but not accusatory.

"I remember Mona," Charlie said. "She died ..."

He glanced down at his hand. The wedding ring was gone.

"My ring?" he asked.

Inez pointed to a small bag on a counter.

"Everything's in there. Yours is okay but Mona's ring was ... was melted ..."

Alice sniffed.

"Oh Charlie ... I'm so sorry!"

But he couldn't think about that now. He wouldn't.

"Hey," he said, "do either of you remember ... monsters? Because I remember monsters that ate people's existence?"

Inez laughed a little shakily. Alice shook her head.

"Oh, Charlie," she said. "Trying to cheer us up with a silly story?"

"I need Joe," Charlie said. "Where's Joe?"

"He's not allowed out of bed yet," Inez said. "His arm is in pretty bad shape, and he had a concussion. Charlie, what's wrong?"

"Have you talked to him? Does he think it was a gas tank, too?"

"Of course it was the gas tank—what else could it be?"

Alice patted Charlie's arm again.

"We need to let you rest," she said. "I'm sorry, this was too much. We should have waited to visit."

"No, I—" Charlie sighed. "I'm sorry. I'm glad you came, really. I'm glad you're going to be okay."

Alice stood and gave Charlie a quick, gentle hug. Inez followed suit.

"We'll be back tomorrow," Inez said.

"Yeah. Okay."

They left. Charlie dropped his head back on the pillow and groaned. What was that gas tank nonsense? Why was he the only one that remembered the portal?

He wrestled with the question for the next few days, finally coming to the conclusion that the forgetting must be something to do with the portal's memory altering camouflage defense. Maybe it kicked back in when they got the portal closed again. But why did he still remember? Was it because he was the one who'd touched the portal initially? Did the words keep his memory intact?

"That makes sense, right?" Charlie asked a little stuffed dog he had found near his bed. It appeared to have been bought at the hospital gift shop. The tag said it was a get-well present from Joe, but the handwriting was Smitha's. "Like ... the portal's closed and it's important that no one remembers it so no one tries to open it again. Sure. Okay. That makes sense."

The dog looked up at him with glassy eyes.

"You're right, though," Charlie continued, petting it distractedly. "Then why do I remember? There wasn't anything about forgetting in the instructions."

Charlie's hand brushed against one of the dog's stuffed ears. It flopped against the back of his hand.

"Yeah, true—there wasn't anything about someone having to die to close the gate, either. So, who knows. Of course ... there is another option. Maybe I'm not remembering anything. Maybe I'm wrong and it really was a gas tank explosion. Maybe I'm actually losing my mind."

The dog did not say anything. Charlie picked it up and brushed its soft fur against his cheek the way he used to do with his blanket as a young child.

"I don't feel like my mind is gone. But do you? If your brain breaks, do you know it? How do I know?"

That was the million dollar question: how did he know? If everyone believed one sequence of events and he believed another—didn't that make him delusional?

But what, really, did it matter? Mona was still dead—but he pushed that thought away, far away. The rest of the family was still in the hospital. Maybe he could just ... close it off, make himself believe, force himself to accept their reality and ignore his. Fake it 'til you make it. Sure. He could do that.

"A gas tank explosion," he whispered to the dog. "Gas tank. No monsters. No portal. No magic words. A gas tank. Yeah."

The dog did not look as if it believed him, but it kept its silence. And Charlie kept his.

SEVENTEEN

I t was a sunny day, the girls looked beautiful and in love as they said their vows, and Charlie couldn't concentrate on any of it.

There was a monster walking around outside.

He tried his best to ignore the thing as the officiant, a reverend from the Metropolitan Community Church, held up the rings and said "Love, like the love between Alice and Inez, has no beginning and no end. These rings symbolize the never-ending cycle of love."

The monster was moving back and forth, in that quick but jerky old movie frame by frame walk that Charlie could never, never forget. It headed behind the pavilion. Nobody else seemed to see it, though. And why weren't they all freezing? Charlie started to turn his head to follow it, caught Joe's eye, and quickly faced the front again.

Now the girls were lighting a candle together. The reverend quoted Albert Schweitzer: "At times our light goes out and is rekindled by a spark from another person. Each of us has cause to think with deep gratitude of those who have lighted the flame within us."

The monster moved back into sight and Charlie glanced over at it. As he did, the Professor noticed. She smiled at him and patted his hand. More proof, as if he needed it, that he was the only one to see those things. If the Prof could see the monsters skulking around she wouldn't be smiling.

Inez and Alice, hands linked, turned to face the crowd. Their faces beamed. The reverend lifted her arms and said, "Alice and Inez, as you have chosen to join together in a bond of holy and loving union and have pledged yourselves to each other in the presence of family and friends, it is my joy and privilege to pronounce you partners in life."

The crowd stood and applauded as the girls kissed again and walked down the center aisle. Charlie stood, too, and used the opportunity to check on the monster. It was heading away now, down the sidewalk that ran along the lake, and soon was out of sight. Charlie sagged a little. Time to relax, until the next time one of those gut-mouthed rubber band men showed up.

They filed through the receiving line one after another, Joe-Smitha-Charlie. Inez and Alice greeted them politely in their post-wedding haze before realizing who they were.

Alice threw her arms around them one by one.

"You guys!" she squealed. "I'm so glad you came!"

"Couldn't stay away," Joe said, hugging her back before moving on to Inez.

"You two look gorgeous," Smitha gushed. "Congratulations!"

"How many glasses do I have to tap before you kiss?" Charlie asked.

Inez laughed.

"I hate that tradition. Bang away, but if you break a glass, you're paying for it."

"You're always ruining my fun, 1B."

"Look, we've got to get through the rest of this line," Alice said. "See you at the reception?"

"I wasn't going to stay," Joe started to mumble. Alice looked like she might actually start to cry.

"No, Joe! You have to stay! Please?"

He looked from Alice to Inez to Smitha to Charlie

"I—well … sure. Okay. Fine."

They all rode together to the reception, piled into Charlie's old Chevy Cavalier. Smitha flipped through a pile of CDs.

"Bowie, Nina Simone, Drive Shaft—Britney Spears? Really?"

"Leave Britney alone," Charlie said. "So, what's up with cutting out early, Joe? You and Angie got a hot date?"

"Ah, unfortunately, no. Angie has moved on to greener pastures."

"Oh geeze, man. I'm sorry to hear that."

"Uh huh," Joe said. "And where's your hot date?"

The car went silent.

Joe stammered an apology.

"Oh, Charlie," Smitha began.

"I had too many choices," said Charlie breezily. "And you can't take just any Tom, Dick, or Harriet to a wedding."

At the reception they all sat together and caught up. Joe had just been promoted to shift manager of a burger joint. Smitha was working hard on her PhD.

"Almost done," she said, then grimaced. "I hope so, anyway."

"And what about you, Charlie?" Joe asked. "Anything new in your life?"

Charlie shrugged, taking a sip of water only because you had to save the champagne for the toast, and he wasn't sure he had enough money for the open bar.

"Got a job," he said. "Got an apartment. Got a tattoo."

"Where?" Smitha asked.

"Tattoo or apartment?"

"Who got a tattoo?" Inez plopped herself down at the table and sighed. "Getting married is exhausting."

Charlie pulled out a chair for Alice but she demurred, fluffing out the skirt of her white dress and saying "I can't actually sit down in this thing."

"Charlie got a tattoo," Joe said.

"You look lovely in it, though," said Smitha.

"She does, doesn't she?" Inez blew Alice a kiss. "Charlie, you sullied your perfect skin with a tattoo?"

Charlie made a face. "Perfect? Tell that to my high school dermatologist."

Alice's mom bustled over, giving the others a brief nod. She had never warmed to her daughter's freshmen year friends.

"Alice, Inez, it's time for the first dance," she said.

Smitha squealed and hurried up to the dance floor to get a picture of the couple as they started to sway to "It Had to Be You".

"I'm going to get a drink," Joe said. "You want something?"

"If you're paying? Absolutely," Charlie said.

While they waited for their drinks Joe leaned against the bar, studied Charlie, and said "For real, man. How are you?"

Charlie eyed the bartender instead of facing his friend.

"I'm getting by," he said. "College was a lot simpler, wasn't it?"

"I was not ready to be a grown up," Joe admitted.

"I don't think anyone is."

"Smitha seems to be doing okay."

"The Professor has been a grown up since she was a baby," Charlie pointed out.

The bartender gave them their drinks. They drank. Joe ordered them a refill.

"Sorry about Angie," Charlie said. "What happened?"

"Nothing, really. It just wasn't working. No hard feelings."

"Ah, well. The course of true love never did run smooth."

The bartender gave them their drinks. They drank. Joe ordered them a refill.

"A burger joint?" Charlie asked. "How's that going?"

"It's a paycheck. You said you got a job?"

"You don't have to sound so surprised."

"You just never struck me as the work type."

"Only until I convince a rich old widow to fall in love with me."

Joe laughed and held up his glass.

"Good plan. To rich old widows?"

"To rich old widows."

They clinked glasses. They drank. The first dance ended and the floor opened up with other couples heading out to dance.

"So, there's no one special?" Joe asked.

Charlie shook his head.

"I know it's hard, man, but it's been five years. That's a long time. Mona wouldn't want you to be alone forever."

"I don't know what Mona would have wanted. I never got a chance to ask her."

The DJ started playing another song, slow and a little sad.

Charlie closed his eyes and felt the heavy weight of the ring that hung on a chain around his neck. Five years was a long time. And he did know that Mona would have wanted him to move on. He just couldn't imagine someone else taking that place.

It was that, and it was the memory of the day she died, the way she died, the fire that burned in his mouth and burned on her skin, the heat so intense his tears evaporated as soon as they left his eyes. And the fact that no one else remembered.

No. Don't dwell on it. Never look it in the face. Lock it away and leave it be.

Someone took his clenched hand. Charlie opened his eyes and the Professor smiled up at him, the warm but slightly worried smile she'd taken to giving him over the past five years.

"You okay?" she asked.

"Sure," he lied. "Sure. Just a little dizzy. One too many, I think. Joe here is trying to liquor me up. I think he wants to take advantage of me later."

The music switched to an upbeat club banger and Charlie tossed back the rest of his drink, took off his jacket, and loosened his tie.

"Come on," he said. "Let's dance."

PART THREE
PRESENT DAY

CHAPTER

EIGHTEEN

Joe woke from dreams of the past. He knew immediately that he was in Ravencrest. The hazy, not quite bright enough sun shining through the curtains was the same. The sounds outside the window were the same. But the room was different, this hastily cleared out guest room in Smitha's house. He was different, favoring the various aches that never bothered him in his younger years. And what waited outside the door was different. Not the family, young and vibrant and so full of life. Just Alice, and Inez, and Smitha.

Smitha wasn't even there when he came downstairs. A note on the table explained that she had a meeting that morning about the worrisome low attendance at the college, and she had to teach a class after that, but she would be home in the afternoon. Joe read the note and shook his head.

"Typical Smitha," he said. "Always hard at work."

Inez, picking at a piece of toast, laughed roughly.

"She worked harder than the rest of us, anyway."

"Water's ready!" Alice chirped as the sharp kettle whistle

cut through the thick atmosphere of the kitchen. Smitha, always prepared, had set out three mugs and three boxes of tea: Early Grey for Joe, mint tea for Alice, and chamomile for Inez.

The tea restored some measure of balance. It was a ritual, an anchor point for their shared existence as a family. A tradition. They'd shared tea on dozens of long, late nights and unwelcome early mornings. Sometimes in silence, sometimes in raucous laughter or full-voiced debate. But always in communion.

"I could make pancakes again," Joe offered half-heartedly.

"No thanks, Joe," Alice said.

Joe made himself toast.

Alice took her mug to the sink and washed it out. Smitha's kitchen was well stocked and economically laid out. There were few decorations but a window above the sink let in morning light and provided Alice a bird and two squirrels to watch. In the distance, but not too far, she could make out the red brick tower of the university's science building.

"This is a nice house," she said as she rejoined her wife and Joe at the table.

"It is," Joe agreed. "Smitha seems to be doing well."

"At least one of us is," Inez grumbled.

"Heh. Yeah." Joe paused. "Are you guys, uh, sticking around today?"

He had heard them arguing last night.

"For a little," Alice said carefully. "Since we're already here. We don't really have a set schedule."

"Yeah. It's Homecoming—I guess there are Homecoming-type things to do?"

"Like what?" Inez asked.

Joe shrugged. Alice pulled out her phone and found the weekend's schedule of events on the university website.

"There's not a lot today," she reported. "A cocktail hour

later. Tomorrow is really when everything happens—the football game, the parade, that sort of thing."

"None of that sounds fun," Inez said. Joe agreed.

"We could ... go for a walk?"

Alice didn't expect anyone to agree to her suggestion—it had been hard enough to convince Inez to stay for breakfast. But Joe immediately went to put on his shoes, and Inez followed.

It was still too early to tell— Ravencrest weather usually didn't settle in until well after lunch—but it seemed like the sun was going to make an appearance, so Joe left his coat behind, venturing out in only a very old RU T-shirt and a pair of jeans.

"You haven't changed at all," Alice said, smiling at him.

"You have! What's all this?" He indicated Alice's skinny jeans, sweater boot socks, and tailored raglan tee.

"I'm not poor anymore; I can afford things that fit. And Inez goes shopping with me."

Inez, waiting by the door in a moto jacket and stoned gray pedal pushers, winked and hit Joe with two finger guns.

Most of the sidewalks in Ravencrest were in terrible shape. The three started out in single file, stepping carefully over the roots that had thrust their way up through the concrete slabs. Runoff from heavy rains and melting snow had dug trenches on the house side of the sidewalk and sloped the ground on the street side so that one misstep in either direction could send someone tumbling.

Fallen leaves crackled beneath their feet. The occasional passing car kicked up tiny foliage tornados that danced around their ankles. The town wasn't very large and it was hard to escape the looming towers and brick and stone edifices of the campus. The trio tried, though, heading from Smitha's house in the opposite direction.

They passed houses and yards, following the sidewalk until it petered out and they were walking on the road itself. The suburban layout—cozy house, backyard, neighbor—thinned into gravel parking lots, factory loading docks, and eventually empty fields. While there was scenery the three were able to find unimportant things to talk about. Joe made the pups laugh by relating how once he tried to climb over a certain fence they passed and hadn't quite made it, to the detriment of that pair of pants. But as the distractions fell behind them, as they walked in their own footprints from years before, their spirits remembered. They began to talk.

"I'm glad you stayed," Joe said. "I wasn't sure ..."

Alice and Inez shared a glance.

"We weren't either," Alice admitted.

"I was pretty mad last night," said Inez. "And this morning."

"At me," Alice said in a small voice.

"Yeah," Inez agreed. "And at Smitha, and at me, and at everybody."

Joe nodded.

"I feel like she betrayed us."

"She did," Inez argued, "she lied to us."

"I guess." Alice kicked a small rock out of her path.

"She did," Inez insisted. "She told us we were meeting for Homecoming. She told Joe it was some sort of intervention for Charlie."

"And where is Charlie?" Inez spread her arms meaningfully, as if they all couldn't feel the absence of their lanky, genial friend. The heart of their group was missing.

"If what Smitha told us is true," Joe mused, "I wouldn't blame Charlie if he never came back here again."

Inez rounded on him.

"You don't believe any of that, do you? Magic portals and monsters?"

"I don't know what to believe," said Joe. "Obviously her story sounds, well, unbelievable. But this is Smitha. She's the most stable person I know."

Even Inez had no answer to that. It was indisputable.

"So ..." Alice looked from her wife to Joe. "So, we believe her?"

Joe paused but shook his head.

"I can't go that far. But I can listen to her."

Inez took Alice's hand.

"And I can forgive her."

They had lunch at Jenny's Tavern. When they were poor college students, Jenny's was reserved for special occasions only, preferably when someone else was buying. Going back as a grown up was a revealing experience.

"This place isn't even that expensive," Alice mused, glancing over the menu.

"Mid-range," Inez judged.

"I'm buying us an appetizer!" Joe declared.

"Appetizer *and* a meal? We've really come up in the world."

As they finished eating, Alice commented on Inez's suddenly paler complexion.

"I just got a little cold," Inez complained, "that's all."

"It is cold all of a sudden," Joe agreed. "They must have cranked up the AC."

"Still," Alice said anxiously, "maybe we'd better head back."

They were followed out the door by a young server, who waved his cigarette at the hostess to indicate he was going for a smoke break.

"Those will kill you one day," she told him. He just laughed.

Outside the server idly watched one man and two women walking away from the restaurant. He smoked and watched until they were out of sight and his cigarette was half gone.

He shivered, as if a sudden cold wind bore into his bones. Behind him, knife-sharp jaws opened.

Inside the restaurant, the hostess looked over the tables and sighed. Short-handed again. They really needed to hire a server. One more would be perfect.

CHAPTER

NINETEEN

Smitha paused on her front step with her key out.

More than a part of her had been hesitant to come home, afraid to walk into more arguing or, worse, that stony silence. But from behind the door she heard laughter, Inez and Alice laughing, and Joe's voice raised in a story.

She turned her key in the lock and opened the door.

"—got their wires crossed so we ended up with enough food to feed the whole damn hall. We were eating leftovers for a week!"

Smitha closed the door and hung up her coat and keys.

"I remember that," she said. "Freshman year, right?"

Joe nodded.

"That was when you had a thing for Loren," Smitha continued. She joined the pups on the long sectional, not missing how Inez stiffened when she sat. Alice smiled at her, however, and eventually Inez relaxed.

"Who was Loren?" Inez asked.

"My roommate," Smitha explained. "Joe had it bad for her. He and Charlie were always hanging around."

183

"Nothing happened with Loren," Joe continued. "We never really clicked. We spent so much time in that room, though, that the Professor must have just gotten used to having us around."

They shared a smile and Smitha's heart warmed.

"Would anyone like some tea?" she asked.

Inez hopped up.

"I'll help."

Smitha got out cups and tea bags and sweeteners while Inez put the water on to boil.

Inez cleared her throat.

"So, um. I'm sorry. About snapping last night."

"I'm sorry," Smitha said. "For lying. I am worried about Charlie, really. And I tried to get him to come this weekend. But not for Homecoming."

"For this ... portal?"

Smitha nodded.

"I know how it sounds. I know, trust me."

"It sounds like you've gone 'round the bend. Too much schoolwork broke your brain."

But she laughed as she said it, and so did Smitha, remembering all the times Inez had claimed that same thing in college.

"If you just saw it," Smitha said. "I think—I hope—you'd remember. I didn't remember until I saw one of those monsters ..."

She might have said more but Inez didn't hear. At the word "monster" her head grew fuzzy, her hearing cotton-closed, her vision fish eyed. She began to fall into nothingness.

Piercingly painful, the harsh whistle of the kettle sliced through the muzzy fog. Inez blinked, focused on Smitha. Her friend hadn't seemed to notice anything.

"I don't want to see any monsters," Inez said softly. She

grabbed two mugs and headed back to the living room. Smitha followed.

Once again tea worked its magic. They talked together about unimportant things, carefully avoiding subjects that could cause any flare-ups. And by the time Smitha brought in the kettle to pour their second cups, she was ready to bring up the portal again.

Inez flinched. Alice frowned. Joe just shook his head.

"Look," said Smitha, "you don't have to believe me. Can you just come with me, though? Come up to campus, to the garden. If we don't see anything, if there's nothing there, I'll—I'll tell Beau I need psychotropics or find a therapist or whatever you guys suggest. But at least come up with me?"

She tried a smile.

"One more walk? For old time's sake?"

And of course they couldn't say no.

"But I remember the explosion."

Joe stared at the rickety gate just behind the founder's statue.

"I remember the tank, fooling around by the tank, and it exploded, and Mona and Charlie were closest to the blast ..."

Alice picked up where he trailed off.

"But I remember this, too. The pool house, right?"

Smitha nodded.

"If you squint, you can sort of see both of them at the same time."

They all squinted, comically tilting their heads and half-closing their eyes. And there it was, the old concrete structure with flaking white paint cracks riddling the outer walls, a rundown recreational facility from an era before their time.

They opened their eyes again and the greenhouse was back, a squat, functional building with an arched roof and heavy, industrial grade, translucent plastic stretched across the top from end to end. A simple wooden door was built into the frame, the only structure aside from the tall wooden beams that supported the plastic.

"Do you guys... remember anything else?" Smitha asked.

Inez looked gray as recycled paper. Joe reached up to dash away a tear.

"I remember—" he began, then stopped. He swallowed hard. "Yeah, I remember it all. Mona ... and the portal ... how could we ...?"

Alice shook her head like a pony.

Smitha gave them a moment to sit with the newly resurfaced memories—but only a moment.

"I remember closing the portal. I remember it closing. So why are the monsters back?"

It had been bothering her since she saw the first one, the one that jogged her own memories. What they did—it should have worked. It should have closed the portal forever and kept the monsters away. But it hadn't, and she didn't know why.

"We did something wrong?" Alice suggested.

"Or the instructions were wrong," Joe said. "Or Charlie misinterpreted them."

"I wish Charlie were here."

Smitha hated that her voice sounded so small.

"Yeah ..." Alice agreed.

"If he doesn't want to be here," said Joe, "then we don't need him."

He reached for the door.

"Be careful," Smitha warned. "One of those monsters could be around."

Joe hesitated, then shrugged and opened the door.

Alice stepped forward but stopped at Inez's hand on her arm. It felt like ice. Her wife's eyes were wide.

"I can't," Inez said.

"'Nez, I'm here. I'm with you."

"I know. I know." She breathed, long and deep, in and out, until she could look into Alice's eyes.

"You good?" Alice asked.

"No," Inez replied. "But I can go in, at least."

They followed the others inside. Long rows of thick PVC pipelined a rough floor, with openings cut into the pipes at regular intervals. Tomato plants were lodged in each opening, winding skyward around single lines of twine which dropped down from a clothesline running parallel to the pipes five or six feet above them. The plants were tall and thick, making it difficult to see much of the greenhouse beyond whatever row you currently occupied.

"Now what?" Joe asked.

"The stairs down to the pool used to be in the back corner, remember?" Alice said. "The ground floor was an ... exercise room or something."

Inez nodded in agreement. "That's right. I remember how odd all those busted bikes and treadmills looked, just piled around the room."

"Back corner, then," Joe said.

"Carefully," said Smitha.

A wave of cold blasted through the humid heat of the greenhouse. The leaves on the tomato plants fluttered frantically as the air pulsed and rippled. A low, slavering growl rumbled over the dirt.

Joe ducked. Inez muffled a shriek and Alice moved in front of her, shielding her.

"One of them is here," Alice hissed. They huddled together at the front of the greenhouse, looking around wildly through dense rows of green.

They waited.

Joe grabbed Smitha's shoulder and pointed. The leaves on the far end of one of the rows were rattling. Not like the others—not shaking in the disturbed air, but rustling as though they were being jostled. As though something was walking through.

Inez crumbled. Joe spun around to see her trembling on the ground, her whole body shaking in tight, convulsive jerks while her breath came in hurried bursts. Alice dropped to her knees beside her and ran a hand over her stomach.

"It's okay, 'Nez. You're here. You are right here in front of me. I see you. I can feel you, see? That's my hand on your stomach."

"What's happening?" Joe hissed.

"She's having an episode," Alice explained. "It's sort of like a panic attack? She ... disassociates? Goes somewhere else. She says she feels like she doesn't exist."

Alice turned her attention back to Inez, whispering into her ear, rubbing her shoulders, reassuring her.

"Should we move her?" Joe asked.

"No," Alice said. "It should be over soon."

Joe turned back to Smitha, who had been watching the plants carefully.

"Anything?"

Smitha shook her head.

"Whatever it was, it's gone."

Joe noticed warmth seeping back into the greenhouse. The tomato plants were still. They were alone.

"Joe," Smitha said. "What are we going to do if a monster does show up? Charlie was the one who knew how to fight them."

"I've got two fists and a gun," Joe replied. "I can take care of things."

He hoped.

Inez sat up and reached up to Joe. He pulled her to her feet.

"Should we go home so Inez can rest?" he asked. "We could always come back tomorrow."

"I'm good," said Inez, shaking her head. "Gonna have to face this sometime, right? We're so close."

"You sure, baby?" Alice asked. Inez nodded.

They moved as a unit to the furthest row of tomato plants and walked single file to the far side of the greenhouse. An old boombox sat on an older wooden table, wires running up to speakers somewhere in the corners of the ceiling. Beneath the table, an open hatch door revealed a descending staircase.

"Everybody ready?" Joe asked, looking around. He was greeted by a series of dour nods.

After Joe dragged the table out of the way, they walked down the stairs: Joe first, Alice and Inez behind him, and Smitha trailing. Four bright cell phone lights offered a shadowy illumination sufficient to ensure nobody fell as they navigated the slick stone steps. Fifty steps further on the stairs finally gave way to a large, open cave—a gaping hole in the Earth's flesh. The floor was uneven and rough. Enormous, jagged projections of rock jutted out from walls and ceiling at every angle. It looked like it had been carved into being by the weapon of a god. Perhaps it had.

In the center of the cave was the portal. It looked just like they now remembered, an unsettling union of ancient beyond words and advanced beyond understanding. It was more than a door. It was a threshold, a thin shimmer in the air, the edges occasionally flickering with green, yellow, and purple sparks that roughly framed its vaguely rectangular outline.

Joe swore under his breath.

The portal shimmered and a Nowhere Man emerged. It erupted through the portal and stopped, snapping its head from side to side, searching.

They saw it.

It saw them.

The creature roared. Nowhere Men emerged from behind dozens of rocky outcroppings. Not the bodiless specters, but the corporeal monsters who had already consumed a soul and stolen its place within Earth's reality. Gnarled arms, thick legs, and thorny, knotted flesh; huge, monstrous brutes that were impossibly strong and fast. The Real Boys. One of them had nearly done them all in fifteen years ago. Now there were twenty or more.

"We're going to die here," Inez said in a flat, hollow voice.

Joe wanted to correct her, or reassure her, but looking around the cavern the best he could do was pull out his compact handgun and shrug.

"Then we'll go down fighting."

Three demon dogs oozed out of the portal. They took their snarling places beside the Nowhere Men, dripping ichor from nightmare jaws.

"We used to be able to fight them," Smitha said.

"Did we?" Alice whispered.

"No. Charlie did." Inez shrank further into herself, her voice growing fainter. "And he's not here."

"We don't need him," Joe said gruffly, and fired into the mass of monsters.

The Nowhere Men scattered at the shot, phantom flapping to different parts of the cavern. One of the demon dogs whined and pawed at its leg where a trickle of blood showed Joe's hit.

"Take that!" Joe yelled, triumphant.

The uninjured demon dogs leapt.

Joe fired again in a panic but missed as one of the dogs bore him down with its weight.

"It's so cold in here," Inez whispered.

"Ethan!" Smitha yelled, trying to dredge her revived

memory for the words Charlie had used so long ago. "Ever! Eva!"

They did not work. The monsters charged.

Smitha closed her eyes.

"*Ehan evna thae*!"

Smitha opened her eyes.

Charlie shoved past her, placing himself between the monsters and his friends. He grabbed the demon dog that was on top of Joe and yanked it up by the scruff of its neck. He could only move it a few inches, but that was enough for Joe to scrabble out from beneath it.

"*Ehan evna thae*!" Charlie yelled again, and his hand burned the demon dog's skin with acid green glow. It squealed and snapped but Charlie held it tight until the evil light died from its eyes. He threw it to the side.

"You came," Smitha said. Charlie turned to wink at her and she noticed the scratches on his face, the fresh blood in his mouth, the big bandage wrapped around his arm.

"About time," Joe growled, but took Charlie's offered hand to haul himself to his feet.

"Fashionably late," Charlie replied. "Now get out of here."

He whirled back and shouted another round at the approaching Nowhere Men. The Words splattered into the nearest monster. It staggered back, gaining them a brief moment of breathing room.

"But—"

Charlie turned to argue with whoever had spoken but saw, at the back of the group, Inez slump against Alice, her eyes rolling back.

"Get her out of here," he commanded.

The Professor and Alice relented, hoisting Inez between them and taking the stairs as quickly as they could. It was slow going, but the Nowhere Men were focused on Charlie, the obvious threat. Joe, however, stayed behind. He pointed over

Charlie's left shoulder and yelled a warning. Charlie spun and let go, knocking another two Nowhere Men backwards. He collapsed and the other monsters pressed forward, sensing his waning strength.

Joe hurdled one of the fallen creatures and landed with a thud beside Charlie.

"Can you walk?" he grunted.

Charlie tried but fell back on his knees. He shook his head.

Without another word, Joe hoisted Charlie onto his shoulders and broke for the stairs. A Nowhere Man slashed his leg, ripping it open just below the knee. Joe stumbled but pressed on. Two more closed in and he raced to split through the gap between them, but he wasn't quite fast enough and took another giant claw across his back, scraping his flesh from shoulder to hip. He bit his tongue and kept running.

One Nowhere Man stood between him and the stairs, another dozen or more were mere steps from his back. Joe put his shoulder down—the one that didn't have Charlie on it—and plowed into the creature with everything he had. He kept his center of gravity low and hit the monster in its chest, driving his shoulder up and through. The thing stumbled, stepped back, and lost its balance just long enough for Joe to barrel past him.

Charlie looked back and saw the Real Boys grouping together around a Nowhere Man that sported a long, jagged scar down the right side of the hatched-shaped face. A chunk was missing from its mouth that left one of its tongues constantly lolling to the side. Charlie shivered. He knew that face. He had made that scar.

"That's right, Goofy," Charlie mumbled, trying to fake bravery. "And I'll do it again."

As far as threats went it was pretty weak, but the Nowhere Men did not pursue them as the two struggled up the stone stairs.

Joe lowered Charlie down to the bench next to the founder's statue and then collapsed on the ground. Inez was laid out on another bench, eyes closed. Alice sat on the ground next to her, holding her hand and speaking calmly as Inez breathed slow, long, shaky breaths. Smitha approached the two men, the worry in her face briefly replaced by relief before returning.

"We can't stay here," she said.

"I'm fine, thanks for asking," Charlie muttered.

Smitha pushed some hair back from his face tenderly but did not relent.

"We have to go," she insisted. "Those monsters could be coming and none of us are in any shape to face them again right now."

A small group of students walked down the path past the benches, thankfully too engrossed in their phones and conversations to spare a glance at the bloodstained adults. Smitha waited until they were well past before continuing.

"There are too many people around, too. We don't want someone to call the police."

"I'm pretty sure I can't walk," said Charlie.

"Come on, man," Joe said. "You've always been up for a walk. What's one more?"

Charlie sat up, hissing in pain.

"Screw you," he said without much venom. The short fight under the greenhouse had taken a lot out of him, more than he was willing to admit.

"Boys," Smitha admonished sternly. "There's no time. Look."

Three dark shapes, just visible through the thick plastic greenhouse walls, moved toward the door with familiar fast, jerky movements.

"Do we fight?" Joe asked.

Everyone looked at Charlie, whose head was lowered.

"Charlie?" Smitha asked.

Slowly he raised his head. There were dark circles under his eyes. Blood reddened his lips.

"Charlie, do we fight?" Joe repeated.

Charlie took a deep breath.

"No," he said. "No. We run."

CHAPTER

TWENTY

They kept just ahead of the Nowhere Men, a few dropped steps the only thing between them and the monsters. They fled in fear and defeat, pure terror pumping adrenaline through them and into their weary legs. The road they followed, running out of town parallel to a set of abandoned train tracks, was a familiar one. Once they had walked it often, in joy or in deep discussion. Now their feet thudded, the only sound between them struggling breaths. The early fall sunset washed their faces in red, the horizon a riot of fire.

"I—I can't—" Alice gasped.

"Have to," Joe rasped out.

Charlie risked a glance behind him. The Nowhere Men were still there, still following close behind. Too close. Closer than before, it seemed. They were slowing, their mere human bodies starting to fail them, but the spectral ghouls had no such hindrances. They were coming, and they would catch up, and then Charlie and Alice and Inez and Joe and Smitha would cease to exist.

"Like hell," he grated, and pumped his legs harder. He took the lead. They were going to make a stand.

"Charlie!" the Professor barked. "Slow—down!"

"Shelter," he replied, and pointed.

A row of abandoned train cars had long ago been parked on an unused section of track. It was less than half an hour from campus on foot, but the college discouraged students from visiting it because of the obvious danger.

Smitha nodded her understanding. She began to fall back, urging the others toward the train cars.

They were almost there when Charlie tripped, his feet losing all coordination. He went sprawling over the loose shale between the rails and scraped his arm sliding to a stop on one of the rails. If he had stayed there any more than a second, it would have been all over. His body, given time to rest, would have shut down. But Joe was there, reaching down and pulling Charlie to his feet. Joe grabbed Charlie's arm and threw it over his shoulder, ducking down to support his friend. Together, Charlie leaning into Joe's broad shoulder, they ran forward at a stagger.

"Close your eyes," Joe whispered. "I know it helps. It's okay. Close your eyes."

Charlie nodded and let his vision darken, trusting Joe to guide the ship while he fought with the familiar pain inside his skull. Alice and Inez had reached a rusted green train car. Its enormous bay door was wide open, and the girls were climbing in.

A brutal, guttural roar shook the train car. It rattled on the tracks, flakes of paint and rust shedding off and falling to stone cluttered ground.

Four heartbeats passed, the trio's feet pounding out in rhythm as they ran through an endless second of silence. It was destroyed by Alice's scream—a sound of pure, barbarous pain that started in a squeal and rose in pitch and timbre until it became an unintelligible howl, a single-voiced cacophony of agony. The car shook again, and a wet thump echoed out of the open door.

The Professor reached the train car and leapt in, Joe pulling Charlie up only a step behind her. The three friends barreled into the car, getting well inside before they stopped to see the Nowhere Man standing crouched over Alice's body. A wet streak of blood down the side of the train car showed where she'd bounced off the wall and slid down. There was a gaping wound in her side, three enormous claw marks tearing through flesh to expose her ribs.

Inez stood frozen against the wall, eyes closed and fists clenched.

The Nowhere Man turned toward the newcomers and roared again, baring a mouthful of needled teeth and writhing tongues. It was answered by a cold vortex filling the room as the other three Nowhere Men, who had pursued the group from town, jerked themselves into the train car.

The monster crouched as though it were preparing to leap, its clawed hands soaked in Alice's blood.

Charlie was ready. He shrugged out of Joe's support and dropped to his knees, reaching into himself and pulling all the power he dared risk. There wasn't much left, he'd barely had time to recover, but he gave it to the Words and sent them out, hurtling toward the hulking nightmare in front of him.

"*Ehan evna thae!*" he screamed, his raw voice ripping the Words out of his mouth. He poured power into it—too much, he was taking too much. The fight in the cavern had emptied him and he risked his own life taking anything more. But what choice did he have? His mouth erupted in boils, his lips split and burned. The heat was unbearable, but at least it pushed the cold from his bones. And the Words were wrong, wrong for this sort of fight. He knew they wouldn't work, not in any useful way. But there were other words lurking; they'd been trying to grab his attention since he returned to the portal.

The green bolts slammed into the Nowhere Man's chest. It rocked back a step and howled, baring a mouthful of tongues.

"Charlie!" Smitha yelled. "You have to move!!"

"Shutupshutupshutup," Charlie moaned.

A memory was stirring. One he'd never paid attention to before. He'd been too busy in the fight at the portal to listen, but now he opened himself up to it, dove in, let it soak into his mind and become his own. He remembered. He needed new Words. What were they? Think. Think. RIGHT.

"*Sha tak ertasa*!" he screamed, and the Nowhere Man's eyes went wide.

The Words demanded power and he gave the very last he had, toppling forward onto his forearms as his legs gave out. He pulled from every corner of being; he felt a rib crack, then another, as he summoned the strength from his chest—his entire body was covered in burns, but the Words were going. They were going. A second blast hit the creature, and this time the spectral form of the Nowhere Man stumbled out of the lumbering body, the familiar not-quite-there shape of it lurching as it scrambled to maintain its hold its physical form. The body fell to the floor of the train car and began to crumble, but the Nowhere Man managed to stay tethered. The air rippled as the specter fought for control. It pushed back in and reasserted mastery, and the body pulled back to life.

"Not strong enough," murmured Charlie through bloodied lips.

"My turn," said Joe, reaching into his jacket and pulling out his gun.

He pointed it at the creature and squeezed the trigger. Two shots missed, tearing through the rusting wall of the train car somewhere behind it. The third smacked into its chest and bounced off, failing to pierce the thick hide. The Nowhere Man grabbed Alice's body by the foot, pulling it towards itself. A giant, muscled hand wrapped around her throat as the creature glared at Joe, defiant.

Charlie coughed up a frothing mix of blood and bile as he drew himself back to his knees. He readied himself to try again.

"Hand!" shouted the Professor.

On instinct, Charlie's hand shot out. She grabbed it and reached out with her other arm towards Joe, who hesitated only a moment before nodding in understanding. He locked his fingers around hers. Charlie looked up at them.

"We're here," said Joe. "We're here. Don't kill yourself."

"Use us," the Professor encouraged.

"You ... sure?" slurred Charlie. "Not ... not sure I can control it."

Joe grinned, a little awkwardly but with a hint of warmth. "I'm your huckleberry."

Charlie closed his eyes again. He felt arms wrap around him. Inez whispered in his ear "I'm here too."

Charlie reached into himself, found the corners of fraying power. There wasn't much left, and if he drew out too much more, he would kill himself. He pulled at the tiniest corner, summoning just enough strength to light the pilot.

"*Sha tak ertasa*," he whispered, his thick tongue barely able to form the Words.

But instead of firing them towards the creature he pushed them through his connection to Inez. She was so afraid, but the fear was not for herself. The power inside of her burned with her fear and love for Alice. He drank from it greedily.

Next Charlie sent the Words to the Professor, letting them flow into her as he had so many years ago. He found her power, still—always—brighter than his own, and took as much of it as he dared, wrapping it around the Words, feeding it to them. He felt the Professor tense up and knew that she was in pain. He sent the Words through her and into Joe.

Oh, Joe, thought Charlie as he reached out and felt the power in his friend. It covered him like a warm blanket, the deep, durable energy flowing over him. He took it, more than he needed, probably, but he had a plan. The Words wanted out and he finally let them loose, his own dribble of power dwarfed by the combined might of his three friends. He saw Joe contort as the Words escaped through him, felt the flaying heat as it washed over both him and the Professor.

The monster's head snapped up as the Words collided with him. The Nowhere Man was forced from its body and hung suspended in the air, its hatchet face hovering above the echoed memory of a black robe, the air rippling around it.

"Ehan evna thae," Charlie spit out. The second Words hit. The Nowhere Man screamed as it was torn apart, rent into a million pieces of non-existence by the ancient Words.

"That's new," said the Professor, so startled as to be nearly beyond fear.

Charlie coughed, then ordered "Again."

He didn't wait but pulled the energy from them again, spitting the green fire Words this time toward the three wraiths. They were thrown against the side of the train car, flakes of paint mingling with the ashes of their shredded forms and falling like snow over the fading body of their massive, Real Boy companion. In a moment the body, too, was gone.

Joe slumped to the ground. Inez dropped Charlie's hand and dashed over to Alice. She threw herself on the body of her wife, sobbing.

"She's alive!" she cried. "She's still breathing!"

Joe pulled off his shirt and wrapped it around Alice, trying to put some pressure on the open wound in her side. He lifted her gently, like a fireman, and headed for the door.

"Come on," he said. "Professor, get Charlie. We need to get them some help. Inez, can you walk?"

Inez nodded.

"You don't exactly look like the picture of health," Charlie chided Joe.

"Can you stand up?"

"No."

"Then I'll carry on giving the orders, thank you."

Together, the five of them exited the train car and headed back towards town.

The Professor looked at Charlie as she helped him limp along. "What happened in there? How did you ..."

"Long story, darling. I'll tell you in the morning," said Charlie. "Right now, I gotta concentrate on staying conscious, unless you want to carry me like Joe's carrying Alice."

"I could if I had to," she answered.

"My hero."

"Not yet," she said, pulling out her cell phone. "I'll take that title once I make this call."

TWENTY-ONE

Smitha braced herself but Beau asked no questions, just helped get everyone into the back of his car and drove them to the community hospital. When they arrived, a small team was already waiting to get Alice and Charlie prepped and moved. Joe collected their insurance information and stood talking to the receptionist, sorting out paperwork.

Inez went with Alice when she was carted through the swinging doors and into one of the patient rooms beyond. Smitha had tried to follow Charlie but she was waved off by her old friend, who insisted his wounds were minor and he'd be "in and out in no time."

She turned her attention instead to Joe, insisting that he have his earlier injuries checked out. As he was being led to another examination room, he glanced back to see Beau peppering Smitha with questions. She waved them all away, begging him to hurry and promising to share everything with him later. He grumbled but agreed and disappeared back through the double doors.

Once Joe returned, fresh bandages and a few stitches firmly in place, he sat with Smitha at a small table in the corner of the mostly empty waiting area outside of the Emergency Room.

"Something was going on there," Joe noted, glancing at Smitha.

"Going on where?" she asked.

"There. I mean, here. With your friend," Joe said, waving at the door through which Beau had exited. "He was worried about you."

"He's a doctor. He works here. That's his job."

"No, this was personal worry. Not professional. I saw it. I *heard* it."

"I told you, he's a friend of mine," Smitha answered.

"Your earlobes are pink," Joe said.

Smitha's hands slipped up to cover her ears.

"Not fair," she said.

Joe chuckled and leaned back into his chair, crossing his arms and raising an eyebrow.

"Alright, fine," Smitha said. "Beau also teaches a few courses at the college every now and then. We've been out once or twice."

"Is it serious?" Joe asked.

"It ... could be. Maybe. It's on the edge of serious."

"On the edge of serious?"

"Well. Serious adjacent, at least."

"What the heck does that mean?"

"It means I'm afraid," she confessed. "No, not afraid, exactly. I don't know what it is. Something is holding me back. He's great, and I think he's ready to jump in, to make it something *real*. But I can't do it. I want to, but I can't."

Smitha sighed and let her guard down.

"Everything since college has been such a fight, you know?" she said. "I was so confident then, with you guys around me. Nothing's felt right since. I had to fight myself to get through grad school. Every single day was a battle just to *care*, just to force myself into doing the thing in life I always wanted most. Then, somehow I ended up back here, just ... just killing time. Just stalling. Waiting for something to finally feel *important* again."

"I never knew you felt that way," said Joe, frowning. "You seemed to be the only one who had it all together."

"Yeah. I don't talk about it much. It's my job to have it all together."

"I know what you mean, though," said Joe. "It's been the same for me. I think it's been the same for all of us. Sleepwalking through the echoes of a life that isn't quite right."

Smitha nodded.

"I mean, look at us," Joe continued. "The girls are the only ones with a successful relationship, and that started in college. In the good times. We've all shifted through a bunch of empty jobs with no purpose and no plans. We've been *surviving*, not living. And poor Charlie ... He's had it worse than all of us. We were hiding from a past we couldn't remember, but he's been living with it all, and the only people who shared it with him—his *family*—none of us remembered. We should have been there for him. *I* should have been there for him."

The reawakening of lost memories finally caught up to Joe in full. He hung his head and cried. He cried for Mona, his lost friend, for Charlie, his lost brother. For the family he'd failed and nearly lost.

Smitha watched him, a hand on his knee, but she did not interrupt. She let him cry, sitting next to him, her presence close to his. Fifteen minutes later, he raised his head, his eyes rimmed red. He clutched at her hand and she welcomed his grip.

"That's the first proper cry I've had in years," he confessed. "I've been divorced twice and I barely let myself process it. I just closed everything off."

"Feel good?"

"It feels terrible. My nose is full of yuck, my head is pounding, and my eyes hurt."

Smitha squeezed his hand.

"But yeah. It feels good," he admitted.

They sat in silence for some time, watching the clock and enjoying each other's quiet company. The silence was broken, as it often was, by Charlie, who came strolling out the swinging double doors of the Emergency Room, a nurse trailing in his wake.

"Good to go!" Charlie announced, plopping down in a chair across the small table from Joe. He clutched at his chest with a grimace that he immediately tried to hide.

"No, you are not!" said the nurse, looking at Smitha helplessly. "He's not."

"Couple of cracked ribs," Charlie said, waving a hand. "Some bumps and bruises. The good painkillers. Nothing I need to stay in the hospital for. The doc said so."

"He did NOT! He said there's nothing else to do for cracked ribs except wrap your chest and let them heal. You have to take it very easy. You need to discuss things with the doctor, and you should probably stay here for evaluation for at least a night so we can make sure none of your other injuries are more severe than we think."

"I'll be fine," Charlie declared. "We have work to do."

"Perhaps the doctor could talk to all of us, out here?" Smitha asked the nurse. "We'll do our best to take care of him."

"I'll go ask," she said, and retreated.

"I need some coffee," Charlie announced before Smitha or Joe could ask him any questions. "Please? I know my mouth is a mess, but I have to have some coffee. Then we can talk. Coffee, then talk."

"Alright, Lorelai, settle down," said Joe. "There's a little cafe down the hall. I noticed it when we walked in. I'll go get ..." he looked at Smitha, who nodded, "three. Three coffees. Heavy on cream, no sugar?"

Charlie nodded in confirmation.

"Black?" he asked Smitha, who smiled.

"Only way to drink it," she answered.

Joe sauntered off.

Charlie studiously ignored Smitha's gaze for a full five minutes before cracking.

"Stop looking at me like that," he said querulously. "I'm not a baby."

"No," Smitha said, "you're my friend who has been very bad at taking care of himself."

Charlie leaned forward over the table, winced again, and leaned back.

"I know you care about me, Smitha," he said. "And I appreciate it, I really do. All the days you were the only one I could count on—it means a lot. But there's more at stake than just me."

"I know, but—"

"Please, Prof. Hear me out. There's a good chance I might not make it out of this. And that's fine. It's ok. Because we have to close this damn portal, and if the only way to do it is by physically jumping in and pulling it shut you'd better believe I'm going to be grabbing it with both hands. I need you to know that finishing the job is my priority."

"What if it's not mine?"

"Then it should be."

Smitha set her mouth in a thin line. This was a Charlie she had never encountered before, and she didn't like it. But she couldn't argue against his position. He was right. The portal needed closed.

But we will all make it, she vowed. *All of us, alive, no matter what it takes.*

Joe returned, empty handed.

"Found the cafe, but nobody was there," he apologized. "I looked around for a while, but the entire hall was pretty empty. Eventually I gave up and came back. Sorry."

"Is there a machine somewhere?" Charlie asked. "I'm telling you, I *need* this coffee."

"Maybe," Joe said, looking around the empty lobby. "I'll ask next time someone comes through."

He shuffled his feet for a moment.

"Hey, uh, Charlie? I'm sorry. For not being there for you. We were best friends and ... I just let you go. We never hang out. I never call. I feel so guilty about not being there for you, but I ... I think I know why. I felt all that guilt about Mona, so I pushed you away. I abandoned you."

He sniffed back the beginning tears.

"No, man. We just grew up," Charlie said, standing up and waving helplessly as his own tears formed. "People grow up and grow apart. You didn't remember. I should have tried more, I should have reached out, I should have—"

Joe walked over and wrapped Charlie in a hug. The two men stood, unmoving, holding on to each other and letting the pain and separation of the last fifteen years bleed away. Smitha wiped away her own tears.

Eventually Charlie lifted his head from Joe's shoulder.

"Hey," he said. "Let's start again. I'm Charlie. Want to be my best friend?"

Joe laughed, feeling a darkness start to lift. "Well, it worked the first time. So sure, why not?"

Smitha stood and joined the hug.

"It's so good to see you two together again," she said.

They broke apart, Charlie wiping his face with the back of his arm.

"Man, now I need that coffee more than ever," he said.

"Sorry," Joe said, "I haven't seen anyone to ask yet."

"Where is everybody?" Smitha asked. "We've barely seen anybody since we came in. This place must be running on a skeleton crew. Weird for a Friday evening, right? Shouldn't there be more people here?"

"Oh no," Charlie muttered. "No, no, no."

"What?" demanded Joe.

"Quick, both of you. Tell me the names of anyone we've seen since we got here. Faces? Ages? I'll take anyone."

"Well, there's Beau," hazarded Smitha.

"Beau?! Dr. Tall and Pretty is Beau? How did I miss that on the ride over?"

"You were pretty out of it," Joe reminded his friend.

"Professor, we need to talk about him. I mean, not now. First, tell me who you remember. But we are going to talk about this. Anyone else? Who else was here?"

"The attendants who pulled the roller bed things," Joe said.

"Anyone else?"

"No," he said, shaking his head.

"Isn't it a bit odd that nobody took our information? Nobody is at the cafe? Have any new patients come in while I was back there?"

They shook their heads. Charlie raced to the closest window, sucking in painful breaths as he went. He cracked the shade and peered out.

Outside the hospital were dozens of large, bulky Nowhere Men in full body, each one a hulking Real Boy. They appeared to be ringing the facility, standing every twenty feet or so as far as Charlie could see.

"Damn it," he hissed. "They're here. They've been taking people right under our noses. Why didn't we feel them?"

"They must be playing it safe," Smitha hazarded. "Taking people only when they're far enough away that we can't sense them."

"They're trapping us in here," Joe said. "They're still scared of Charlie, probably more so if they know he's figured out how to properly kill their bodies now. Nothing else can hurt those things. I shot one, and it bounced right off. Even back ... even the first time, I was only able to hurt one when I hit it where Charlie's magic had opened it up."

"So, they're massing strength," Smitha said. "They're pinning us down in here and gathering an army. We escaped at the portal and the train, so now they're just coming with numbers. There's no way we can take down that many of them."

"The pups!" cried Joe. "We have to go get the girls!"

The air wavered and rippled. Charlie spun around to see two Nowhere Men rushing through the main doors. Without thinking, Smitha and Joe each grabbed a hand. Charlie reached into them and spoke the Words.

"*Ehan evna thae!*"

Lightning leapt from him. The Nowhere Men were in a small line, with one trailing just behind the other, and the Words ripped through both of them, unraveling them.

"They're getting antsy," Charlie said. "They're trying to flush us out. We need to hurry!"

The trio crashed through the swinging doors separating the waiting room from the Emergency Room itself. This part of the hospital was still fully staffed; the Nowhere Men apparently hadn't ventured this deep in. A series of hurried conversations led them into a nearby wing and down a long second floor hallway to the room where Alice had been moved. To their great relief, both of the girls were there.

"How's she doing?" asked Joe, glancing from Alice to Inez.

"We've got trouble!" Charlie announced simultaneously.

"I'm okay," said Alice. "Not great, but okay."

"She'll be fine," Beau said as he walked through the open

door to join them. "Those cuts were deep, but clean. We were able to close them back up without much trouble, and since they went down her side, nothing else critical was damaged. She's lucky."

"Thank you, Beau," said Smitha.

"Smitha, can we talk now?" Beau asked. "I'm glad she's okay, but I need to know what happened."

"It's hard to explain," Smitha started.

"No, it isn't," said Charlie, interrupting. He pulled open the curtain and pushed the doctor up to the window. "Look down," he ordered.

Beau, confused, did as he was ordered. He covered his mouth with his hand, the blood draining from his face.

"What are those things?" he stammered.

"That's what cut open Alice," Charlie answered.

"There's another one out there?" Alice demanded from the bed. "Is that what you meant by 'trouble'?"

"More than one, Alice," said Inez, who had sidled up to the window. "There are a lot of them. Dozens, maybe. What's happening?"

"What the hell are those things?" asked Beau again.

"Do you want me to answer?" asked Smitha. "Do you want the real answer?"

He looked into her eyes, noticed the hard edge there, and felt his spine crawl with fear. But he nodded.

"Fine, but no questions," Smitha said. "You can ask questions later. I don't care if you believe me or not, just hold your questions until there's time, understood?"

He nodded again.

"Those are monsters from another world," Smitha said. "They came through a magic portal on campus. There are a lot of them, and they want our world. We know how to stop them, and they know we know, so they're trying to kill us."

Beau looked at her, bit his lip, and swallowed all his questions except one.

"What can I do?"

"We need to get out," Joe said. "All of us. Maybe they'll follow us and leave the hospital alone."

"Doesn't matter if they do or not," said Charlie. "If we don't end this, it's only a matter of time before they get everyone."

"I might be able to get you out of here," said Beau. "There's a parking garage for employees beneath the building, and it has interior access. But we're going to need to be very careful with Alice. She's sewn up well enough, but too much movement could pull those stitches wide open again."

A scream ripped through the hallway. A minute later, another followed. Then a third.

"I think somebody else noticed your friends," said Beau.

The hospital descended into panic. Somebody pulled an alarm and multiple calls to the police and 911 were placed from cell phones throughout the building.

Beau answered a call on his work cell phone.

"That was the chief of medicine," he explained when he ended the call. "We're implementing emergency procedures. The police are on their way. If you are leaving, you need to go now. You won't be able to get out soon, even through the garage."

He threw Smitha his keys. "You know what my car looks like. It's in the back row. Hang a left at the end of the hallway, then take the first right, and the stairwell will be the first door on your left. You'll need this," he added, unbuckling a key card from the three or so hanging from his belt by a lanyard and handing it to her. "It'll get you in the door."

"Come with us," Smitha urged. "You can drive."

"There's barely enough room in my car for five," he said. "And I'm needed here."

Sirens wailed outside as police cruisers pulled into the main lot.

"Take care of Alice. Be very careful moving her. No twisting," Beau said, looking at Alice. "Try to avoid crouching and don't rotate at the waist unless you can't help it. Turn your whole body. Now go!"

Smitha stood on her toes to kiss his cheek. "I'll call you later," she said, hoping against hope that she'd even remember he existed later.

They hurried to follow Beau's directions, Joe and Inez supporting Alice between them and moving her as quickly as they could risk. Smitha identified his car and they piled in, Charlie in the passenger seat and Joe with the girls across the bench seat in the back. Smitha reached down to adjust the seat, sliding it forward so she could reach the pedals, and then fired it up and headed for the exit.

A Nowhere Man stood silhouetted in sunlight at the top of the ramp where the garage emerged to ground level. Gunshots rang out from somewhere above, and the barking shouts of police communication followed.

"Hold on!" Smitha yelled and pressed the gas pedal to the floor. The car's back tires fishtailed for a moment until they found purchase, but Smitha kept the vehicle pointing straight up the ramp. They flew into the Nowhere Man at top speed.

The nose of the vehicle crunched as it smashed into the creature, throwing it backwards. Airbags popped out and slammed into Charlie and Smitha. Alice yelped in pain as she was thrown forward into the back of the driver's seat.

Charlie cursed and retrieved a small knife from his pocket, hacking at Smitha's airbag until it deflated enough for her to see another Nowhere Man staring at her through the windshield. She threw the car into reverse and, miraculously, it still functioned, peeling away from the creature.

"Charlie?" she begged. He was already winding down the

window. He leaned out, fingers spread towards the Nowhere Man like a cartoon wizard about to cast a spell. He dropped a bit of power into the Words—not much, he barely had anything in the tank, but enough to do the job—and yelled.

"Sha tak ertasa!"

There wasn't enough strength there to do any real damage, but the Nowhere Man recognized the Words and the accompanying blast of lightning, and it dodged out of the way. Smitha slammed the gas again and the battered car flew past the monster and out into the hospital's main parking.

The guns were already silent. Three police cars sat in the lot, surrounded by Nowhere Men, but they saw no officers as they sped past and headed for the road. The air was a mass of distorted ripples, and cold fear settled into their bones.

"It wasn't just the solid ones," said Inez as they pulled away. "There were so many of the... the hungry ones, too. I saw police cars. Somebody must have called them, but I don't remember them showing up. They must have been ..."

"Yeah," said Charlie. "They must have been."

TWENTY-TWO

They sped from the hospital, Smitha pushing Beau's car to hurry.

"Where are we going?" she asked Charlie.

"I'm not sure," he confessed. "Somewhere quiet. Somewhere without a lot of people, just in case..." He paused and cleared his throat.

"The fewer Real Boys the better," Inez filled in from the back seat.

"Right." Charlie cocked his head. "Actually, Smitha, could we get into one of the academic buildings? I have an idea."

"Sure," she said. "I have a key. But—"

"Great. Head for campus."

Smitha's phone dinged.

"That's Beau," she said. "Let me see what it says."

"Is that a custom ringtone?" Charlie asked. "You have a custom ringtone, but you still haven't kissed him? Professor, have I taught you nothing?"

"Now is not the time, Charlie. Please give me my phone."

"No. You're driving. Safety first." Charlie picked up the

phone himself. "And now is exactly the time, Smitha. There's a reasonable chance that there will never be another time after tonight. This might be the very end of time. Kiss that man."

The phone dinged again.

"What's your code? I'll tell him to meet us at your office."

This is not his fight, Charlie."

"This is everyone's fight, Prof. Your Beau is part of this now."

Smitha smacked the steering wheel in resigned frustration. She told Charlie her code.

A few minutes later Smitha parked Beau's car in the visitor parking lot closest to the academic building that housed her office.

"Keep the engine running," Charlie told her, "in case we have to jet before the good doctor gets here. Alice, how are you doing?"

She gave a shaky thumbs-up.

"Great. Hang in there, pup."

"Charlie?" Inez asked, her voice as shaky as her wife's hand. "Why didn't it work?"

In the front seat Smitha could see Charlie's jaw tighten.

"The first time, I mean," Inez continued. "Why didn't the portal close?"

Charlie shook his head.

"I didn't do it right," he said softly. "I don't know what the right way is, but I must have done something wrong."

Smitha took his hand and squeezed it.

"We'll figure out the right way together."

Charlie squeezed back.

"It was almost right," Joe offered. "I remember feeling it close, just before Mona ..."

"Before she died," Charlie said flatly. "When she died, the chain must have broken."

"So, we did get it mostly right?" Joe said.

"Yeah. Six people, sharing their energies, one wizard in the back who knows the Words, and one focus point up front, touching the portal itself."

"So, we need six," Inez pointed out. "And even when we had six back then, we failed. Now we don't have Mona, who was always the strongest of us."

"We have a sixth, if he's willing." Charlie looked at Smitha. "I'm sorry, Prof, but I think we need to have Beau in the chain."

"I won't force him," Smitha said firmly. "But ... yes. I think we need to ask."

"And as for strength," Charlie continued, "that's why we're here. I think we can up our game a little."

A car pulled into the parking space next to them. Beau turned off the engine and stepped out.

"Whose car is that?" Smitha asked as the family piled out.

Beau shrugged.

"It was in the parking lot with the door open and keys in the ignition."

"Beau! Did you steal a car?"

He grinned sheepishly.

"I technically just borrowed it. I intend on taking it back when we're done here."

"A little dangerous, Doc! I like it." Charlie bumped Smitha on the shoulder and grinned at her shocked expression. "What's a little minor felony at the end of the world? Come on, Prof. It's Take Your Family to Work day."

They filed into Smitha's office. It wasn't large enough for everyone to be fully comfortable, but it had the same warmth and charm, the same imprint of her welcoming energy, that Smitha's house exuded. They wanted to be surrounded by it, so they made do. Beau settled Alice on Smitha's office chair. The group unanimously made Charlie take one of the other chairs. After a brief scuffle Joe found himself put into the other one. Smitha perched on the corner of her desk. Inez settled at Alice's feet. There didn't seem a convenient spot for Beau so he leaned against a bookshelf, arms crossed, watchful.

"Nice setup, Prof," Charlie said, looking around the office. Alice picked up the framed picture from Smitha's desk. She smiled.

"That was a good day," she said, turning the frame to show the others. Charlie took it and studied it. It was from his wedding day. He remembered asking the scared-looking freshman to take their picture. Joe stood next to Charlie, arms slung around each other's shoulders. Both of their bowties were crooked and badly tied. Inez and Alice flanked the group, grinning young– very young– smiles. Smitha stood next to Alice, and between Smitha and Charlie ...

He lightly touched each of the faces, lingering on the smiling girl whose arms were wrapped around Smitha. Mona.

"The best day," he said.

Joe patted his shoulder. Charlie put the picture down and turned to Beau.

"So Doc, are you sure you're ready for this?"

Smitha replaced the picture, nervously straightening the already-straight desk. She had thought, often, of what it would be like for Beau to meet her family. She had run through many scenarios. Faceless monsters did not feature in any of them.

"No," Beau said honestly. "Whatever you're going to tell me about those monsters at the hospital, I am definitely not ready."

"Here's the quick and dirty version," Charlie said. "There's a portal on campus. It leads to different worlds. We tried to close it with magic when we were seniors. Well, seniors and freshmen. Whatever. You know what I mean. It didn't work. We have to do it again. The monsters are trying to stop us. With me so far?"

Beau glanced at Smitha. If this was a joke, some sort of elaborate prank, he knew he would see it on her face. She was open with her feelings, to him, and he felt sure he would be able to tell, to catch a look or a smile or something. There was nothing like that. In her deep brown eyes, he saw fear. In the set of her mouth, he saw determination. Her friends—no, he corrected himself, her family—looked the same. He turned back to Charlie.

"Yep," he said. "Tell me more."

As Charlie laid out the details for Beau, sparing him none of the messy nitty-gritty, Alice sat back in the office chair and closed her eyes. The pain from her side was intense. If she didn't move much it stayed a mostly manageable throb. Getting up to the office had taken its toll, though. But there was nothing to be done. She was going to muscle through and do her best to make sure no one caught on to how bad it was. Inez's back pressed against her legs, a reassuring weight. Alice let herself drift off into a hazy half-sleep. The picture on Smitha's desk was foremost in her mind. She remembered that day. The wedding, the carnival, sprinting through the warm-cool spring night at Inez's heels.

When she shook herself back to the present, Charlie was finishing up his explanation.

" —so like Inez said earlier, either we die tonight trying to close the portal or we die in a couple of days when those monsters find us."

Beau still stood against the bookshelf, arms crossed. His head was bowed.

"We need a sixth," Charlie said. "Uncle Sam wants you, if you're willing."

"You don't have to," Smitha was quick to add. "You don't have any responsibility here."

"I think I do," Beau said slowly. He looked up and pointed at Alice. "You're my patient." He pointed to Joe, then Charlie.

"You're hurt, and you. It sounds like you're expecting there to be more injuries. I can't in good conscience let you go get yourselves hurt or killed without offering my help."

Joe let out a huge breath. Charlie leapt up, hugged Beau, and sank back in the chair, holding his ribs.

"I am so glad you said that," Charlie said. "I honestly had no idea where we would get another person if you had said no."

Beau brushed past them and walked over to where Smitha still sat on the desktop. He took her face in his hands and knelt down until he could look in her eyes.

"Are you okay with this?" he asked.

"It's your decision," she said softly.

"It is. But I want your input. Do you want me there?"

Smitha bit her lip and glanced at Charlie. Charlie knew what she was asking.

"It was worth it," he said, his gaze straying to the picture on her desk. "Even though we didn't close the portal all the way, even though I lost her...it was worth it."

Beau knelt down so that he was looking up into Smitha's face. His thumb traced her cheekbone.

"Do you want me there?" he asked again.

"I do," she said, and leaned down and kissed him.

Alice giggled.

"Pups, look away," Charlie commanded. "Give her some privacy."

Smitha pulled away from Beau.

"I'm sorry!" she said. "I'm so sorry, I shouldn't have—and they were all watching"

"I told them to look away," Charlie said.

Beau kissed Smitha on the forehead. He was smiling.

"It's fine," he said. "Smitha, really. It's fine. All of it. It's fine. It's good."

They kissed again.

"I really hate to break this up," Charlie said, "you have no idea how much, I have been trying to get her to do that for ages, but there are probably hundreds of Nowhere Men hunting for me right now. We need to get a move on."

"Yes, sorry," Beau said. He straightened up but took Smitha's hand and held it as he asked "So, what next?"

"I have an idea about that," Charlie said.

Across from Smitha's office was an empty classroom. The motion sensor lights turned on as they entered. Charlie stood at the front and everyone else took seats in the front row. They sat expectantly while Charlie surveyed them.

"Is this what it feels like all the time?" he asked Smitha. "This is power. I love this."

"You'd be a great professor," Smitha said.

"Damn straight. Now listen up, class. This is Wizarding 101."

"Wait, what?" Joe, who had adopted the slouching posture he had used for four years, sat up straighter. "But you're the only one who can sling magic."

"Why?"

"What do you mean, why?"

"No, I see what you're getting at," Smitha said. She leaned forward on her elbows, also unconsciously mimicking her college years stance. "It's not like you're inherently magical."

Charlie paused.

"I am, actually," he said, "I'm a beautiful unicorn of a person. But in the very literal sense, no, there's nothing special about me that would make me the only one able to use the Words. There's only one difference— I actually know them."

"No, you know how to—what, how to get the power out or something." Inez frowned, trying to figure out how to phrase what she meant. "It's not just saying the Words, right? You have to put some oomf behind them."

"True, but I think I can teach you that, too." Charlie

turned to Smitha. "Prof, do you remember the first time I pushed the power through you, senior year?"

She nodded.

"And the rest of you, you've had the power running through you. I think, if I teach you how to say the Words right, you'll be able to figure out how to use them."

Charlie turned to face the whiteboard behind him and looked around for a dry erase marker.

"I've got some in my office," Smitha said, getting up. "Be right back."

There was a brief awkward silence as the door closed behind her.

"So," Beau said, "you've been trying to get her to kiss me?"

"For months," Charlie confirmed.

"I see." He flushed a little. "She's been talking about me for that long?"

"She's been talking about you for years, Doc."

"Oh. That's good to know."

Charlie sat on the desk in front of Beau.

"Listen, Doc. Smitha is special. She's the best of us."

Joe, Inez, and Alice nodded.

"We want her to be happy. She deserves to be happy. Can you make her happy?"

Beau met Charlie's gaze and was surprised at what he saw. From all of Smitha's stories, from the pictures she'd shown him, he'd gotten the impression that Charlie was sort of a goof, never taking anything seriously, the life of the party with not much else going for him. In person, though, Charlie was different. A goof at times, yes, but there was an edge to him, a sharpness that took one even more by surprise because of how unexpected it was. He'd always wondered why Smitha was so close to someone so very different in personality. Looking into Charlie's green eyes, he knew.

"I can try," he said. "I will try."

"Good," Charlie said. Smitha came back into the room and he hopped off the desk to take the marker from her. "Thanks, Prof. OK, kids, let's have some learning."

The strong smell of dry erase marker filled the room as he wrote three words on the board.

EHAN EVNA THAE

"This is what I use on the Nowhere Men. The monsters," he clarified for Beau. "You've all heard me say them before. Except you," he said, nodding to Beau again. "These Words will kill the ghostie versions of the Nowhere Men. They don't do much to the Real Boys, but it still spooks 'em. They're a good place to start, anyway. Now, like Inez pointed out, you've got to put some oomf into the Words. Don't do that right now! Keep your oomf to yourself. I want to make sure you've got it right before we start flinging lightning around. So— softly. *Ehan.*"

He motioned for them to repeat him.

"*Ehan,*" they chorused dutifully.

"*Evna.*"

"*Evna.*"

"*Thae.*"

"The."

"No, no. Listen. *Thae.* Tha-e. *Thae.*"

"*Thae.*"

"Good. Say them again."

After a few repetitions Charlie was satisfied at their pronunciation.

"Gold stars all around," he said. "And two gold stars for me. Now, here's the hard part. This time when you say them, don't just say them. This time I want you to push it out. When you feel a tiny surge of power, you know what it feels like, then feed into it until it grows, then use it to shove the Words out. Don't aim at anyone."

Beau raised his hand.

"I don't know what it feels like," he said.

"That's right!" Charlie slapped his scraped-up forehead, a move that made everyone else wince in sympathy. "I forgot that you're new. Here, take my hands."

This time Charlie walked around the desk and knelt in front of Beau. He held out his hands. Beau reached out and took them.

"Is it going to hurt?" Beau asked.

"Yes."

"Okay. I just wanted to know."

Charlie closed his eyes and felt for the power. It was there, waiting as it always was, anxious to be released. And there was Beau, also waiting. Charlie could feel his energy, steady and strong. It was a good match for Smitha's. The thought made him smile. Still smiling, he gathered up the Words and, whispering them, pushed them through the point where Beau's hands touched his. Green lightning danced down his fingers and up Beau's arms.

Beau stiffened, gripped Charlie's hand more tightly, but kept silent. Charlie pulled back on the reins a little but kept the channel open.

"Your turn," he said. "Say it."

"I don't know-" Beau began but stopped. "Actually wait. I think..."

He frowned. Charlie felt him start to draw power.

"Whoa, hold on there, cowboy. Not so much. Just a little."

Beau drew back, narrowing the channel to a thin artery of power running between them.

"There you go," Charlie said. "Now—the Words."

"Ehan. Evna. Thae."

A tiny thread of green sparked between Beau's lips. It dropped forward like trails from a weeping willow firework and landed on the desk, sizzling a tiny hole in the polished surface.

Joe whooped. Beau opened his eyes and saw Charlie grinning at him.

"Congratulations. You're a wizard, Doc," he said.

Beau rubbed his hand across his lips, feeling the small raw spot. Charlie gave him a sympathetic look.

"No kissing for a little bit to let that heal. Charlie's orders." He stood and clapped his hands. "Okay, class. Your turn. Find your power—on your own to start with, I think—and then see what you can do with the Words."

The room at first was silent as the others followed Charlie's example and closed their eyes. Still in teacher mode, Charlie put his hands behind his back and paced around his students, soon adding the second phrase—the one that ejected Nowhere Men from their bodies—beside the first on the white board. When he reached the back of the room, he dropped the act. Moving as quietly as possible, he dropped down to the floor and spread himself out, gingerly settling his body to give his aching ribs at least some cushion. He couldn't stop the low hiss of pain. Everything hurt, and he felt empty of energy. His head was fuzzy and, for some reason, he was ravenous. Maybe they could pick up something on their way to the portal. How late was the student union open? What time was it, even? What day was it? Everything was running together, yesterday and today and the past and the future.

And yet, for all that, he felt better than he had in ages. Emotionally, that was. Physically, he was pretty sure he was dying. But his family was here, and he had a purpose, and he was being useful and had a plan and he thought, he really really thought, that they had a chance of doing the thing right this time. It wasn't going to be without cost, but it could all end, once and for all. He could be done.

And then what? What was he if not stuck in the past, terrified of monsters no one else could see, questioning his sanity?

Well. Enough time for that later if this worked out. And if it didn't, no need to worry about it.

He smelled burning and tasted copper in the air. Something sizzled and Alice yelped.

"Careful," Charlie said fuzzily from the floor, just as a general warning. Then, as his wizardlings practiced, he fell asleep.

He walks down a century of stairs into the gaping sharp maw of a stone giant. Ahead of him is the winter, tiny pieces of ice swirling up on cold winds to stick, freezing, on his face. Behind him is the fall—he can still smell the rich dark earth, the ripeness of the growing things longing for the harvest. He is in the waiting time, no longer one and not yet the other.

His hand is against the wall, his fingers trailing down wood slick with ... water? He hopes it is water.

One finger snags against a rough indentation in the wall. He stops, turns, looks.

There is writing on the wall.

His fingers trace the loops and turns. They twine together, a puzzle that his waking mind would not be able to untangle.

But now he is asleep, and now he sees.

It is not a language. It is a picture.

Six circles link together, each one a part of two others. Not one stands on its own. Linked together, they form one giant circle.

Around the circle of circles are small dots, many small dots, chiseled so sharp into the stone that tiny darts of granite dust prickles the tip of his finger. One arc of the circle touches a rectangle. The rectangle is not a carving—it is a hole, empty black as far back as his questing fingers can fit.

It means something. But everything means something to someone at some time. This may not be his.

The cold of winter is increasing. Ice crystals sting his cheeks.

Someone is saying his name.

CHARLIE WOKE UP, GOOSEBUMPS RUNNING UP HIS chilled arms.

"They're here," Joe said. "We've got to go."

CHAPTER
TWENTY-THREE

They ran, although for some it was really more of a stagger, out into the darkness.

We are going to lose, Joe thought, looking around at the pained expression on Alice's face, the way Charlie favored his side. The only one of them in perfect shape was Beau, and Joe supposed that wouldn't last for long.

It had rained while they were in Smitha's office. The damp grass of the quad soaked their pants legs. It was late, or early, depending on your point of view, and though there were a few lights on in windows in the dorms that lined the quad, no one else was out walking. Joe couldn't keep himself from thinking that maybe there had been someone, or a few someones, who had gotten caught by Nowhere Men. There was no time to worry about that now, no point to it. The battered family was drawing close to the portal.

There were no monsters waiting for them in the clearing. There were no monsters waiting for them in the greenhouse. Charlie kept pushing them ahead, pushing them on, needing to finish the job as quickly as possible. Smitha and Beau brought up the rear, the doctor craning his neck to look around at the building that should not have been there. And then they were at the top of the stairs, and then they were pounding down the stairs, down into the cave that rose up to meet them. The disguise had broken down even further since their last visit. Stalactites jutted down to nearly brush their heads. Their feet slipped on rough cut stone. Tiny clouds of dust were tossed up with every footfall. Inez sneezed—the air was filled with must, a cloying, old smell that tickled the nose and made Charlie wrinkle his face until he was almost sporting a growl.

When they reached the bottom of the stairs, they skidded to a stop, nearly knocking into each other.

"Holy–" Joe breathed.

"Well," Charlie said, "I don't know what we expected."

The cave was filled with Nowhere Men. They were gathered around the portal, grotesque faces bathed in purple and yellow sparks from the threshold. As one, the monsters turned and looked at the group. At Charlie.

"Oh no ... they're real." Smitha put a trembling hand on Charlie's arm. "Charlie, they've all got bodies. They're all real."

"Um, guys?"

Beau pointed up the stairs. More Nowhere Men, Real Boys with real bodies, were coming down.

"There's no way out," Alice whispered.

"I don't want out," Charlie said. He raised his hands and cracked his knuckles. "Come on, kids. Let's rumble."

He made a swooping gesture, yelled the Words, and from his outstretched hand green lightning crackled into the cave and sent a monster reeling.

"Go go Power Rangers!" Joe whooped. Charlie winked at him.

"You guys are ridiculous," Inez said.

"Um, is the hand gesture part of it?" Beau asked.

"No," said Smitha. "Charlie's just showing off."

"It's what I live for, love," Charlie confirmed. His heart was so full he was afraid it was going to burst out of his chest —full of power, full of adrenaline, full of love for the people around him. He wiped a bit of blood away from the corner of his mouth, grinned, and faced the monsters. Joe stepped up beside him and readied his hands in a martial arts movie stance.

"Attaboy," Charlie said.

Inez and Alice pressed their backs against Charlie and Joe's, facing the monsters that continued to come down the stairs. Beau and Smitha looked back and forth, both hands outstretched in different directions, ready to assist at whichever front needed it.

"It's clobberin' time," said Joe, and whispered the Words that sped lightning across the room to throw a second monster out of its body. The Nowhere Men surged forward, and the fight was on.

For a moment, one moment, it seemed as if they had a chance. Although Charlie's power was the most effective, everyone was now able to strike the monsters. The Nowhere Men had not been expecting an attack on so many fronts and several were thrown out of their bodies and unmade before they quite caught on to what was happening. Once they regrouped, though, the monsters swarmed forward, pressing the group front and back. Charlie took a few steps forward to meet the attack—Smitha ducked to avoid a pair of swinging claws and popped back up facing a different direction—Inez shoved Alice backward to keep her from being sliced—and just like that, the formation was broken. The monsters swept in, forcing them further apart from each other in two wedges that were overwhelming in their numbers.

The cavern lit up with flashes of green lightning, rang with powerful Words and unearthly screams when the Nowhere

Men were hit. Charlie could taste copper so strong he might have been sucking on an old penny. Their lips cracked and bled; their fingertips reddened, blistered, blackened. And still there were more monsters.

Joe, standing alone, was dodging a Nowhere Man's claws and trying to spit the lightning at it. He didn't see the other creature coming after his left side. Charlie did, and leapt at the monster, bearing it to the ground with his weight. Its wildly swiping claws caught him across the cheek, but he ducked closer to its face and growled *"Sha tak—"*

Before he could finish the monster heaved up and threw him to the side. A second monster, seeing its opportunity, shot out with its claws. Charlie thudded against the rocks, his head cracking hard. He lay still.

"Charlie!" Smitha screamed. Beau caught the panic in her voice and started sprinting toward Charlie's crumpled form. A monster loomed up in his path and he swerved, tossed a few Words at the monster. It fell back but another was there, and a third. The monsters saw that Charlie was down and were beginning to jerk forward, their aim to destroy the most dangerous of their adversaries.

Alice, mere hours removed from a hospital stay where her entire left side was stitched up, fought with the frantic energy of the doomed. She reached into Inez, pulling strength and mixing it with her own, flinging Words of power. They had been driven into a corner when the wedge split their party. For a minute, the Nowhere Men had ignored them, focusing the bulk of their efforts on Charlie. There were still so many of them. Too many. Alice and the rest were burning through their reserves too fast, and it wasn't nearly enough. Inez felt a tug as Alice reached into her for power.

"Sha tak ertasa!" screamed Alice, sending the Words arcing across the room in a blast of green lightning to slam into a Nowhere Man looming over Charlie's prone form.

The body of the monster shuddered as the specter within was forced out. Smitha, bloodied and limping a few feet behind Charlie, was ready. She gripped Beau's hand tightly; her knee gave way as she released the Words, but Beau was ready, propping her up and helping her stay on her feet.

"*Ehan evna thae!*"

The purple lighting leapt from Smitha and splashed into the terrified Nowhere Man, unmaking him in a matter of seconds. One more down.

Two Nowhere Men spun to face Alice, now attentive to the threat she represented on the other side of the room. They came at her quickly. She pulled more strength from her bond with Inez and forced Words through her blistered and raw lips.

"*Sha tak—*"

One of the Nowhere Men had picked up a fist sized rock and, before Alice could process what was happening, threw it across the twenty feet separating them. It smacked into her cheek with a meaty pop, knocking loose several teeth, and forcing Alice to the ground. Her vision clouded as she fought to maintain a grip on consciousness. Inez was behind her. Inez was in trouble. She had to stay awake, had to fight. She stood, looked around, and collapsed, hard, her body bouncing off the stone floor of the cavern and ricocheting her head into the wall behind.

Inez crawled to her. Joe leapt in front of them as the two Nowhere Men closed and in desperation wrapped himself around one of the two. In a desperate gamble, he reached into the monster and searched for power as the monster drew him against its barbed rib cage.

Inez buried her head in Alice's chest, sobbing and frantically muttering. Alice's stitches had failed, as Beau warned they would, and she was bleeding heavily from the wound in her side. The left side of her face had been heavily bruised by the rock, and it looked like she'd lost a tooth or two. She looked at Inez through swimming sight.

"You can't die," Inez was babbling. "I need you. I don't know who I am without you. I don't know how to live without you. Stay here, baby. Please, stay. Get up. GET UP, Alice. Come on, baby, you're okay. You have to be okay. I can't be okay if you aren't okay."

Alice gurgled, coughing up blood as she tried to answer. She raised a hand and brushed it against Inez's face.

"Please, Alice. Please."

"I love you," Alice managed through a mouthful of blood.

"No!" Inez screamed, her voice echoing through the room. "No. That was a goodbye. No goodbyes. I love you too. I love you, and I need you. Alice, I need you. Alice, I don't know who I am without you. I'm so lost. I'm so afraid. If you go away, I'll just vanish; I'll disappear. I only exist because you believe in me."

Joe howled in fury and triumph as he pulled every ounce of power from the Nowhere Man he had embraced. The Nowhere Man fell to the ground and Joe whirled to face the second, crackling with power.

"*Sha tak ertasa!*" he yelled, stretching out one hand and ejecting the specter from the monster as it swiped at him with a giant arm.

"*Ehan evna thae!*" he followed a second later, flinging out his second hand and shredding the specter as it exited the body.

His timing was tight. He killed the Nowhere Man just as it closed on him, but not before its massive claws raked three ugly gashes across his chest. He winced and turned to help Smitha in her defense of a still prone Charlie. There were over a dozen Nowhere Men still standing; Charlie and Alice were down, Inez was useless, and Beau was gamely clinging to Smitha's hand. The defense of the world was forgotten as Joe and Smitha pulled tight to each other, standing back to back over Charlie's body with Beau nearby. This was now a fight for Charlie. A fight for their friend. The Nowhere Men closed in.

"I love you," said Alice again, her eyes closing. She repeated it like a mantra, the small ledge to which her fingertips had gripped as the looming abyss of unconsciousness gaped beneath her. "I love you."

"I need you!" Inez sobbed in response. "I need you so I know who I am."

Alice's eyes focused for a moment, and she pulled Inez close to her. "You're me," she whispered. "I'm you. 1A and 1B. I'm not going anywhere, 'Nez. I can't. We're one."

Alice slumped over. Inez, desperate, clung to her chest, and startled when she realized Alice was still breathing. Inez opened her eyes and looked up. A dozen Nowhere Men were ringing Joe and Smitha. The fight was nearly over. They were losing. Alice was dying.

Alice was dying. Her Alice. Inez looked down at the thirty-two-year-old woman in front of her and saw an eighteen-year-old girl, awkward and gorgeous in baggy jeans and faded blue hair. She saw Alice perched on her bed in apartment 1A, saw her sitting on the sidelines of dozens of soccer games, saw her huddled beneath a blanket on a tattered old couch. She remembered the look in Alice's eye the first time they met. A fierce hunger, a longing. A look which told Inez that she was everything Alice would ever need.

Inez took Alice's hand and held it, turning it over in her own, studying every line and crease. She knew it as well as her own. Better, probably, as she rarely examined her own hands but held Alice's constantly. She pushed the Words though her hands and into Alice, drawing strength from her beloved, and found within her a mixture of potent energies.

Relationships change people. As two beings meld their lives together, they affect one another; they bend and shape and grow in and around and through, sometimes twisting together, sometimes verging wildly apart and, in the very best of cases, combining into one.

There was an alchemy to the binding of Alice and Inez; a metaphysical fusion that merged two souls together and created something well beyond the sum of their individual parts. They had separate identities, but they shared a fused core, a relentless, glowing fire of love they had spent fifteen years feeding with joy and trust and laughter and fidelity and everything else they shared.

To Inez, the fire was a sun. She fell into it, losing herself in the heat and light and finding herself again in the boundless, borderless union between her and her wife. As she fell, she seized the Words, wrapping them in the heat of her own sun, feeding them from the bounty of her eternal and unbreakable bond. Alice was finite and Inez was finite, but the connection between them, the miniature sun built of relentless, unconditional love and fierce devotion, felt eternal and limitless.

Inez, taking Alice with her deep in her soul, stood. Beau was on the ground now, and she couldn't even see Joe within the mass of Nowhere Men. Smitha stood alone, crouched but determined, shouting defiant Words of power at the descending hoard that was slowly swallowing her, sacrificing everything within her as the last line of defense.

Crackling with power, Inez strode forward.

"Go get 'em, baby," whispered Alice from behind her.

Inez turned around long enough to offer Alice a smile laced with confidence and illuminated by blue lightning. Alice saw the gladiator in her eyes and let herself slip away again, knowing that Inez would take care of her.

"*SHA TAK ERTASA!*" Inez roared in a mighty voice, power unleashing from her in a wave of electricity that washed over every Nowhere Man remaining. A dozen spectral bodies roared in anger as they were forced out of their physical forms. They turned on Inez, furious, and fell on her as one.

"*Ehan evna thae!*" she shouted, pointing forward and shredding one of her attackers. "*Ehan evna thae!*" she shouted again and again, ripping lightning bolts through the cave and destroying Nowhere Men one at a time, watching with satisfaction as they were unmade.

But they were coming too fast and Inez had misjudged her power, spending so much of it on the initial attack. She fired, taking down another, but the next got through and pinned her arms to her sides, drawing her forward. She held her head and looked it in the eye as it pulled her in, recognizing the feeling of herself slipping away but determined to fight. She reached inside herself again, searching for any power that remained.

"*Ehan evna thae!*" yelled a voice not her own. Smitha! The monster that had been holding her splintered into unbeing, and the two remaining Nowhere Men hovering close at its sides quickly followed.

Then Smitha was on her, leaping across the room, balancing precariously on her one good leg and launching into a hug. The Nowhere Men had fallen. They were alone with the portal and their four fallen friends.

Joe dragged himself up a moment later, shaking his head and apologizing. Alice was coming in and out, while a revived Beau attempted to put together a makeshift wrap out of his coat to hold Alice's side shut. Inez sat beside her.

"You saved me," Alice whispered.

"She saved all of us," said Smitha.

"What about Charlie?" asked Joe.

"He's alive," said Beau. "Unconscious, but still with us. He should be okay, although I suppose we will have to wait for him to do anything else. Honestly, we should all rest and heal before ..."

Smitha leaned over and kissed him. "No time, Beau. We have to end it now. As soon as Charlie wakes up."

"But we're falling apart," Beau protested. "I have no idea how you were doing all that you were doing, but I felt it when you reached inside me, I know how much you took. There's not much left, and according to Charlie, it takes an enormous amount of power to close that thing." He gestured towards the portal.

"We have to try," Joe grunted.

"But if we fail, we die. If we wait and rest, regain our strength, there's a chance we might survive and close the portal," Beau argued.

A noise like the sound of a hand reaching into water caught their attention and all eyes turned to the portal.

An enormous, spectral Nowhere Man stepped through. A giant scar split open one side of his face from jaw to eyeball.

"Aw, hell," said Charlie fuzzily. Still half-concussed, he climbed unsteadily to his feet.

Inez instantly leapt to her feet.

"Go home!" she yelled. "Go home or go to some other world; you can't have this one. Go back through that Portal right now or we'll kill you, too—don't think we can't! Look around, all your buddies are gone. Dead. We did that. GO. BACK."

The Nowhere Man turned his hatchet shaped face to the side, locking the gaze of his single good eye onto Inez. It screamed, its jaw unhinging to reveal a mass of tongues flicking and writhing within the ungodly noise. The air, rippling around his distorted presence in reality, quavered so hard it threatened to break, and the fearsome chill reached an intensity that, even with the Words inside their heads, made it difficult for anyone to move. Their bones felt frozen, petrified by frigid, raw dread.

Charlie shook it off and screamed back, unleashing Words

of tremendous power. His early fall, which initially threatened to devastate the entire plan, now seemed a blessing; unlike the others, he'd barely touched his reserves. He was ready for a fight.

"*Ehan evna thae!*"

The Nowhere Man was prepared, and was very, very fast. It dodged adroitly to the left and the vivid lightning of the Words splashed harmlessly against the stone wall a dozen feet behind him.

"I know who you are!" said Charlie, the confidence in his voice making the statement sound like a threat. "I've beat you already, and this time I'm going to finish the job!"

The Nowhere Man blanched in anger and screamed again; the pressure of fear and ice increased. Charlie's teeth rattled in his head, and he had to fight for control of his jaw as it bounced and trembled in clattering panic.

Inez felt herself begin to disassociate. The fearsome despair, the foreboding helplessness, was too much for her to face. She felt the call of the hiding place behind her own eyes, the empty room within her mind where she was safe from the paralysis of choice. It beckoned her with reassuring, beguiling insouciance.

Joe staggered to Inez's side, resting a hand on her shoulder to steady himself, the gash marks across his chest still oozing blood through his shirt. Inez felt the weight of his presence land like the crackling warmth of a bonfire. Then Smitha was on her other side, slipping an arm around her waist and pulling her close. If Joe was a bonfire, Smitha was the morning sun, her strength and confidence, her unyielding love, leading Inez back to herself.

"*Ehan evna thae!*" cried Charlie, firing again, missing again.

The Nowhere Man jerked aside, this time heading straight in at Charlie instead of falling away. It grabbed his arm as he dove away, and for a fleeting moment, Charlie felt himself being pulled inward. He twisted, wrenching himself free of the invisible hand and falling to the floor, where he rolled twice to create a few feet of separation between him and the Nowhere Man before standing up again.

The Nowhere Man spun and moved again but appeared to notice Alice for the first time and changed direction, swerving towards the prone girl.

"You're done!" Charlie raged, taunting the monster. "Even if you get me, there are five other people here who can do what I do, now. And some of them might even be stronger than me. So go ahead. Take me. TAKE ME! They'll kill you as soon as you build your body! *Ehan evna thae*!"

Again the Nowhere Man dodged and refocused on Alice.

Inez reached into Joe and Smitha, felt them offer their strength to her as they recognized what she was doing. The Nowhere Man was bearing down, and she prepared to make a desperate attack.

"Beau, run!" Charlie screamed. Beau, who had stood to insert himself between Alice and the descending Nowhere Man, shook off the terror as best he could and forced his legs to throw him sideways. It was an inartful leap, and only covered a few feet, but it was just enough to get him clear.

The Nowhere Man fell on Alice, not even stopping to pull her up, but rather collapsing onto her like a child belly flopping into a pool. Its ribs connected with the horrifying thunk of a large meat tenderizer pounding into a butcher's steak.

Inez screamed, a nearly inhuman siren of primal fury. Joe retched, vomiting across the stone floor and flinching in maddening pain as the working of his stomach muscles pulled at the open wounds on his chest and abdomen. Smitha hugged them both, pulling them toward her and whispering words of comfort.

Charlie had seen Nowhere Men steal a life before. He'd seen this very Nowhere Man try it on Inez. It wasn't an instantaneous process—it took several long, precious seconds. Seconds in which the Nowhere Man had no choice but to stand still. And because of Inez, he knew that if he was fast enough ... the girl ... his friend ... the one from downstairs, would survive. She was already fading. Her name was gone. Charlie had one shot.

"*Ehan evna thae*," he said, his voice soft and sharp as honed steel. The Words, full of love for his family and malice towards the Nowhere Men and hope for humanity leaped from him in a sizzling rainbow of electric light and cascaded into the Nowhere Man.

It screamed. Not in pain or anger, but in pure, broken fear. It fought as the Words tore through it, howling and thrashing as it dissolved into eternal unbeing, but it could no more resist the power of the Words than a boat could resist a tidal wave. Within seconds, it was gone.

TWENTY-FOUR

"Alice!" gasped Inez, her throat raw and her voice raspy. She tore herself free from Smitha's grip and stumbled over to her wife, falling to her knees beside her.

Alice's eyes were open. She smiled. "I thought of you," she said as Inez knelt down. "It tried to make me forget myself, but I fought it. It didn't know that I keep a part of me in you."

Inez kissed Alice, soft, careful, but full and on the mouth. When she pulled back, Alice reached up and wiped blood off Inez's lip.

"Sorry," she muttered. "Not quite the same as strawberry lip gloss." Then she shook, pain and fatigue rippling through her body. "I was almost gone," she said, grasping for Inez's hand and squeezing it tight. "I was fighting as hard as I could, but I was almost gone."

Charlie knelt down beside Inez and pushed the hair from Alice's eyes.

"I never would have let that happen, kid," he said. "Hey, Doc?"

"Yes?" asked Beau.

"See what you can do for her, okay? Scarface there was their leader, and if he was back that probably means his army is close behind."

"What are you saying?" Smitha asked.

"I think the invasion is coming. Soon. Now."

"Show time?" asked Joe, a cautious tone to his voice.

"As soon as we can risk it," Charlie nodded.

"We're pretty spent, pal," Joe answered.

"We're stronger than we were fifteen years ago," Charlie challenged.

"I don't know how you possibly think that's true," Joe said. "I've had a pretty crummy fifteen years. I peaked at twenty-one."

"Garbage," Smitha answered. "You're still here. Happiness and success are not the only roads to strength. Sometimes they cripple it. Charlie's right. We've all fought like hell to keep our heads above water for the last fifteen years. We've kept going. We're stronger."

"I don't feel stronger," Joe muttered.

"I do," Inez said. "Especially surrounded by all of you. This is where I belong. With all of you. This is where I am strongest."

Alice nodded. She spoke slowly through her pain but forcefully. "Me too. We survived. Maybe for this. Maybe for today. Maybe because this stupid portal put magic words in Charlie's head, or maybe because the world needs us to be heroes. Or maybe just because we still need each other. Maybe we survived for each other. And now we're together and whole again, and maybe that's all we've ever needed. I feel stronger. I mean, I feel like I've been ripped open and I'm slowly bleeding to death. But I feel stronger. This wasn't about needing to come back together for the portal. This was about needing the portal to make us come back together."

Smitha smiled. "Don't die, Alice. We need you. All of us. We need to make up for lost time."

"Speaking of time," said Charlie loudly, "we do not have any more of it. There will be no making up for lost time because we are about to lose all the world's time, forever, if we don't get this done. This is it, right now. With us. Together."

The air was still as Charlie looked at Joe. They sat in silence while Joe shook his head back and forth. The rest of the gathered family watched him struggle with his doubt. Charlie wanted to push him, to tell him to hurry, to tell him again that time was up and they had to move, but he let Joe think. Let him process. Smitha bit her lip, Alice and Inez held hands, and Joe opened his mouth to speak.

"I'm your huckleberry," he said.

Smitha snorted, her pure, rising laughter bouncing off the stone walls and filling the underground cavern with the sound of joy unfettered.

Joe stalked over to the portal and stared at it, momentarily lost in the memory of the last time they'd attempted to close it. He let himself think of Mona for the first time in years—really think of her, not just remember her in passing, or reflect fondly on a memory. He thought of her as his friend, as an active part of his life, as a piece of himself as he had been a piece of her. He thought of her with Charlie, the mad, kinetic joy they shared when they were together. He allowed himself to miss her. For the first time since the funeral, he thought of Mona and cried.

By the time Smitha arrived, Joe's hands were firmly planted on the base of the portal where Mona had been fifteen years ago. Smitha tugged gently at Joe.

"I'll never understand how you look so handsome when you cry. Most people look like squished tomatoes."

"It's really not fair, is it?" asked Charlie, coming up behind Smitha.

The three of them stood together, wordless, while Joe's hands still rested on the Portal.

"It's not your job, you know," Charlie said, breaking the reverie.

"It is. It should have been last time, too. Cost you your wife. My turn this time."

"Shove off, ego boy," said Smitha with a hint of a smile. "I'll do it. I'm in better shape than either of you are at present."

"I wouldn't trade Mona for you," Charlie said. "Even if I knew she was going to die, I wouldn't have asked you to take her place. You mean just as much to me as she does."

"And I abandoned you, too," said Joe with a shake of his head. "You lost both of us."

"Start that again and I will break every bone in your body," Charlie growled. "I've had enough of mopey Joe. We've all got enough regrets to fill this cave, okay? That's life, man. I love you, and that's what matters. You love me. Better days are coming."

Joe smiled. "Okay, but I'm still not moving. It has to be me."

"How do you figure?" asked Smitha.

"It's obvious," said Joe. "Charlie is the engine, he has to be at the back, like last time. Everybody else has somebody. You've got Beau now, the girls have each other. I've just got me. I have the least to lose."

Joe gasped for air as Charlie tackled him, bodily shoving him away from the portal and driving him to the ground. Charlie sat on top of him and jammed a finger into his chest.

"You didn't hear a word I said, did you?" Charlie demanded.

"What do you mean?" Joe asked.

"I mean I need you. I need you. You're not my boyfriend or my husband, but that doesn't mean you aren't important.

You're not alone, you moron. You've never been alone. I don't want to lose you. Or you," he added, whirling to throw an accusatory glare at Smitha, who had taken Joe's place in front of the portal.

"Can I do it?" asked Beau, approaching the portal and taking Smitha's hands. He tried to lead her away but she shut him down.

"I know you mean well, but do not shepherd me," she growled.

"That's not what... I mean, I wasn't ... I'm sorry," said Beau.

"Good," said Smitha.

"Nobody's got to do it," Charlie said. "At least, not alone. We can do it together."

"That's not how it works," Joe protested. "We know the rules. You have to be at the other end. You have to say the Words and push them through all of us. We've learned the basics, but nobody else knows the closing Words. And you're still much better at controlling them."

"About that," Charlie said. "I think we may have gotten it wrong."

"We—what?" Alice demanded, limping up to join the conversation with the help of Inez.

"You shouldn't be walking," Beau said, concerned.

"I shouldn't be breathing," Alice retorted. "Yet here we are. Charlie, you were saying something about getting it wrong?"

"Maybe," Charlie said. "Listen, I had a dream. There was a giant and a bunch of circles which were us, and everyone else, and there was ... okay, it's not important, okay? I don't have time to break this all down. The bottom line is, I think we got the instructions wrong. Or maybe the instructions themselves were wrong, I don't know."

"What are you saying, Charlie?" Inez asked.

"I don't think we're supposed to be in a line. Or, at least, I don't think that's the only way to do it. That made Mona bear the brunt of everything. What if we stood in a circle, instead?"

Joe nodded. "But the line let you focus the power, too. Push it all through one point."

"You're thinking about it the wrong way," Inez interjected. "A line is limiting. A circle is endless."

"You're following this?" Joe asked.

Inez nodded. "It's like when I connected to Alice. I didn't just rip the power out of her. I ... I don't know, it's hard to explain. I rolled the power back and forth between us. Tied it all up together around the Words. It felt easier to control that way."

"Show me," said Charlie, excitedly, grabbing her hands.

"Are you sure?" asked Inez. "Don't we need to save everything we have for the big job?"

"We don't have enough," Charlie said. "We know that already. We could have come in here fresh as daisies in the morning sun, and we wouldn't have enough. Show me. If I'm right, we might pull this off."

Inez grabbed his hand and, after a brief thought, grabbed Alice's hand as well, waving at Charlie to take Alice's other hand and close the loop.

She whispered the Words, reaching into Alice again as she had less than an hour ago. This time she was not cautious, but exuberant, anxious for affirmation she found within her wife. It was nearly impossible to distinguish between them, to tell where the power from one gave way to the power from the other. They were a single unit.

She felt for Charlie. He was familiar too, his energy deep and electric. She pulled power from him and into herself, and then, as she did with Alice, gave of herself as well, letting the mingled energies flow from her to Charlie, and to Alice, felt them as they connected to each other and came back to her, a live current of power no longer in three separate strands but twined together as a braided rope, nearly indistinguishable as unique elements.

She let the Words go free, using only the smallest draw from the power they'd built up. Electric energy splashed harmlessly onto the floor a few feet away.

Charlie whooped and laughed, capering around the room. He grabbed Joe and led him in a manic waltz, spinning and dipping him as they went. Joe laughed, too, compelled by the joy on Charlie's face.

"I think she's got it!" Charlie cried. "By George, she's got it!"

Abruptly he stopped and grabbed at his side.

"That was a mistake," he said, wincing, but his eyes still sparkled with hope.

There was still a fight over who would stand where, with Smitha and Joe unable to shake that whoever was touching the portal would be at greater risk. Ultimately, Charlie and Smitha, against the protestations of Joe, each laid a hand on the Portal—Charlie on the left and Smitha on the right. Beau stood beside Smitha and Joe beside Charlie, with Alice and Inez together opposite the Portal.

"Ready?" Charlie asked. Everyone nodded. "I love you all," he added. "Even you, new guy. Thank you for being here."

Beau nodded and Smitha smiled.

"Love you, too," Joe said, squeezing his hand. "All of you."

"We love you all," Alice said.

"Love you," Smitha whispered.

"Ok, Waltons," laughed Charlie. "Did everybody get a turn? Everyone feel loved enough? Do we need to go individually by name?"

"You started it," Smitha teased.

"Beau didn't say he loved us," Alice said with a mock pout.

"I barely know most of you," Beau protested. "But … I understand what Smitha sees in you. I see how she comes alive around you. I hope to be a part of that, some day."

"No time like the present," Charlie said. "Baptism by lightning, as it were."

Beau offered a tight smile. He leaned forward and whispered in Smitha's ear. "I love you."

"So, you'll tell her, but not us?" Alice teased.

"You weren't supposed to hear that," Beau said, his face turning red.

"I didn't. I guessed. You're not exactly an enigma, Mister Doctor."

"Can we maybe get on with this before the world is invaded by monsters?" Charlie asked.

"Oh, fine," said Alice. "But you're not off the hook! We'll pick this up later."

"If this … if it doesn't go well," Charlie said. "If this, you know, ends here—"

"Nothing is ending," Smitha said. "This is our new beginning."

"But if it does—"

"It won't," said Joe, firmly.

"I just need you all to know that I'm—"

"We know," said Alice.

"We're okay with it, too," Inez said. "With this being the end. But it won't be."

"What's a guy got to do to deliver a monologue around here?" Charlie grumped.

"Save the world?" Smitha suggested.

"Worth a try," said Charlie, cracking a smile for the ages. He fed the Words with all the power left within him and whispered "*Metsa kodru rima mkaba.*"

He reached to Joe, reached through the portal to Smitha, and joined their power to his. He moved to Beau, the newest addition, and to Alice and Inez, taking strength from each of them and feeding it through the circle, letting it flow through the portal and through each of them. Rather than smashing them all into the Words, as he had done fifteen years ago, he threaded them into each other, following the example Inez had given him. Joe's resolute camaraderie, Smitha's soaring compassion, Beau's cautious but willing service, Alice and Inez's twin joy. He wrapped them together in a mighty braid, a rope fifty times as strong as its individual strands, and let it soar around the circle.

The expenditure took great effort from each of them. Already beaten and bruised from a day of brutal combat, tanks half empty from the exertion of using the Words to defeat the guardian Nowhere Men, they each buckled under the strain of the Words. Even sharing the load, the physical cost was tremendous, and the Words burned like fire as they passed from hand to hand. Charlie felt the breaking point approach.

The Portal thrummed with energy, the yellow and purple and green lights surrounding it surging with light each time the Words passed through. As it had done many years ago, the Portal began to draw closed. It puckered and shrank, becoming the size of a hula hoop, a dinner plate, a saucer, a nickel. Again, just before closing, it froze. Power was required to close the Portal—tremendous power—to shut the door and seal it for eternity.

Charlie urged the Words on, following the flow of the energy and feeling for any strength he could borrow. His friends were spent, already giving everything within themselves to the effort. If he pushed harder, someone would die. Instead, he focused on the Words, sending them through the circle again and again, hoping the recycling power would eventually be enough. It was not.

"It's okay," Joe gasped from behind him, spitting blood as he spoke. "I feel it, too. Take whatever you need."

"No!" Charlie cried. "You'll die."

"Gotta try," Joe said. "Better me than the world."

Charlie reached into Joe, found the flickering flame of power that was keeping him alive. He turned away, unable to take it. At last, he looked into himself, past the fifteen years of pain and scars to a door he'd locked long ago; a room he'd sworn to never open. He reached for it and quailed. As the Words flowed through him again he felt his friends with him, felt their strength and support. Felt the missing strand. He opened the door and stepped in.

"Hello, baby," Mona said. "I've missed you."

Charlie fell into Mona's arms, dropping his head to her chest and sobbing. She wrapped her arms around him and whispered in his ear.

"It's been a long time, Charlie," she said.

"I killed you," he answered. "I couldn't bear it, Lisa. I couldn't bear life without you."

"You're never without me," she answered, pushing his chin up with a finger and kissing him. "I am a part of you. You are a part of me."

"I'm sorry," Charlie said. "I'm sorry you died. Sorry we never got the life together that we planned. It—it wasn't long enough, it—"

"No," Mona agreed. "But would it ever have been enough?"

And Charlie had to admit that she was right.

"Now come on, Lover Boy," Mona said. "Let's finish the job."

Hand in hand, Charlie and Mona walked through the door.

Charlie's eyes snapped open, his heart pounding. He'd

locked away a piece of himself when Mona died, and when he opened the door, her energy flowed into him. He added it to the Words as they flowed past. He felt Joe jerk beside him and heard his soft tears as he started to cry. Inez yelped in happiness and Alice actually called out Mona's name. Smitha, on the other side of the circle, merely smiled and nodded as she let the Words flow out of her and into the Portal.

The lights dimmed and then faded completely. The portal winked closed.

TWENTY-FIVE

As they left the greenhouse, the rising sun bathed their faces with warmth. After the cold of the Nowhere Man-filled cavern, it felt beautiful. A bird sang. Another answered, and suddenly the air was alive with song.

"I am starving," Charlie announced.

Smitha burst into tears.

Immediately she was surrounded, encased in embraces.

"Hey now," Charlie whispered in her ear. "We've done it. We've won. It's over."

"Mona," she managed through sobs. "That—that was Mona."

"Yeah." Charlie laid his head on Smitha's shoulder. "It sure was."

They stayed locked together, a knot of tired, broken adults, leaning on each other for stability and bleeding all over, until Smitha's sobs subsided.

"You know," Joe said, sniffing, "she never did like to be left out."

Charlie laughed, a loose, light sound that was closer to his old self than anything the family had seen in the past day.

"No, she didn't. Something as big as saving the world, you think she would miss that? Not a chance."

"I'm hungry, too," Joe said.

"We should all go get medical treatment," Beau pointed out.

"Sure, but first I'm hungry," said Charlie.

"Eggs N'at is open pretty early," Smitha said. "They don't deliver but we can pick some up and take it to my house." She looked around at the group. "Maybe we should get cleaned up first, though."

"And we probably shouldn't be hanging around here when everyone starts to wake up," Joe pointed out. "The way we look, someone's bound to call the cops and I don't really want to answer any awkward questions before I get something to eat."

"I really think we should take care of our injuries, too," Beau added. "Alice, let me take you to the hospital in the car. You shouldn't be walking."

"I don't want to walk, either," Joe complained.

"I can take four of you. It's a small car."

"I'm not leaving Alice!" Inez protested.

"If someone calls for Eggs N'at they could have the order ready and we could pick it up on the way."

"Eggs N'at is not on the way."

"But we'll already be in the car."

Charlie and Smitha left them arguing and began walking home.

IT WAS A LATE DINNER BEFORE THEY MANAGED A meal together. Beau was not a forceful man, but he insisted on Alice going back to the hospital where he personally oversaw her care.

Joe eventually joined Charlie and Smitha at the Professor's house, and Inez stayed with Alice. In a quiet moment between check-ins, Inez slipped into the hospital bed beside Alice and held her hand.

"Somehow, this is not what I imagined our first homecoming weekend would look like," she said.

"I didn't think we'd ever come back for one," Alice admitted.

"I called Donna, while you were getting stitched up again. Explained that you were in a bit of an accident. You've got all next week off, and more if you need it."

"Ugh," said Alice. "Thanks. I hate to miss a week of pay, but thanks."

"I'm off, too," Inez said. "I know we shouldn't, it'll kill the budget. But after I called your job I just ... I just called mine, too, and I explained, and Riley said they had plenty of coverage and it'd be fine. I can pick up some extra shifts next week so my paycheck won't be too light, and—"

Alice kissed Inez.

"Thank you," she said. "It'll be fine. We're fine. We can survive a few weeks if we need to. Let's worry about it later."

"I just want to take care of you," Inez said. "And ... and I thought it would be nice to have a whole week together. It's been awhile since we've had more than an evening."

Beau finally agreed to release Alice a few hours later—but only because he was going with them and could keep a close eye on her. Beau, not technically on the calendar for today anyway, let his colleagues know he was leaving around eight pm, and the three finally headed to Smitha's house for dinner, which Smitha had assured Beau via text message would not begin until they arrived.

At the house, Joe, Charlie, and Smitha spent the long day catching up properly. Joe filled them in on the disastrous details of his second marriage. They talked and laughed and spun stories and asked questions and revived old jokes and even tried out a couple new ones. The years melted away through the course of the afternoon as they found each other again.

"Beau says they're leaving, and will be here soon," Smitha said, waving her phone in the air as the evening began to give way to night.

"Great," Joe said. "I'll call Eggs N'at."

Charlie shook his head.

"No, man, this is no longer time for Eggs N'at. Tonight, we feast."

Joe grinned.

Charlie called Sun Garden for Chinese: Joe called Blue Isaac for ribs. Smitha had an app on her phone for Giancarlos. The Lamppost had closed down since their senior year, but Smitha had some pancake mix in her cupboard.

"Do you mind going to pick up the food?" Charlie asked Joe. "I'll help the Prof make pancakes."

"I don't need help making pancakes," Smitha protested. "Go with Joe."

Charlie hesitated, glancing over at Joe. Joe smiled tentatively.

"Yeah, ok," Charlie agreed. "Call me if you need help with the batter or anything."

Smitha watched the two men get into Joe's truck and leave. She knew Charlie well enough to know that he was afraid the time with Joe would be awkward. They hadn't been alone together all weekend—probably hadn't been alone together since before they lost Mona. Some of their banter, their relationship had returned, but there was still a distance.

Well, they would work it out. They were best friends, and even though they had grown apart, it was impossible to ignore the years that had come before, impossible to ignore the fight they had just fought together. They would be fine.

Smitha turned away from the window. She got down the box of pancake mix and a large bowl. Then she put the kettle on.

The truck ride for Joe and Charlie was awkward, at first. They looked out the window a lot, fiddled with the air and heat, cleared their throats. Joe, surprisingly, broke the silence first.

"So that really was Mona?"

Charlie nodded.

"Yeah. Well, her energy, or something like that. I guess it's been a part of me that I just closed off, you know?"

"It was good. To feel her again. I am sorry, you know ..."

"Joe, we've been over this—" Charlie began, but stopped himself at Joe's hangdog expression. There was something in his friend's eyes that he had missed before. Charlie looked closer and realized: Joe didn't need absolving again. He needed time.

Unbuckling, Charlie scooted to the middle seat. The truck dinged at him until he put the new seat belt on.

"Joe—I know. And it's going to be okay. For both of us. But we can't walk away from each other again. I'm not saying you have to move in with me or anything. My apartment is not big enough for that. But, you know, if you have any problems, just call. I'll pick up."

"And if I don't have any problems?"

"Call anyway."

"You sure?"

Charlie reached over and gently squeezed Joe's arm.

"Twenty-seven quarters sure."

Joe laughed.

"I still have him, you know. Conoisseurus Rex—I think he's in a box somewhere, but I never threw him out."

Charlie grinned happily.

"I knew you'd love him."

"I did. I do." Joe laughed again. "Do you remember that one time we took him with us to that little restaurant? What was its name?"

"I have no idea. It was so gross, I'm pretty sure it shut down two weeks later." Charlie joined him in the laughter. "I remember the look on the waitress's face, though, when we tried to buckle him into a highchair."

"We were ridiculous."

"Were? Mate, I'm as loony as a tune, didn't you know that?"

Joe slung his arm around Charlie's shoulder and hugged him tight for a moment.

"And I wouldn't have you any other way."

When they got back to the house Smitha had several stacks of pancakes ready. The table was set, and she was standing at the griddle waving a spatula and humming to music that played in the background.

"Honey, we're home!" Charlie said.

They started unpacking the takeout bags. The grease and butter smell of restaurant food mingled pleasantly with the light pancake aroma.

"The pups aren't here yet?" Joe asked.

"No," Smitha replied, "but they should be any minute now."

"If they don't make it soon there won't be anything to eat. Joe and I will pick it as clean as Pharaoh's fields after Moses." Charlie picked up a pancake, folded it in half, and took a huge bite. Smitha swatted at his hand.

"Put that down and get me another plate for the sausage, please. That cabinet over there, on the lower shelf on the right."

As Charlie reached up to the cabinet, Smitha noticed a ring, shining on his right hand. She glanced at Joe, who nodded. Charlie had taken the ring from its chain and put it on his hand in the truck on the way back home.

The door swung open, and Inez bolted through.

"Can we get the couch ready for Alice?" she asked hurriedly. "Beau's bringing her in, and he says she needs to stay off her feet, but I know she's going to want to be with everybody."

Smitha put the spatula down and wiped her hands on a dish towel.

"It's ready," she said. "I knew the two of you would end up sleeping on the couch somehow. There are blankets beneath the coffee table and a couple of pillows stacked up behind it."

Inez grinned.

"Thanks, Professor."

Beau came through the door and deposited Alice gently on the couch. She looked much better after her rest and treatment at the hospital, although it was clear that she wasn't completely back to normal. Inez hovered over her anxiously, arranging pillows and asking if she needed anything.

"Actually, yeah," Alice said. "Make me up a plate? A little of everything. You know what I like."

"Yes, please!" Smitha said. "Everyone eat, before it gets cold!"

"Wait! The toast!"

Charlie made sure there were full glasses all around. He lifted his own and said, "Here's to the six of us."

Beau tipped his glass in Charlie's direction slightly, acknowledging the inclusion. Smitha, standing next to him, tapped her glass to his.

"And here's to victory," Smitha said. "And to family. And ... and to Mona."

They clinked glasses again and drank. A moment passed in shared memory, a glint of renewal mixed with familiar sorrow. They smiled at each other, each holding Mona in their heart.

"That's enough of that," Joe said, clearing his throat. He opened every container, filled his plate, and motioned for the others to begin.

Smitha stood back and watched, hugging herself a little in joy. This was what the big old house was made for. The living room, which often seemed too empty with just her rattling around, was perfect for six adults. They filled the space with noise and laughter and light. Her family.

Charlie, leaning against the breakfast bar, caught her expression. He put down his plate and wrapped her in a huge hug.

"This is perfect," she said, leaning her head against his chest.

"Well, it's only a matter of time until someone spills something," Charlie said.

Night gave way to a pre-dawn haze as they re-lived old memories and built the foundation for new ones. Despite their overwhelming weariness, nobody wanted to be the first to go to bed as they sought to wring every moment out of the first night of a friendship truly reborn.

Alice and Inez were on the couch, Inez willingly doting on her wife and careful to keep her as comfortable as possible. When Charlie, now standing at the center of the room and eating a third plate of dinner which he was referring to as pre-breakfast, launched into a tale about Alice coloring her bangs purple to match Inez's soccer cleats as an ill-conceived romantic gesture, Inez caught Alice by the chin and kissed her deeply.

Joe lounged in a rocking chair beneath the window, rarely talking but smiling more than he had in fifteen years. He'd occasionally fill in a detail or object to the shape of a particular memory, but mostly he just watched Charlie, in his element as a storyteller, and thought about how much he'd missed him and how good it was to be back.

Smitha and Beau shared an oversized loveseat, initially sitting side by side, but as the night wore on Smitha nudged ever closer until she was curled up on his lap. Beau loved the stories, soaking in everything he could about a young Smitha and her friends.

Sometime around 4 am, Joe caught Charlie's attention and put a finger to his lips, nodding at Alice and Inez, who had fallen asleep together on the couch. It was such a familiar sight Charlie's eyes welled with joy. He pulled a blanket over the two of them as Beau and Smitha stood and stretched out.

"I should get going home," Beau said. "This was an amazing night. Thank you all for including me."

"It was the best night," Joe said, nodding. "I've needed this for a long time. Not the whole fighting monsters, almost dying, and saving the world parts. Just the ... seeing you all again. I feel whole."

Joe smiled and hugged Charlie. Smitha joined, and after a beat Charlie's arm shot out and dragged Beau in as well. Then they broke, Beau heading toward the front door and the others to their respective beds for a long overdue rest.

"Hey," Alice whispered, cracking an eye open. Everyone turned to look at her. "What are you guys doing for Christmas?"

ACKNOWLEDGMENTS

This book started with Charlie.

Well, with a version of Charlie. It took a bit of exploration and discussion for us to find the version of him who shows up in these pages. In fact, when we first started talking through this plot in early 2019, he was just called "Lead Wooby". (For the record, Smitha was "Professor Lady", Mona was "Dead Make Out Friend", and the rest were "Players 3-5".) But once we found Charlie, the heart of the family, everything else fell into place. Charlie is the foundation that every character and story beat rests on.

Life threw a lot of things our way while the book was being written, including young kids who hated to sleep, career changes, and a global pandemic. We wrote during lunch breaks and in preschool pick-up lines, on paper and on our phones, sending messages back and forth like lifelines in the middle of the night. Sometimes we were working on the same piece at the same time – there was a particular sort of writer's high when we would chase around the page, picking up each others' thoughts sometimes in mid-sentence. We've been telling stories together since we started playing *Deadlands: The Weird West* our freshman year of college and basically have never stopped.

We both love music, but one album that particularly rose to the top during the writing was "Odessey and Oracle" by The Zombies. It is, in many ways, the soundtrack of this story. You should check it out.

Thanks to Jean for taking a chance on our group of

misfits, to Staci for thoughtful and helpful edits, and to the rest of the Creative James Media family for being so welcoming. Many thanks to Rhonda Parrish and Amanda C. Davis, excellent authors in their own rights, who gave invaluable editing and plot advice. Thanks also to our own family, the ROS, who made writing a close group of college friends almost too easy. Meg would also like to thank the Cajun Sushi Hamsters writing group in Cleveland, for writing wisdom, advice, encouragement, and celebratory champagne.

We wouldn't be here without the love and support of our spouses Lucas and Holly, as well as our kids.

From Mark - This book doesn't exist without the active encouragement of Holly, who is in all ways my truest and best friend. If there is such a thing as a dragon in human form, it is my wife. I often describe her as being made of lace and steel. She's simultaneously delicate and powerful. She's made of magic. She shouldn't exist, but her willpower is so unstoppable that she must exist anyway. She is a creature of legend, a gorgeous and deadly thing from a different world that somehow slipped through the spaces between spaces to manifest in our own. It's hard to lose faith when you've got a dragon in your corner.

From Meg - Lucas is the straight line to my squiggle. He is grounded, sensible, solid, and a heck of a lot of fun. Lucas reminds me of what is real and what is important when I go too far on my flights of fancy. He is the most supportive spouse I could have asked for, often sending me away to make sure I get my writing done. Thank you for always being in my corner, hubband. *Mi amas vin.*

ABOUT THE AUTHORS

Mark Beall and Megan Engelhardt met at band camp a week before the start of freshman year in college and became fast friends. In the many years since then, they have taken long walks in the middle of the night, played many tabletop RPGs, enjoyed countless cups of midnight tea, gone to the beach, podcasted, been deeply invested in Eurovision Grand Final performances, and, of course, written novels. Mark is the founder and operator of Retrograde Orbit Radio and Retrograde Orbit Dice and Leather. Megan's writing has appeared in several publications including Asimov's, Crossed Genres, and Daily Science Fiction. Mark lives in southern Pennsylvania with his wife and their kid. Megan lives in northeast Ohio with her husband and their four kids.